Praise for the no...

ON THIN ICE

"Grabs readers from the first word and doesn't let go until the last page is turned. Ms. Erickson really delivers a first-rate story with characters who'll have you begging for more. They're so well-drawn, readers will even feel sympathy for the villain. I highly recommend this book to anyone looking for a great story written by a top-notch author."

—*Old Book Barn Gazette*

"Erickson creates a masterful suspense with *On Thin Ice* . . . fascinating characters . . . As the tension builds and the pages turn faster and faster, the reader will be swept away in a dangerous world . . . Very highly recommended."

—*Midwest Book Review*

"Exciting romantic suspense . . . The lead characters are a wonderful duo struggling between their demons and love. Readers will enjoy Lynn Erickson's latest."

—Harriet Klausner

"A highly suspenseful novel. Erickson makes you feel as though you're walking the tightrope with Ellie as she searches for the killer . . . a must-read." —*Rendezvous*

continued . . .

SEARCHING FOR SARAH

"Erickson builds suspense by expertly weaving romance into multiple thrilling story lines." —*Publishers Weekly*

"Intricate suspense and deft characterizations make *Searching for Sarah* a top-notch thriller. Don't miss out."
—*Romantic Times*

THE ELEVENTH HOUR

"A fabulous romantic suspense . . . the lead characters are charming . . . Counterpoint to the sizzling romance is a brilliant who-done-it." —*Painted Rock Reviews*

"Layers of depth . . . what a ride!" —*Rendezvous*

"A thrilling read . . . exciting . . . compelling relationships . . . a winner." —*Romantic Times*

NIGHT WHISPERS

"Erickson skillfully navigates the fraught task of portraying the mind of a stalker with multiple personalities . . . The narrative is shadowy and suspenseful, leaving the reader with a creepy, unsettled feeling of expectation."
—*Publishers Weekly*

ASPEN

"A deliciously juicy romp through the winter playground of the wealthy and powerful . . . A complex and truly interesting heroine . . . Suspenseful and tumultuous . . . a sharply plotted page-turner."

—*Publishers Weekly*

ON THE EDGE

LYNN ERICKSON

BERKLEY BOOKS, NEW YORK

If you purchased this book without a cover, you should be aware that this book is stolen property. It was reported as "unsold and destroyed" to the publisher, and neither the author nor the publisher has received any payment for this "stripped book."

This is a work of fiction. Names, characters, places, and incidents either are the product of the author's imagination or are used fictitiously, and any resemblance to actual persons, living or dead, business establishments, events, or locales is entirely coincidental.

ON THE EDGE

A Berkley Book / published by arrangement with
the authors

PRINTING HISTORY
Berkley edition / July 2002

Copyright © 2002 by Carla Peltonen and Molly Swanton.
Cover design by Ann Manca.
Cover art by David Stimson.

All rights reserved.
This book, or parts thereof, may not be reproduced in
any form without permission.
For information address: The Berkley Publishing Group,
a division of Penguin Putnam Inc.,
375 Hudson Street, New York, New York 10014.

Visit our website at
www.penguinputnam.com

ISBN: 0-425-18541-9

BERKLEY®
Berkley Books are published by The Berkley Publishing Group,
a division of Penguin Putnam Inc.,
375 Hudson Street, New York, New York 10014.
BERKLEY and the "B" design
are trademarks belonging to Penguin Putnam Inc.

PRINTED IN THE UNITED STATES OF AMERICA

10 9 8 7 6 5 4 3 2 1

This book is dedicated to Tap Richards and Flint Smith, and all the valiant climbers we have known, living and dead.

THE SICK ROSE

O Rose, thou art sick!
  The invisible worm
That flies in the night,
In the howling storm,

Has found out thy bed
  Of crimson joy:
And his dark secret love
Does thy life destroy.

WILLIAM BLAKE
1757–1827

ON THE
EDGE

PROLOGUE

She died in his arms at 6:05. The sun was shining, the sky blue, the mild autumn breeze cooling the sweat on his brow. She'd had so much to live for.

"You'll get me down," she kept saying to him, weaker and weaker, and he couldn't leave her, couldn't carry her out of the boulder field in her condition. He had no cell phone, no radio equipment. Even if by some miracle another climber spotted them, it would take two hours to get to the phone at Maroon Lake.

Bridget didn't have two hours.

He hadn't prepared properly; he'd left too much to chance.

It was going to be a simple one-day outing, a walk in the park to him. But to her . . . She was afraid of heights; he knew that. It was the first thing she'd blurted out when they'd met, and he'd told her what he did for a living. "You're *that* Erik, oh my God, a mountain climber! And I'm scared to death of heights."

"It hurts," she whispered.

"Sure, it hurts, but you're tough. A few minutes. I'll get you to the hospital before you know it."

"It's hard to breathe. You'll get me down, won't you?" Weak, the air pressed out of her lungs, the blood leaking in. She had a puncture wound, he knew that from the bloody froth he wiped from her mouth with his fingers, with his lips, kissing death away.

"Yes, I'll get you down. Don't talk, darling." *Lying, lying.*

"Hold me." Barely audible.

He'd never panicked before in his life, not on Everest when his group had been stranded in a storm, not on Aconcagua, not on the Eiger or Kilimanjaro or McKinley. Not in weather bitter enough to freeze exposed skin in seconds, in wind that cracked the sides of tents like pistol shots. He was always coolheaded, knew precisely what to do. That was his job, his calling, his religion.

But here, in the bright Colorado sun, in the jumbled boulders below the ice chute only a few miles from Aspen, he was in a firestorm of panic. She was dying, her chest crushed, bleeding internally, and he couldn't do a fucking thing.

She'd overcome her fear for him, practiced on easier slopes. Had he pushed her? Had he forced her? Was this, this—the pale sweating skin, the weak breathing, the eyes focusing on something far away, the heavy, flaccid dying flesh—his fault?

Would she be here if it weren't for him? Christ, no.

"Erik," her lips barely moving, "I loved you."

Loved? Did she know her life was already over?

She'd been so brave, hiking in that morning, a crisp, clear fall day, perfect weather, perfect conditions. He'd chosen South Maroon Peak because it was the easier of the two Maroon Bells, even though it was over

14,000 feet high. They'd rock climbed to the ridge and walked to the summit from there. She'd been pale but determined on the ascent, giddily excited at the top. He'd been so proud. Lovely, courageous Bridget.

But she'd been slow on the climb up, and the early-autumn darkness would soon be upon them. He'd thought, he'd weighed the choices, and he'd decided; they would descend the snow chute to save time instead of walking down the ridge, the easier but longer route.

He had crampons and ice axes and ropes in his backpack. At the top of the chute, they put on the crampons and looped their ice axes over their wrists.

"Follow me," he said. "Step exactly where I step."

To him, it was like walking down stairs, kick in your heel, transfer weight, kick in the other heel one step lower. The slope was forty-five degrees, steep but not impossibly so.

He should have remembered that most climbing accidents happen on the way down. Gravity was a stern taskmaster.

It was automatic to him, the positioning, the need to keep your center of balance out a bit from the face of the mountain so your feet carried all your weight, but Bridget was new to the game. Her instinct was to hug the mountainside.

It was September, and the snow was soft, with snow-melt channels running down its surface. His crampons got balled up with the sticky snow, and he had to knock it out from between the sharp spikes with his ice ax. He showed Bridget how to do it, too.

He remembered that he'd been sweating like a pig, the sun, the hot Southwestern sun, sweat in his eyes.

Not cold like most climbing. Funny, he'd been think-ing, when she fell.

His brain had computed instantaneously what had happened. Bridget's crampons had balled up, her feet had gone out from under her. At the time, all he'd heard was a little strangled cry of fear, then she shot past him on her back, almost taking him with her.

He'd watched, and he saw, but it didn't register for a moment. Then he yelled, "Self-arrest! Self-arrest!"

She'd tried, as he'd taught her, tried to turn from her back to her stomach and stop herself with her ice ax, but she got twisted and dug the tips of her crampons in, which flipped her. Then she was hurtling headfirst down five hundred feet of slick snow. So fast, so un-believably, frighteningly fast.

He'd heard her scream. "Erik!" Fear, stark, undiluted terror.

He was already moving, far too swiftly for his own safety, as she fell, knowing, hoping, his mind speeding with permutations and combinations, taking up and dis-carding. Phone? No phone. Other climbers? All de-scended, on the way home.

Speed, trajectory. She'd been far below by then, still sliding, and for an instant fear shot through him before he shoved it down.

God, God, goddamn. He'd been panting, nearly lost his purchase once; only instinct saved him.

When he'd reached her, he knew it was no good. She'd slid all the way to the bottom of the chute and hit naked boulders. At her speed, Christ, it was a won-der she was conscious. She hadn't struck her head, but her chest, and her ribs were crushed and digging into her lungs, and blood was filling them and she couldn't breathe and he couldn't do anything but hold her and wipe the lifeblood away and lie to her.

He watched, helpless, when the last ragged breath seeped from her lungs, and he held her to his chest long after she was dead.

The sun slipped below the shoulder of the mountain, and he stood and hoisted her death-heavy body and began to walk out. It took hours, and her body grew heavier with each step, but he trudged on.

His eyes stared straight ahead, and no one could have deciphered what went on behind their sharp blue depths. But he was looking at the future, the way his ancestors had done from the prows of their dragon ships, and he saw his fate with a clear, unflinching gaze.

ONE

Meredith Greene would remember with stark clarity the first time Bridget Lawrence walked into her office. She didn't know it then, but later, when tragedy struck, she would realize that Bridget's appointment with her was the fulcrum upon which the rest of her life balanced. It was not fate. No, because she herself, with her own will, tipped the future down the tumultuous slope it would slide, steeper and steeper and faster, until she was swept inevitably along.

It had been a typical June day in Aspen. A perfect Colorado summer day in the morning, the sky sapphire, a few graceful white billows over Independence Pass at the head of the valley, and then the buildup of clouds in the afternoon, promising rain.

Bridget Lawrence's call for an appointment had not been unusual. As a psychologist, Meredith had treated patients for a variety of phobias, using desensitization or flooding techniques. Yet there had been something in the young woman's voice on the phone, something curious. Most prospective patients spoke guardedly, often defensively, as if no real problem existed despite their seeking treatment. But Bridget's voice had been filled with exuberance and hope.

Meredith's third-story office was situated in an older building that sat on Aspen's Main Street next to a movie theater. She would have preferred a ground-level entrance, but at rents in the thousand-dollar-a-foot range, her desire was a pipe dream. She'd decorated the place in calm colors, with plants and posters of mountain scenery. Two small rooms, a waiting room and her inner sanctum, where her patients revealed their secrets, their problems, their fears. She couldn't afford a receptionist; her answering machine performed that function.

Bridget arrived on time, three o'clock in the after-noon. She was in her late twenties, Meredith guessed, a few years younger than Meredith's own age, a pretty girl, dark-haired, with fine features and the athletically honed body of so many Aspenites.

Meredith had the client fill out the necessary forms, took a copy of her insurance card, then led her into her consulting room.

"Now," she told her new patient, "tell me how I can help you."

The young woman leaned forward; her dark eyes met Meredith's intently. "I'm afraid of heights," she said. "You've got to help me get over it."

A fear of heights. Acrophobia. A common enough problem. "Is there any particular reason?" Meredith asked. "I mean, many people have acrophobia, and they live with it quite easily."

"Yes," she said. "A very good reason."

Meredith waited.

Bridget closed her eyes, as if deciding something

momentous. "I met a man. We're in love. I've never felt like this before. I think he's the one."

"Yes . . . ?"

She sat back, let a sigh out through her nose. "He's a mountain climber."

Ah. Well, there were plenty of those in Aspen, that was for sure. "All right, Bridget, I see where you're going."

"He's not just any mountain climber. He's famous. World famous. Erik Amundsson." She looked at Meredith eagerly, awaiting her recognition of the name.

"Yes, I've heard of him." *Everyone* had heard of him.

"And he wants me to climb with him. But I'm afraid, God, it's awful. I can hardly stand to ride ski lifts. My heart pounds and my mouth goes dry and I can't catch my breath and I get so dizzy I think I might jump just to end the agony. But he loves the mountains so much. . . ."

"Bridget, does he know you're here?"

Solemnly, she nodded. "He thinks it's a great idea." She fixed Meredith with her liquid, dark eyes. "Can you help me? And fast, too, before the summer's over?"

Good God. "Well, I can certainly try to help you, but these ingrained phobias are difficult to deal with, and I can't guarantee you'll get over your fear of heights by the end of the summer."

"I *have* to."

"Why, Bridget? Do you feel your boyfriend will leave you if you can't climb with him?" She felt a stab of unprofessional anger in her heart. She certainly knew about macho men who selfishly led their women into danger.

"Oh, no, Erik wouldn't leave me even if I never make a climb. He loves me, but it'd be so much better, don't you see? We could *share* everything then."

Meredith sat quietly for a moment, then she spoke. "Is he forcing you to undergo therapy?"

"No, no, it's not like that. It was my idea."

Meredith remembered that day in remarkable detail. It had etched itself indelibly in her brain; she could close her eyes and the scene came back to her as if it were happening *now*, over and over again, reinventing itself anew each time.

A cool breeze had stirred the wood-slatted blinds in her office, and the air smelled of new leaves and the hint of a shower to come. Somewhere a car horn sounded, and the room darkened as the cloud shadows that had hugged the peaks slid across the valley floor.

"It was my idea," Bridget had said, "entirely my idea."

Distant thunder reverberated off the surrounding peaks, and the blinds rattled. How many times that summer would the question form in Meredith's mind: *Whose idea had it really been?*

Yes, she would always remember the ripening June day Bridget had walked into her office. The fulcrum day.

It was September now, the beginning of September, the trees just touched with color, the sky blue, the high peaks surrounding Aspen brushed with an early snowfall. Midday was warm, but the night would be cold, and frost would form on the grass by morning. A beautiful day, a fitting day for an outside memorial service.

She had decided to go; she wasn't sure why. Sadness, guilt, professional interest, all entered into her decision. She didn't have to attend, but she felt it necessary, in some unfathomable way. For moral support, she'd asked her friend to go with her. Good natured as always, Tony Waterman had said yes.

The park alongside the Roaring Fork River was crowded. There must have been more than two hundred people in attendance, mostly young. Casually dressed, some in running or biking gear. Tables had been set up, laden with food. Even if the item was only a bag of chips, everyone had brought something. She had baked brownies. Cried as she'd set them in the oven.

A girl Bridget's age was standing at the center of the throng with a wireless microphone. At first, Meredith couldn't hear what she was saying, but the group gradually quieted.

"You're here because you all loved Bridget. You're honoring her just by your presence. And isn't it wonderful how many friends she had?" The speaker's voice broke.

Meredith felt her eyes tear up. She squeezed Tony's hand hard, felt his answering pressure. As a psychologist, she had to admit to herself exactly why she was so terribly upset, why her emotions were so out of control. She knew about therapists who had patients commit suicide. They often suffered emotional distress. But Bridget's death had been ruled an accident. *An accident*. Just as her own mother's death had been ruled an accident.

A tear ran down her cheek; she dashed it away.

She'd never been this distraught over a patient before. What was wrong with her?

The girl with the microphone was speaking again, but she didn't hear. She was thinking, her mind swimming through the murky depths of her own motivation, of Bridget's, of Amundsson's.

There he was. He stood beside the girl who was talking. Tall, lithe, his fair head held proudly, his face stony, as if making a mockery of this memorial.

For God's sake, she wanted to sob, *this is your fault. An accident? You took her up on that mountain, and you might as well have murdered her.*

Everyone who lived in Aspen for any amount of time knew someone who'd been killed in a climbing accident. She was well aware of that. It was the risk climbers took. But Bridget, God, she wasn't a climber. She was merely a poor young woman who'd fallen so in love she'd do anything to be with her man, even the one thing she was most afraid of.

But the worst part of it, the part that tore at her insides with bloody talons, that kept her awake at night, that gave her nightmares in which she was falling, falling, sliding forever, was the fact that she herself might have enabled Bridget to die.

Tony put his arm around her. She realized she was trembling. Maybe she could have stopped Bridget. Had she encouraged her too much? Had she led her patient to believe she'd made more progress than she actually had? Had she been firm enough when she'd told Bridget she was far from prepared for a serious climb?

Or perhaps she could have done nothing at all to prevent Bridget from following her lover up that mountain.

"She was so brave," the girl was saying. "She had a passion for life."

She had a passion for Erik Amundsson, Meredith thought. *That's why she's dead.* She stared straight at the man, stared so hard he must have felt the vitriol in her gaze. He was as still as a statue, a head above the crowd, in a blue and green plaid shirt with the sleeves rolled up over arms ropy with muscles, and big hands. Bridget had told her what he could do with those hands. Meredith shivered. She stared at him so hard, her eyes watered.

He wore a beard, trimmed short and shot with gray, even though she knew he was only thirty-nine. All those close calls, she supposed.

And then, taking her by surprise, as the girl next to him rattled on about Bridget, he looked straight at her. His eyes, blue as the sky under sandy brows, fixed on her, and she felt herself go cold. He didn't know who she was, of course not, and she wondered if he could read her thoughts. She refused to look away.

Then the connection was gone, and he was as he had been, implacable, untouched by emotion, and she had to wonder whether she'd imagined that momentary meeting of glances.

Erik Amundsson didn't know her, but she knew a lot about him. Not just from Bridget. Amundsson was a well-known climber, as notorious among Aspen locals as among the international mountaineering crowd. He'd summited every big peak in the world. He had a reputation for superhuman strength and endurance, for courage and a cool head under pressure. He'd done solo climbs that he shouldn't have returned from. He'd saved climbers in trouble countless times, his own clients and those of other guides. Hell, he'd saved the guides, too.

Ten years ago on Mount Aconcagua in the Andes, he lost three clients in an unearthly storm. He'd taken a lot of flak for that, Bridget had explained in one of their sessions, but he'd saved the other five people, who'd been disoriented and half frozen in that fearsome storm. He'd lost two fingers to frostbite on the expedition. Bridget had told her she loved to kiss his mutilated hand with its missing fingers.

"Take it easy," Tony whispered in her ear. He always knew how she felt, could see right through her.

"I can't," she whispered back. "Look at him, standing up there as if he were the poor bereaved husband, for God's sake. He should have known. *I* should have known."

Tony was aware of her opinion of Amundsson, but there was so much she couldn't tell him. The entire summer's worth of therapy sessions that were doctor-client privilege. Oh yes, she knew things about the man his mother couldn't possibly know.

She knew intimate details of his lovemaking. She knew he had a dominating nature, a towering ego. He'd controlled every facet of Bridget's life. She had sat in her office week after week listening to details of Bridget's obsession for Erik Amundsson.

"Hey." Tony's voice was low, his mouth close to her ear. "You're taking this too personally. It's not your fault, for chrissakes."

Taking it personally. He didn't know how true his words were. Tony knew about the tension between her and her father; Tony knew her mother had died twenty-five years ago. What Tony didn't know was the blame her father bore for her mother's death. And that un-acknowledged blame had created a hard stone at her center, where every soft emotion bashed itself to death.

"Meredith."

"I'm not taking it personally," she whispered back, a bald-faced lie.

She fixed her attention on Amundsson again. She waited, hoping he'd say something when the girl finished, but when the speaker broke down sobbing, he only patted her back calmly, his expression carved in granite.

Safely held in Tony's embrace, she studied Amundsson. The thought flashed through her brain that she was being childish, but she didn't care. Someone had to acknowledge the tragic mistake this man had made.

He was looking out over the crowd now, his gaze arrogant, bored.

Can't people count? Three dead in South America and Bridget made four. How many more people would die in his trust?

"Let's go," she said. She couldn't stand there any longer, willing poor Bridget back to life, blaming Amundsson, blaming herself.

"Already?" Tony asked.

"Let's just go," she said tautly.

They walked on the Rio Grande Trail that followed the curve of the Roaring Fork River. Once, over a hundred years ago, trains loaded with silver ore and passengers had chugged along this route. The tracks were long gone, and now bicyclists, joggers, women with strollers, and dogs used the paved trail.

A century ago, all the trees had been cut for shoring up the many silver mines that honeycombed the mountains above the boomtown. Now there were tall cottonwoods, aspens, and pines shading the way.

Tony kept his arm around her as they finally headed up a path toward her office, and she was grateful for his understanding. Her heart still pounded, and she felt nauseous, sick with sorrow and regret.

"You want me to drive you home?" Tony asked.

"No, no, I'm okay. I just . . . It's so awful what happened, so senseless, and he stood there as if . . . as if he had nothing to do with it. God, Tony, this is driving me nuts."

"I know. But it's over. You did your best, and it's over. Jesus, Meredith, it's not like it was your fault."

"Maybe it was," she said dully.

"Stop it."

"I can't."

"Look, did you tell her she was cured of her fear of heights? Did you ever tell her that?"

"No."

"Did you tell her she was ready to climb?"

"No, but . . ." She desperately wanted to tell him about her mother's death, about her father and her sister and all the years of pain she had suffered, blaming her father, hurting . . . but she couldn't because she had trained herself to appear strong to the outside world. She had trained herself to rise to every occasion. She did all she was supposed to do, meticulously and capably, and she had done so from a very tender age, taking care of her younger sister, Ann, when their mother had been killed in a car accident.

She'd managed brilliantly, but the effort had left its mark. She had a need to be in command of situations, not overtly or noisily, but quietly and relentlessly. She did not get along with her father, whom she blamed for her mother's death. After all, it had been *his* idea to drive to Denver that snowy day. Her mother had been terrified of driving on mountain highways in storms, but Neil Greene had prevailed.

She was conscientious and unpretentious, self-confident and utterly honest, except about that spot deep inside her that was like a clenched fist.

She'd grown up on her family's ranch, where cattle and horses were raised on a spread thirty miles from Aspen on Missouri Heights, a broad plateau above the Roaring Fork River. Until her mother died, hers had been an idyllic childhood. And with her degree in psychology, she was certainly aware of how her life had been impacted.

"The hell with your guilt trip, Meredith," Tony was saying as they crossed Main Street. "You're beating yourself up for no reason. Did it ever occur to you that climbers can fall even if they *aren't* afraid of heights?"

"Yes," she whispered.

Tony stopped and turned to her. His square face was uncharacteristically concerned. "I don't like what's happening to you. It's affecting your whole life. It's affecting *us.*"

"I know." She looked down at her feet, unable to meet his gaze. "I'll try to work it out. I will. I swear."

"Good." He tipped her face up with a finger. "That's my girl."

"Yeah," she said, trying to smile.

She lived two doors away from Tony in Woody Creek in a set of town houses that had been built as upper-end employee housing. Affordable places to live were in desperately short supply in the entire county, as Aspen's economy required large numbers of employees. The Roaring Fork Valley was narrow, space was finite, the Forest Service owned most of the mountainous terrain rimming the valley, and the lifeline of the town, State Highway 82, called "Killer 82" by locals, was continuously clogged with commuters.

Woody Creek was an old ranching settlement, five miles from Aspen, set on the bank of the Roaring Fork River. There were still working ranches in the area, but there were also suitably impressive starter castles, a crowded trailer park, and the Woody Creek town homes for middle-class professionals and young families who could not afford the million dollar and up homes in Aspen proper.

She and Tony had seen each other from afar for months before actually meeting, getting into or out of their cars in the parking lot, going for a jog or a walk. Emptying the trash.

Tony was a friendly guy, quite charming, which was a great asset in his profession. He was an investment broker, working for the local office of Merrill Lynch. He exuded absolute integrity and confidence. He was broad across the shoulders, strongly built, with floppy dark blond hair and a heavy jaw, a wide mouth, and hazel eyes.

He was a good-looking man, and she had noticed him. She'd noticed also that he wore no wedding band and didn't seem to have a steady girlfriend.

Their relationship developed gradually, no *coup de foudre,* no grand passion, just two people who enjoyed each other at first, had a lot in common, got along like best friends. In the past, Meredith had attracted needy men, and sooner or later, she realized she didn't respect them enough for a healthy relationship. But Tony was strong enough to handle her.

Love came incrementally, but it was good. Tony was the one, she thought. After all these years of dating, of being single, of her married sister Ann asking her if she'd met anyone, at thirty-two she'd found Tony. They'd discussed announcing their engagement this coming Christmas.

She drove straight home from her office. Tony had another client and said he'd be home in a couple of hours. He'd bring pizza.

She went into her town home and tossed her keys and bag on the kitchen counter. She felt exhausted, mentally done in. She sank onto her couch, kicked her shoes off, and laid her head on the back, a forearm over her eyes.

Physician, heal thyself, she thought. *Okay, fine, but how, goddamn it?*

She was still sitting in the same place when Tony arrived at seven, carrying a Domino's pizza box.

"Hi, sweetheart," he said. "Feeling better?"

No, Meredith wanted to say. "Yes, sure, lots better."

He set the pizza down on the table and sat beside her on the couch. "I want my old Meredith back," he said.

"I know. So do I."

He leaned over and kissed her cheek. "Come on. Food."

She sighed mentally. If Tony had a fault, it was a tendency to be selfish at times. He'd gone to Bridget's memorial; it was over for him. Time to move on. Forget that. She was still churning with pain and doubt and could have used a little more understanding from him.

After dinner, he started getting amorous. She knew the signs, the way his eyes became heavy-lidded and his hands brushed her body. Normally, she accepted his needs, even if she didn't get as much from their sex as he did. She knew she wasn't a passionate person. Meredith Greene was never going to be hot in bed. Even in college, she'd been considered prudish. She'd thought a lot about her sexuality and had come to understand her need for control was too great, too necessary for her survival for her ever to shed her inhibitions. She supposed that was okay. You couldn't—and sometimes shouldn't—tear down barriers that served you well.

Tony pulled her close. She knew his moves, every single one of them, knew the order in which they'd occur and how she'd feel and what he'd do then and—

"Tony, darling," she said, laying her hands on his chest between them.

"Um?" He put his lips to her neck, nibbling. He knew she loved that.

"Please, Tony, oh, I'm so goddamn sorry, but I'm just . . . I'm such a mess."

He raised his head and looked her full in the face. "Jesus, Meredith, I thought you felt better."

"I thought so, too. It's that memorial. I can't . . . I can't get it out of my head. I'm sorry."

He frowned and let her go. They had formulated unspoken rules in their relationship: no overnights unless invited. She didn't ask him to stay. Then she relented, feeling so bad, so remorseful and confused and hurting.

She held her arms out. "A good night hug?"

He gave her a hug, a quick kiss on the top of her auburn hair, a murmured good night. He was pissed. He wanted everything all sunshine and roses, and she wasn't ready, and he didn't know how to deal with it.

Relief swamped her when he was gone. Then regret shoved it aside. God, she hated this: the ugly, seething, uncontrollable emotions that assailed her. She wished she could be like Tony, less introspective, simpler.

She brushed her teeth and got into bed. It wasn't even dark out, but she didn't have the energy to do anything else.

She imagined Tony alone in his mirror-image town home. Still fuming. She could see him so clearly. Then, without a bridging thought, Erik Amundsson appeared in her mind's eye. He was standing beneath a cottonwood tree, head and shoulders above the crowd. She saw his blue eyes, the way the weather had lined his skin, the gray-shot beard, the sun coming dappled through the trees to gild his fair hair. She could understand why an impressionable girl like Bridget had fallen for him. He attracted lots of women, Bridget had told her, groupies, camp followers. He was quite a ladies' man.

But there was more to him than his looks. She had recognized it that day, and she'd understood Bridget's obsession better. He had an aura, a look to him, almost otherworldly. A blankness to his expression, no, a sense that he was not *there,* that he was on some mountaintop, fighting a life-and-death battle with the elements.

And an arrogance, which she supposed climbers who challenged the highest peaks must possess, an arrogance that radiated from him like the too-strong scent of an expensive aftershave.

God, she was as obsessed by Amundsson as Bridget had been. She hated that. But she couldn't stop picturing him, going over and over what she'd say, given the chance, what pithy one-liners she'd launch at him. Would he stay so cool then?

She lay there, her beloved Tony two doors away, and her brain was filled with another man.

TWO

In Aspen, situated at 8,000 feet, winter gave way to spring reluctantly. Some years it snowed until June, and the weather was as changeable as a woman's fancy. It was April, and the ski season was nearly over, the sun hot one day, then obscured by a blizzard the next.

It was called the "mud season" by Aspenites, and large numbers of them left for southern vacations when the ski lifts shut down.

Meredith couldn't afford to leave for the off-season, even though Tony had tried to entice her with a Cancun getaway. She wasn't in the mood to have fun, in any case. She'd be a lousy companion.

Everyone thought she needed a vacation; maybe she did. But running away couldn't cure what ailed her.

It had been seven months now, seven months since Bridget's death, seven months since the excruciatingly painful memorial, and she was still suffering episodes of guilt and anger and depression. She'd consulted Sandra Cohen, a colleague, at Christmas. Talking it out had helped, but only temporarily, like going to a chiropractor and getting an adjustment for your back, which invariably went out again the next day.

Her pain, her immature, self-indulgent suffering, had driven a wedge between her and Tony. It had put a strain on all her relationships—her friends, her family—and it had compromised her ability to treat her patients.

She and Tony had not, after all, become engaged at Christmas. The whole scene had been awful, painful to both of them. She'd had to confess she wasn't 100 percent sure. She hadn't known how to tell him that she loved him but wasn't sure she was *in love* with him. The truth was, she'd still been too distraught over the death of her patient and was doubting every facet of her life, every decision, no matter how large or small.

Tony had reacted first with anger and wounded pride. Then he'd had an affair. That had hurt. Terribly. Though, of course, his straying had been her fault. When he'd wanted to start seeing her again in the end of January, she'd reluctantly said she'd give it a try, but in her heart she knew it would never work out.

She guessed they were friends now. And that seemed to be okay with them both.

In truth, she didn't much like herself these days, but she clung to the notion that her problems would pass. She held onto that belief ferociously, and it had gotten her through the worst times.

It was a Friday. A warm day for April, gray skies, snow melting in rivulets everywhere, pulled by gravity until it trickled into the Roaring Fork, swelling the river as it raced toward the mighty Colorado, forty miles downstream. The air was heavy, the trees running with sap, their branches still bare, but life was ready to explode in every bud.

Tony was going to pick her up at four; she'd leave her car right there at her office. No need to clog the highway more than it already was. She was looking forward to the weekend. Saturday, she'd drive down valley to her family's ranch and work with her patients in the equine therapy program. She had to give her father credit for donating the ranch and horses to the program; Meredith donated her time. Equine therapy complemented her training in psychology, and she got enormous pleasure from helping her patients, who were mostly children. The horses used in therapy were carefully trained and very gentle. Most of the children involved had some sort of brain damage or coordination problems. Sitting on the horse's back as it was led around the ring, riding helmets on, dazzling smiles on their faces, literally on top of the world, the kids relaxed and they took on the rhythm of the walking horse.

There were all sorts of scientific explanations for the efficacy of the therapy; the horse provided sensory processing and functional mobility sequencing to improve posture, normal muscle tone, and developmentally appropriate movement. The patient was challenged to build new motor responses. Speech, ambulation, and upper extremity use could be expected to improve.

She'd finished her last session an hour ago, a woman who was having a great deal of trouble handling a grown son who was dependent and manipulative. They were getting somewhere, settling on some ground rules the woman could live with. Meredith felt good about that.

She was writing up her notes, doing busywork, ready to close up shop for the weekend, waiting for Tony.

She was still consumed with anger over Bridget's death, the same unresolved anger she felt over her mother's death. Anger and a sadness that formed in her stomach and rose painfully into her throat. Out of the blue, weeks, months, years after the person died. Sandra had told her that anger was an appropriate emotion in both cases, but that she'd have to let it go eventually, because it no longer served a useful function.

She knew that. For God's sake, she'd studied similar case histories in school. She knew how anger could taint a person's life. It had tainted hers.

She simply didn't know how to get over it. Forgiveness didn't seem to be in her repertoire. If you forgave a guilty person, she reasoned, then his victim counted for nothing, and she couldn't bear that.

Tony found her sitting behind her desk, staring sightlessly out her window.

"Knock, knock," he said. "Is the doctor in?"

"I keep telling you—"

"I know, you're not really a *doctor*." He looked at her expression, then frowned. "Tired?"

"No, not really."

"Good. I've got a deal for you."

She looked up. "What?"

"A party. Big affair at Kemil al Assad's house."

"A *party?* Oh, Tony, I know you don't want to go alone, but God, I hate those things."

"Shush. It's not like this has to be a real date, if that's what's bothering you."

She cringed inwardly.

"I'm just thinking it wouldn't kill you to get out a little more. And, besides, the food will be great. I might line up some clients. You might, too."

"All those pretentious assholes."

"Kemil isn't an asshole. He's a nice guy. A physical fitness nut. He skis and golfs and climbs. He can't help it if he's a prince. And he's on our side when it comes to terrorism, that's important."

"Oh God, Tony—"

"Look, he invited the whole office, and I pretty much have to go. I'd like you to come along, but if you really don't want to, fine."

"You're mad now."

"I'm not mad, Meredith."

"Who'll be there?"

"Hell, I don't know. Most of the rich and famous are already gone for the season. Kemil likes rubbing shoulders with locals. I'm sure his skiing buddies will be there. His climbing pals, too. I heard Amundsson is invited."

A shock, like a splash of cold water, hit her, and she felt her cheeks drain of blood. "Oh," she said, "that really makes me want to go."

Tony shrugged. "Hey, he's a good friend of Kemil's. They climb together a lot."

"Kemil's lucky he isn't dead," she muttered.

"Aw, come on, Meredith."

"Okay, I—"

"I imagine Kemil wants Amundsson to meet his rich

friends so they'll hire him to guide them. That's the way it works."

She barely heard. A thought had struck her, a ghost of an idea, a sudden stabbing notion. What if she went to the party and confronted Amundsson? In front of all the wealthy men who looked up to him, the icon. She saw herself crossing a crowded room, standing before him, and hurling her poison dart, the truth. The truth, goddamn it. "You are responsible for Bridget Lawrence's death," she'd say.

"Okay, I'll go," she told Tony. "You're right. I need to get out. It might even be fun."

"And the food'll be great," he repeated, the standing joke of the not-so-rich in Aspen.

She was quiet driving home with Tony, reviewing the possible scene in her mind over and over. Should she turn on her heel and walk away after she said her piece? Or should she stand her ground and wait to see if he had anything to say for himself?

Flickers of tension ran through her. Anticipation. And the question: Did she have the guts to face up to Amundsson in front of everyone?

She showered and took more time than usual with her hair, not that much could be done with it. She had straight hair, shiny dark auburn, which she had cut in layers, so that it was easy to care for. She wore her standard outfit, knowing that people would come dressed in everything from faded jeans to outrageously expensive sportswear. No man would wear a suit, God forbid, and the women would display cashmere and well-cut slacks and long skirts with side slits under thousand-dollars sweaters.

She had bought the dress the year before. On sale,

naturally, at one of Aspen's high-end boutiques. It was an ankle-length black wool knit, with a turtleneck and long sleeves, perfectly plain. Her party dress. She knew it would work for the prince's party just as it had for Christmas dinner at her father's or New Year's Eve with Tony's visiting family.

Gold loop earrings, a bracelet, that was it.

She checked her appearance in the mirror and hardly recognized herself. Her cheeks had patches of hectic pink and her eyes were feverishly bright. She knew it was the upcoming confrontation, and she wondered if once she'd unloaded her anger on Amundsson, she'd finally be cured of her problems.

She smiled at herself in the mirror and felt empowered. She'd be the avenging angel, setting things right, making Bridget Lawrence matter.

And Tony would be pissed as hell at her.

She stood in front of the mirror and wondered at how little she cared about Tony's reaction. *Not good*, something in her brain whispered, and a small frisson shook her. *Not good,* her conscience said again.

She'd left the door unlocked for him, and she heard it open and close.

"Hey, all ready?" came his voice from downstairs.

"Oh, sure, yes, I'm ready," she called, and she squared her shoulders for battle.

THREE

Most of the time, Meredith loved Aspen, although there were certainly drawbacks to living here: the high cost of housing, the tourists who filled the town to bursting in the winter and summer seasons. Yet there was nowhere else on earth she could savor city so- phistication that was only five minutes from glorious wilderness. But mostly, she loved the people in Aspen. Old hippies, ski patrolmen who quoted Sartre, sports minded all, healthy and seeking excitement and fun. Young mothers and retired couples, divorcées, tennis stars, movie stars, car racers, pro skiers, rodeo riders. Older, weather-beaten ranchers who could dance a mean two-step. Young professionals who'd chosen to brave the challenges for a lifestyle beyond compare.

Where else could she listen to classical music in a tent in the middle of a mountain meadow and see the graceful shadows of aspen trees through the white can- vas? Where else could she have her pick of great dance, jazz, and blues, homegrown theater, a ride up the Silver Queen gondola in the summer to hear a chamber music quartet play Bach?

Aspen had everything she wanted or needed.

It also had a large number of nouveau riche, who'd arrived to partake of the attractive lifestyle. But she did not belong to this crowd. They made her uncomfortable, with their ostentatious jewelry and face-lifts, the opulence of their houses clinging to Red Mountain above Aspen. They invariably drove Range Rovers and lived on their cell phones. They ran their empires by computer and flew off on a whim in their private Learjets to Palm Beach for golf or cycling in France or shopping in New York. And then their mansions stood empty for months at a time, behemoths tended by cadres of gardeners, house cleaners, plumbers, window washers, and hot tub maintenance crews.

She knew what this party at the Saudi prince's would be like. A crush of people, 200 of the prince's very best friends, some token locals such as Tony and her, uniformed caterers serving gourmet tidbits: dim sum and piles of iced jumbo shrimp, scrumptious pâtés, some ethnic specialties such as falafel and hummus. She was more likely to know the caterer than the guests.

Except for Erik Amundsson. She knew him.

The house Tony drove her to that night could be seen from anywhere in town, perched on the side of Red Mountain. The architect had designed it to look like a cozy mountain cabin but on a colossal scale. It was built of logs and native stone, with huge, soaring ceilings and tree-trunk beams. A two-story plate glass window displayed the view of the town below and the whole of Aspen Mountain across the valley, with its ski runs and gondola that snaked up the face of the mountain, rising 3,000 vertical feet. On the Fourth of

July, on Winterskol in January, during World Cup races, fireworks exploded above the mountain, blooming in splendiferous array over the town. From the prince's aerie across the valley, the display had to be magnificent, the best seats in the house.

She knew all about Prince Kemil's residence; everyone in Aspen did. It had been so massive, with so many bathrooms, the sanitation district had trouble providing enough sewage capacity. The local papers had reported every juicy detail: One Christmas, because of the large number of people staying at the house—including all three of Kemil's wives, it was rumored—the sewage had backed up. "Just too much shit in that big house," the worker bees had snickered.

And then the prince had been forced to pay the city building department $500,000 for exceeding the energy code. A monstrous hot water tank, radiant heating, a snowmelt driveway and sidewalks, too much, too big. But Kemil could afford it.

There were several young men in the prince's driveway to valet park the guests' cars. The house lit up half the mountainside, the double teak doors wide open, music spilling from inside.

The party was in full swing, a sea of people, waiters maneuvering with trays of hors d'oeuvres and champagne circulating through the crowd. A jazz trio in a corner, guests clustered around the open bar. She could see that the bar was accessible to the deck outside, so that in warmer weather the throng could wander inside or outside and barely be inconvenienced.

There was a huge chandelier fashioned of elk antlers hanging in the foyer, faux rustic furniture, priceless Navajo rugs trampled by hundreds of feet, original modern masters on the walls, any one of which she would have given her right arm for, and buffet tables groaning under platters of gorgeously arranged food.

She automatically scanned the partygoers for familiar faces. Yes, there was an old high school friend, now married to a developer. And there was one of her ex-patients. And her father's stockbroker. But mostly, the faces were unfamiliar.

She heard snatches of conversation. One-upsmanship talk of whose private jet was bigger, whose lady friend was being considered for what movie, who had hiked forty-five minutes out to Highland Peak to ski the notoriously avalanche-prone Highlands Bowl that day. The usual Aspen banter.

"Tony," she said, "don't leave me in this crowd."

"I won't. I'd like to find Kemil and introduce you, but I don't see him."

They both took glasses of champagne from a tray. The waiter was young and tan and fit, with pale sunglass marks around his eyes. A skier. He'd work parties at night and ski all day.

She sipped at her champagne and studied the people in the cavernous room. She couldn't see Amundsson. Maybe he wasn't there yet; maybe he wouldn't show at all. Maybe he was in some corner or in another room.

One of Tony's clients waved and came up to them. She'd met him once before, she thought, at a party Tony had taken her to last autumn. Evidently, he was filthy rich.

"Hello, Tony, my man. Great party, isn't it? Kemil knows how to throw one, doesn't he? Hey, have you met my wife Janice?"

Janice was twenty-five years younger than Tony's friend. A trophy wife. Meredith wondered where the discarded ex was.

Tony introduced them. Ollie, the man's name was Ollie, that's right. They chatted a bit. Janice seemed nice enough, but she felt so at odds with the woman's lifestyle; they had nothing in common.

"Listen, Tony, I want you to meet my old friend Jerry. I told you about him. He's here tonight. He's got a lot of money from a business he just sold. You might be able to offer him some possibilities, right?" Ollie was saying.

"Well—"

"Come on, he's over by the bar. It'll just take a sec." Ollie glanced at Meredith, smiling at her with a mouthful of perfectly capped teeth. "You won't mind, will you, Melanie?"

She smiled back. "Meredith."

"Yes, of course, I knew that. Meredith. Sorry. Tony, how about it?" Ollie held his hand around Tony's arm.

"Okay. Meredith, I'll be quick. You don't mind, do you?" A sheepish grin.

"Go on," she said. "I'll be fine."

He left her, Ollie and Janice on either side of him, Ollie's hand still clamped on Tony's biceps. The spoils of war carried off by the victor.

She decided to move around. No sense standing like a stick. She slid a canapé from an offered tray and nibbled at it as she moved toward the plate glass window. She could look out at the night, her back to the party, and no one would bother her.

The view was incredible. The lights were on in town, spangles of bright diamonds crisscrossing the floor of the valley. The background was white, snow covering everything but the ebony ribbons of streets. Shadowed white, every hue from the palest pearl gray to black velvet, a world of chiaroscuro.

And then she noticed just below her, on the deck overlooking the valley, there was a heated swimming pool. An amazing pool, whose outer edge of water slid into space, no walls to hold it in, no walls to obstruct the prince's view when he swam. Where did the water go? Down the side in a shimmering sheet, to be collected somehow and pumped back up? *My God.*

She turned, searching for Tony, wanting to show him the pool, but she didn't see him.

A man approached her, smiling. "Nice view, isn't it?" Friendly, a short man with a generous nose and a bantam rooster's cockiness.

"Yes, it is."

"My name is Dean."

"Meredith."

"Hi, Meredith. Do you live in Aspen?"

"Yes, born and raised here."

"Wow, not many of you around anymore. I'm a part-timer. But I sure love it here. Did you ski today?"

"Unfortunately, I had to work."

"Work, hm, that sucks. The skiing was terrific, spring corn snow. The best." He cocked his head and asked, "Do you know Kemil?"

"Well, not really, but my friend does. And you?"

"Oh sure, we go way back. Skiing, bicycling, climbing."

"He's quite the sportsman, I hear."

"Yeah, he's a nut."

"And you, Dean?"

"I'm a nut, too." He laughed.

She liked Dean. He had an unpretentious way about him.

"Well," he said, "nice talking to you. I think my wife wants me." And he raised a hand, saluted her, and disappeared into the crowd.

Tony. Where was Tony? Was Ollie still holding his upper arm in a vice grip and dragging him around to meet more prospective clients? She craned her neck and stood on tiptoe to see over the heads.

Her eyes scanned the crowd, sweeping across the room, until they stopped short. She blinked, but he was still there. Amundsson, standing quite close, just on the other side of the window.

How could she have missed him? The tallest man in the room, dressed casually in a well-worn blue denim work shirt and black jeans. At odds with the elegantly attired guests but somehow untouchable in his indifference.

He was talking to another man, a thin, intense-looking guy with dark hair. They both had glasses of beer, not champagne, and she studied them for a while, as people swirled back and forth.

Chad Newhouse. That's who the dark one must be. She watched the two men interact, took in their body language, and she had a flash of recall from one of her sessions with Bridget: "God, I adore Chad, you know?" Bridget said. "He's got this dry sense of humor. But, I don't know, he's just *there* an awful lot. Sometimes I think Erik and I will never be alone. I mean, Chad can hardly go to the bathroom without getting the okay from Erik." And Bridget had laughed, an unforgettable, high-pitched laugh that was infectious.

She had told Meredith a lot about the relationship between the men. They had been best friends and climbing partners since Erik had first come to the States from Norway, and they both worked for a local mountaineering outfit called Summit Expeditions.

Bridget had said, "They trust each other. Erik says it's because they have to depend on each other for their lives. Really, I mean you can *die* up there."

Yes, Bridget, I know.

She studied the pair for some time. Chad—if it was Chad—did most of the talking, gesturing with his hands. Erik listened. He was preternaturally still, like a stone. He nodded upon occasion, his eyes deep in their sockets. Raised his beer glass to his lips once, licked foam off his mustache. She could see his Adam's apple move as he swallowed.

Yes, he was as still as an inanimate object, but the arrogance radiated from him, nevertheless. It was as much a part of him as his skin.

She stared and she assessed and she thought, *I should go over there, tell him what I think. It's a perfect opportunity, and Tony isn't around.*

But she didn't move. He fascinated her, the way an unfamiliar object can fascinate. Curiously, she wanted to study Erik Amundsson, to *know* him, to gain a glimmer of why Bridget would have blindly followed this man to her death.

After a time, several people came up to the climbers. Young mountaineering types. Amundsson was their hero; they were in awe of him. She could see their delighted grins and firm handshakes. My God, Amundsson's hand was huge. The better to grip bare rock or haul a fallen climber from a crevasse, she supposed.

He looked at her then, his eyes fixing on her as they had at Bridget's memorial, but this time they rested on her.

Should I do it now? But the moment again slipped away, and she felt awkward standing there alone, staring at the man. She turned to go, to meld into the crowd, but paused when she saw a man approaching Amundsson.

He was young, no more than thirty, dark and very handsome in a saturnine way, black hair, black eyes, a black mustache and goatee. Something exotic about him.

It had to be Prince Kemil.

He greeted Amundsson, shook hands with him, grinned with a flash of white, utterly charming. It was said he had three wives, but they were certainly not in evidence at the party. She wondered about that, a perfectly modern man, but with multiple wives. How did he manage?

Amundsson responded to the prince, the first hint of emotion she had seen him display. He smiled faintly, distantly, still on his lonely mountaintop, but allowing someone else to share it with him for a moment. They spoke, the group that gathered around them listening respectfully, and then the prince left, sallying forth to joust with other worthy knights.

Amundsson reminded her of the alpha male of a wolf pack, alone and revered, a born leader, dangerous and skilled in his profession. Yes, a wolf, with keen, narrow eyes, a powerful leanness, long arms and legs.

And this wolf, too, was dangerous. She wondered if

he'd ever loved Bridget. She doubted it; he could love
nothing but himself and his mountains.

She recalled things Bridget had divulged to her in
therapy sessions. Amundsson had come to the States
from Norway when he was a teenager, looking for adventure. He'd lived in the foothill town of Boulder for
a time, hanging around with the rock climbers the city
was noted for. Then he'd moved to Aspen, surrounded
by fifty-four 14,000 footers, where the challenges
loomed close over him.

He'd told Bridget he could trace his ancestors back
to ninth-century Vikings. He had even recited Norse
poetry to her. At the time, Meredith had wondered if
his recitations were a come-on or if he were truly a
romantic at heart.

He was listening to another climber now, his head
bent slightly to the shorter man. She observed, trying
to fathom him, but she couldn't. He was a cipher.

She would not lie to herself. There was a primitive
magnetism to the man. That arrogance, the strength in
the ropy muscles, the far gaze. She could feel it even
from a distance.

She sipped at her champagne and eyed this man
among men. And there it was again, his lingering
glance at her, his blue eyes touching her, resting on
her light as a feather for a heartbeat.

Now, she thought. *Now, in front of his hero wor-
shipers.* But still she didn't move.

Her skin crawled, the hair raised on the back of her
neck. He was looking at her again. She was not used
to men staring at her. She was nice looking, not flashy.
She had great eyes, pale green and dark-lashed, and
good cheekbones. But Amundsson's gaze was like an

unwanted caress, an insult. Damn him. Did he recognize her from Bridget's memorial? Did he read the interest in her expression? Maybe he was even toying with her.

Where was Tony? Suddenly she wanted Tony's familiar comfort. What was she thinking, confronting an utter stranger at a party? Lowering herself to his level. She was disgusted with herself, with the whole stupid idea. Meredith Greene as the avenging angel. What crap.

She put her empty champagne flute on a tray held by a passing waiter, and she turned to go. She'd find Tony and ask him to take her home. She'd find Tony and—

There was a hand on her arm, stopping her. She pivoted, thinking it was Tony, starting to say something to him, but the words never reached her lips. The hand belonged to Erik Amundsson, a large, hard hand that was missing two fingers. She looked down, her heart banging against her ribs, at the hand, then moved her eyes up to meet his—wintry blue under sandy brows. Knowing eyes, farseeing and clear. Seeing right through her.

"Let's get out of here," he said.

She looked at him, looked back at the hand wrapped around her arm, then she laughed, a false laugh of disdain. "I'm sorry, but I really don't—"

"Look," he cut in, "you want to talk. This isn't the place."

"I want to *what?*"

His hand remained, strong, warm. Too warm. "I never figured you for a liar," he said.

There was no insult in his words, only information,

but she was confused. He never figured her for a liar? But he didn't even know her.

"You have something to say to me," he went on, "so let's go. You have a coat." It was not a question.

She was about to refuse, to ask him if he was crazy, she wasn't going anywhere with him. Instead, she made a decision of pure impulse, and an instant fierce flame of commitment made her say yes. He led her toward the front entrance. Her feet moved; there was no turning back now.

Her coat appeared magically, as if he knew exactly which one she'd worn. Then he suggested she make her excuses to the man she'd come with, embarrassing her because she hadn't thought of it, and he waited by the front door while she found Tony.

"Meredith, hi, listen, this is Bill Thomas, he's putting together that development next to the market in Basalt and . . ."

She shook hands with Thomas, nodded, smiled, said the requisite things. Her arm burned where Erik had gripped her, and she was jumping with impatience to be away.

It took a minute or two to get Tony aside to explain she had a ride into downtown, where she'd pick up her car at the office. She'd need it over the weekend, anyway. "I'm awfully tired," she said, "I'll phone you tomorrow. Okay?"

"Look, I can go right now," he began, but she insisted he stay and schmooze. She smiled, kissed his cheek, and saw Erik's face.

By the time her coat was on and the cold night air struck her cheeks, she'd forgotten entirely how she'd gotten out of there and even exactly what she'd said to Tony.

They waited together in the cold night as a young man fetched Erik's Jeep. She tried to think of something to say, but nothing came to mind. Why didn't she get her questions off her chest? But the words wouldn't form in her brain; it was as if she'd forgotten the skill of speech.

She was acutely aware of him next to her, tall and broad, a blue fleece vest over his shirt. She was shivering, but he seemed oblivious to the elements.

When his car came, he didn't open her door. She got in by herself, not surprised, not wondering. The moves were being called by something beyond her, beyond them both.

"Cold?" he asked.

"A little."

"Takes a few minutes for the heat to come up." He had a faint Norwegian accent, a mere lilt in his pronunciation of certain words. His voice was a deep baritone, smooth and sure.

She finally dared verbalize one question that was ricocheting around in her brain. "Why did you think I wanted to talk to you?"

"The way you were looking at me." His attention was on the road ahead.

"Do you know who I am?"

"Yes." He gave her a sidelong glance. "Just as you know me."

Bridget. Bridget was the link. Why didn't she confront him now? But the time was wrong.

What am I doing here? she thought in a lucid moment. *Curiosity, that's it.*

Liar.

He drove, and once he put his hand proprietarily on her knee for a second. It was his right hand, the whole one. She stared at it, then at his profile.

She almost told him to stop the Jeep and let her out. Instead, she sat rigid, gazing unfocused at the road, her heart pumping. She was appalled at herself, and yet she was unable to stop, as if her path were ordained.

FOUR

The Red Mountain Road snaked down to the river, then rose again into the core of Aspen. She assumed he'd park somewhere on Mill or Galena or Hopkins, and they'd walk to a quiet bar and talk.

That would be her opportunity to fling her questions at him, when he wasn't expecting them. But she had a feeling Erik Amundsson's defenses were never down, and the words she had framed in her mind over the last seven months were jumbled, and she couldn't concentrate on anything but the lingering heat on her arm.

He turned west onto Bleeker Street before they'd even crossed Main. She thought, the Hotel Jerome Bar. Sure. That's where they were headed, but he drove behind the hotel and directly into the West End residential section of town, where stately cottonwoods lined the old streets and shaded the Victorians built by silver barons in Aspen's boomtown days.

On Lake Avenue, he pulled into an alley, parked, and killed the engine.

She didn't ask where they were.

"I rent a garage apartment here," he said, nodding

toward a detached three-car garage that sat perpendic-
ular to a graceful Victorian mansion.

Still, she said nothing. A thought flamed through her
mind, *I must be crazy,* but it was quickly extinguished.

This time he opened her door for her, swung it out
on its mud-caked hinges, and helped her down onto
the pavement alongside the garage. Her brain must
have been severed from her body. She allowed herself
to be steered to a set of steps that led up to a door on
the side of the garage: Erik's apartment. She didn't
even know him. Had not spoken more than a dozen
words to this man, and she was allowing him to take
her to his home.

Halfway up the steps, she paused, her breath coming
quickly. A voice in her head cried out to regain control
of the situation, to make him take her to a public place
where she'd be safe.

"Afraid?" she heard him ask.

"Of course not," she replied, challenged, and her feet
took her up.

She had no idea what to expect when he unlocked
his door and pushed it inward. What met her eyes surprised her. Everywhere she glanced, from the hall to
the alcove serving as a kitchen to the spacious living
room and beyond to what must have been a bedroom,
was climbing gear. Mountains of it. There were spread
out maps, and rolled up nylon tents and sleeping bags
and camp stoves. There were colorful parkas and vests
and gloves and boots and backpacks. Ice axes, crampons, pitons, orange nylon ropes coiled like snakes,
carabiners, goggles, skis.

"Oh," she said.

"Yeah," he said. "The tools of my profession."

"Oh," she said again.

"I have beer or red wine."

"Ah, wine, please."

"I'll get you some."

But he didn't move. He simply looked at her until she couldn't breathe, his eyes glacial blue, so sharp and clear she was mesmerized, a doe caught in headlights.

Then he helped her with her coat, coming around behind her as she slipped it off her arms. She could feel his breath on her neck. She didn't move; neither did he. The universe narrowed to his scent, his exhalations that tickled the fine hairs on her skin. Her breast rising and falling, the drumbeat of her heart.

Eventually, he went to find two glasses and the wine. She embraced the reprieve, trying to collect herself. It was no good. Her head filled with images of Erik hauling the gear up snowy slopes to the craggy heavens. Had that bright blue parka been atop Mount Everest?

There was a unique smell to his lair. Not a single odor but a combination. There was woodsmoke and camping fuel and man sweat and something exotic, something foreign like a spice that she couldn't quite decipher. Tea? Jasmine or smoky Lapsang souchong?

What *was* she doing here?

Bridget, yes, she was here to confront this egotistical *god* about his role in her patient's death. She clung desperately to the thought.

Then he was back, handing her the wine. He didn't offer to clear the cluttered couch so she could sit. He merely stared at her till her flesh rose in bumps, and then he clinked his glass to hers.

"To you, Meredith," he said, pinioning her with his eyes, and he drank.

She sipped. She sipped carefully, and she thought, of course, he'd known all along who she was and exactly what she wanted to say to him.

Then he stole her thunder. "To answer your question," he said, so matter-of-factly she gasped, "Bridget slipped on an ice chute. When you challenge the mountains, it can happen. It was an accident."

She started to say something, then cleared her throat and spoke again. "Accidents are avoidable."

"Sometimes they are."

"But not that time?"

"No, not that time." He met her look unflinchingly, unapologetically.

"And that's all you have to say about it?"

"Yes."

She couldn't believe it. All these long months and weeks and hours with the questions beating at her, and that was it? Bridget slipped and died and it was an accident?

My God, he was just like her father. What was it about these men that made them refuse to accept responsibility?

"Bridget pointed you out to me last summer. Were you aware of that?"

"No, she never mentioned it."

"I suppose this will shock you," he went on, "but the minute I first saw you, I wanted you."

It took time for his statement to sink in. She couldn't find a thing to say. Not a word.

"We belong together."

"You don't even know me."

"I know you," he said, then he reached out and took her glass and set it along with his on a bookshelf. Her mind was frozen, and her body began to shake, to tremble with a mixture of fear and shock and a wild, animal need that she did not recognize.

Panic assaulted her suddenly. She had to get away from this strange man who read her mind and controlled her thoughts. She moved aside, but he moved with her and held her arms, his eyes devouring her.

He spoke, soft words that rumbled in his chest, the way you'd calm a frightened horse. "You're trembling. Don't be afraid. It was only a matter of time until we were together. I won't hurt you, Meredith. I will worship you, if you let me."

And he began to kiss her.

She pulled back, terrified, her eyes meeting his, pleading, telling him, begging him not to do this. But he kissed her again, this time thoroughly, and she sagged shamelessly into his arms and felt hot stabs of desire pierce her body, her very core, her soul. She felt her control peel away like dead skin. She was open, vulnerable, and the risk she took gave her a power she'd never experienced. She opened like a flower.

No man had ever fully undressed her. And certainly not standing awash in lamplight in the middle of a living room.

She let him strip her clothes away, piece by slow piece, until dress and bra and panties lay in a sighing heap at her feet. He stripped her and touched her reverently and looked on her nakedness as if she were a goddess. His words were soft and coaxing, and his tone became low and gravelly with need.

She trembled. *Oh God,* she could hear her inner voice cry, *what's happening to me? What's happening?* But she didn't stop him.

He eased her onto the floor, cushioning her hips and shoulders with down parkas and fleece jackets. He did all this slowly and methodically, while she shook uncontrollably.

He handled her with infinite consideration, touched her as if he knew her body more intimately than she did. He kneeled, fully clothed, beside her and bent his head to her breasts while ripples of desire spread in her womb. She moaned. Frightening herself. Trying to hate him. Wanting as she'd never wanted before.

He pulled back and kissed her again. His beard felt scratchy, different from Tony, she thought, then all was chased from her head. He ran a hand through her hair, caressing it, his eyes still on her, not letting her escape or retreat for a moment. She was there with him, feeling as he felt. Down her neck, fingers trailing delight, his lips at the hollow of her throat. Her pulse beat against his lips, his mustache brushed her skin, tingling, gentle. She was suffused with wonder at the sensations, brand-new. She thought once, *This is how it is supposed to be. I didn't know.*

When she believed she could stand no more, he found another spot on her body with his mouth and drove her beyond the horizon of craving until she cried out for release, which he brought her to with his disfigured hand.

He allowed her no time for rest but shed his clothes and pulled her hips up to meet him. He was long and lean and hard-muscled, gentle and firm, yielding and demanding. She'd never had multiple orgasms, had always known she was too mentally controlled to let go to that extent. But that was before tonight, before Erik. Another lifetime.

The heat built in her as his fingers bit into the flesh of her hips in rhythm with his thrusting. The heat became a delicious pain and then he stopped, pulled out, and savaged her breasts with his mouth until she was insane with longing.

Over and over, he brought her to the edge of release, then skillfully denied her, then took her to the brink once more until they cried out together on the floor of his living room amid the accoutrements of his profession.

In his bedroom he put his head to her belly, then lowered it slowly. She tugged at his hair frantically until his mouth found her, and again she was lost, shamed and lost and joyously rising on a new tide. Panting and crying out.

He possessed her in manners she had barely imagined. He made her laugh and once she cried and many times she held his head to her as he took her on an odyssey of raw pleasure. Shame melted in the heat of her newfound passion.

"God, I want you," he said again and again. "I'll never let you go. Kiss me, Meredith, yes, kiss me there."

Afterward, they lay on his bed, body to body, his long, hard length against her. She ran a hand over his chest, surprisingly smooth and hairless. Like satin. She took his hands between hers and kissed each finger, kissed the scars where the last two fingers of his left hand were missing. He held her and kissed the top of her head, and she felt that anything this good had to be right. She'd been asleep all her life, and he'd awakened her. He's kissed her awake.

• • •

At dawn, passion-bruised and weak, she stumbled into the shower. Beneath the hot, stinging spray she leaned against the tiles and wept. How could she have done this? *How?*

Then the curtain was drawn aside, and he was there.

"No, no," she pleaded, even as he stepped in and drew the curtain closed again. "Please, no, Erik, you don't understand."

"I think I do," he said, and he forced her into his arms, held her, and stroked her wet hair for an eternity. Finally he kissed her. Kissed her brow and eyelids and her mouth. He kissed her breasts, licking the hot water from them. He kissed her belly and held her buttocks in his callused hands. Then he straightened and lifted her in his arms, her legs wrapped around his sharp-boned hips, and he pressed himself into her, over and over until there was nothing but sensation.

FIVE

She walked the few blocks to where her car was still parked at her office and drove home, her head buzzing with exhaustion and a plethora of questions. Her stomach churned with guilt and shame, yet conversely, she was filled with rapture. How was that possible? How could she have done those things with a stranger simply because he'd asked her to? No, because he had *told* her to.

Her mind could not accommodate itself to the reality of her behavior. It hadn't been her, that woman in her skin.

She took the Woody Creek Road, deserted this early on a Saturday morning, looking at her hands on the steering wheel and remembering the feel of Erik's skin, the slight roughness of the down on his arms and legs, his chest, that had only a sprinkling of fine blond hairs. Her entire body was flushed from his beard; he'd possessed every inch of her.

Suddenly she realized she'd let her car drift over the center line of the winding road, and she jerked the wheel to the right. *My God*, she thought, *I'm really losing it*. She anxiously checked the road ahead and the rearview mirror. Had anyone witnessed her lapse?

But no, the way was clear, and behind her there was only one car, pretty far back, a dark SUV. Someone else returning to the fold after an all-nighter?

When she arrived home, she unlocked the door to her town house and stood, keys in hand, staring at the living room. She saw the place with new eyes. Neat, lots of books in shelves, a tidy stack of magazines on the coffee table. Plain blond furniture, a green sofa she'd purchased at the high-end secondhand shop in town, her kitchen just beyond, with white-painted cabinets, the walls white, a green-striped ceramic bowl filled with fruit on the counter. A couple of forgettably tasteful mountain prints hung on the walls. And she wondered at the woman who lived here, in this too-tidy environment.

The only real color was the green sofa and four throw pillows in red and green plaid, two at each end of the couch, positioned precisely.

A motel room, an office reception area, a generic place. Not a home.

And, oddly, no longer a sign of Tony in the entire place.

What would Erik think of her home? It was so different from his, which was only a room to sleep and store equipment. A camp, his apartment was a camp.

She stood there and saw her place for the first time, and then she again became acutely aware of Erik's scent that still clung to her black dress, her hair, her skin. Her pores were filled with his essence.

She tried breathing deeply. It was no good; she was awash with the memories of the man. Worse, she wanted him still. If he were to walk in the door, she knew she'd cling to him, draw him so deeply into her their bodies would fuse.

She sat on one of the three blond wood barstools at the counter separating the kitchen and living room, chin in hand, shoes kicked off. She was spent. Completely exhausted from the endless night of passion. And sore. My God, so this was what it felt like, every muscle and nerve battered, a dull ache between her legs, a distinct rawness. She was empty inside, hadn't eaten a bite since Kemil's party, the couple of canapés she taken from silver trays. Yet she wasn't hungry. Her stomach was too queasy, her nerves jangling against the walls of her belly. And lurking behind it all, behind the soreness, the tiredness, the twitching nerve endings, there was that secret thrill for what she'd experienced.

She wouldn't delude herself; she was full of lust for Erik Amundsson.

With no gap in thought, she remembered that day in her office, Bridget sitting across from her. It was July, yes, July third, she knew, because the town parade and fireworks were the next day, and amazingly, it was snowing out, big, wet, cold snowflakes leaking out of a leaden sky. She was listening to Bridget, but somewhere in her mind was the notion that she needed to get home soon and shake the heavy wet stuff from the branches on the apple tree she'd just planted. A freak midsummer storm . . .

"So, Bridget, I'd like to be clear on this. You tell me you love Erik, and that he loves you."

"Oh, yes, this is the real thing."

"Is being in love the same to you as loving someone? For example, I love my sister, but I am not *in* love with her. Do you see where I'm going with this?"

"Yes. And I am in love. One hundred percent."

"And Erik?"

Bridget paused. Did Meredith detect a cloud crossing her face? "He never actually says, you know, 'I'm in love with you,' but he does tell me he loves me, especially, well, when we're in bed."

"I see. And other times?"

"Um, I think he has." Bridget studied her fingernails. "The truth is, he's pretty reserved, you know, he doesn't talk a lot about his feelings. It's a Scandinavian thing, you know."

"Of course. But today you started our session by telling me a woman confronted you at a nightspot last week and told you Erik was seeing her. You said you were upset."

"You're damn tootin' I was upset. I still am."

"Go on."

"Well, Erik says it's nothing, that the woman hangs out with Chad Newhouse and some of the other local climbers, you know, a groupie, but Erik told me she came on to him and not the other way around."

"So there was no relationship?"

Bridget shook her head. "I believe him."

"But you're still upset."

"Sure. I mean, women are always trying to get his attention. I know he's seen a couple of them in the past. He's human, after all. But those were flings. A man like Erik, well, he lives on the edge. His blood runs pretty hot. But I can tell, I really can, he loves me. It isn't just bullshit."

Meredith nodded. But, as always, she wondered about the great Erik Amundsson. How sincere was he?

And she'd thought, as the snow piled up outside, *Is it love or is it pure physical need?*

She looked down at her toes now and wiggled them. Even her toes were ultrasensitive. But then Erik had also made love to her there.

She couldn't help an inadvertent smile then, remembering, still feeling his mouth on her ankle, her feet, the roughness of his beard, scratching and tickling until she'd laughed and squirmed and begged him to stop. He'd stopped, eventually, and pulled his hard length up alongside her and raised her to a sitting position and taught her yet a new way to make love.

The smile on her lips broadened. For all the mortification she was feeling, for all that secret delight, she had to acknowledge that he'd awakened something inside her, permitted her to experience for the first time true abandonment, a release of her iron control.

How bizarre. Erik Amundsson had allowed her to let loose her wild side. The very man who had ruined the past eight months of her life, caused her sleepless nights and professional doubts, and destroyed her relationship with Tony.

The smile dropped from her lips. *Tony.* He'd seen her leave with Amundsson last night. Of course he had. He would have every right in the world to be furious with her, walking out on him like that, *ditching* him, for God's sake, like some high school girl on the prowl.

Then she remembered how she had felt in January when he'd slept with that woman. It had hurt, damn it, even though she and Tony weren't really a couple anymore. It had still hurt like hell, and she'd just done exactly the same thing to him.

She didn't have to torture herself for long, because

her doorbell rang shortly, and before she could even react, Tony opened the unlocked door and came in.

"Jesus, Meredith," he breathed, "where in hell . . . ?"

He looked at her. His eyes moved from her swollen lips to her wrinkled dress, her shoes kicked aside haphazardly, and back to her face. His mouth formed a tight line.

She swallowed. *The truth,* she thought, *tell him the truth.*

"Well?" he said. "You know I saw you leave with him. So don't bother to—"

"Look," she began, and she had to lick dry lips. "Yes, I did leave with Erik."

"Christ almighty."

"But, I . . . That is, *we* went into town. We talked."

"Till eight A.M.?"

"Well, no, of course not, we . . . that is, *I* picked up my car and drove to the ranch."

"You what? Come on, Meredith, give me some fucking credit here."

With great effort, she met his stare. She'd never lied in her life before—okay, little white lies, she'd told plenty of them—but this was a whopper.

"We talked about Bridget." That, at least, was the truth. "And then, I guess I was upset. I just wanted to drive around. I ended up downvalley, and it was late, and I went to the ranch." She was making the story up as she went along. It was a ridiculous fib but . . .

"And you slept there?" His tone dripped skepticism.

"Yes. In my old bedroom. You know, up on the second floor." *Oh, God.* She cringed inwardly, waiting, waiting for what seemed an eternity, for him to throw the fabrication back in her face.

He didn't speak though, and time stretched out in turgid seconds that piled up in her belly until she was sure she'd be sick.

"Well? Say something," she finally blurted out.

"What do you want me to say? That you look like hell?"

"Thanks."

"I mean it. Your face is all puffy."

"I'm sure it is. I was crying."

"With Amundsson?"

"Why are you giving me the third degree? I told you what happened," she said.

"I'm questioning the whole damn thing because I know about Amundsson, and I sat up half the goddamn night trying not to picture you with that arrogant son of a bitch."

She could have said, "Like I was up all night last January when you slept with that bimbo?" But she couldn't choke the words out.

Instead, she said, "Tony, we're not engaged. We're not even going together anymore. You really have no right—"

His hand slashed the air. "You made a fool of me. Jesus Christ, Meredith, everyone saw—"

"So *that's* what's really bothering you."

"You were my date last night."

"I'm sorry," she murmured. And she was. She felt bad for him, but inside her, a voice clamored to be heard. And it said, *I'm not sorry. I loved every minute. I gloried in them. I came alive. For the first time in my life, I was truly alive.*

"Okay, okay. Maybe I overreacted."

No, you didn't, she thought. Then she felt like a

whore. Worse, because at least a whore went about her work honestly.

She studied her toes again and wondered why she hadn't told him the truth in the first place. The truth was difficult to cough up, okay, but in the end, a lie caught in the throat and just grew and grew until it choked you. No wonder she'd always been so honest. Of course, it was never too late.

She looked up. "Tony, listen," she began, but his expression had softened, and she chickened out and let the moment slip away.

He took a step toward her. "Hey, this is stupid, right? Why don't we kiss and make up?"

Surprising her, a ripple of distaste ran along her spine. She eased off the stool. "Look, I really have to—"

But he moved closer, and before she could stop him, his hands were on her back, his fingers spread, kneading, the fabric of her dress, abrasive on her skin.

A bubble of panic rose in her. "Tony," she said.

"What?"

"I have to . . . I've got, oh God, that's right, I have equine therapy in an hour."

He kept his hands on her back. Swore softly. "You have a few minutes."

"No, I have to get a bath, get my riding stuff. Tony . . . really."

Finally, mercifully, his hands released her, and she felt her flesh shrink.

Somehow, she got him to leave. Somehow, she managed to swallow all the lies and to climb into a hot tub—her second bath that morning. The first, she recalled with acute clarity, had been interrupted.

She washed her hair again and soaped herself all

over, feeling the soreness lightly. She knew then, knew irrevocably with both wonder and fear, that she would never want a man to touch her again unless it was Erik.

She turned up the Greene Ranch driveway, not even recalling how she'd arrived there. She'd driven the thirty miles from Aspen countless times, but never before had she spaced out the entire trip. *My God,* she thought, a little frightened, a little bewitched, remembering, her mind again consumed by images and sensations and Erik's face, his hands, his mouth . . .

The long driveway was so familiar; she knew every pothole, every fence post. The ranch house nestled in its copse of staid cottonwoods, the weathered barn squatted with its tall double doors open and today, as on every Saturday when the weather was good, several cars were pulled up near the barn.

Her equine therapy patients.

Okay, she promised herself, *I won't think about him. Not anymore. Not until I'm done here.*

She parked and got out of her Subaru. It was chilly, the sky blue. Here at the ranch all the snow was melted because it was a couple thousand feet lower in altitude than Aspen. It was generally warmer, too, with summers that were downright hot. But now in April it was still cool, and she'd worn a fleece jacket over her turtleneck.

She knew she should go into the house first and say hi to her dad, but she didn't want to. Goddamn it, she just didn't want to. He would probably stop by the ring while she was working with her patients, and she'd say hello then, tell him she'd been late and hadn't had time.

Excuses, oh yes, she might not be good with lies, but she was a champ at excuses.

Two patients were already waiting for her, Terry and Sean, and their parents, whom Meredith had trained as side walkers, the people who stayed alongside the horse, a hand on the rider's leg for safety. The other parent led the specially trained horse while she put the patients through their exercises.

"Hi, Meredith!" Terry said, a darling ten-year-old girl with cerebral palsy.

"Sorry I'm late," Meredith said.

"No problem," Terry's father said.

"Can I ride Pace?" Sean asked. He was six, a thin, intense boy who had mild developmental disability from a premature birth.

"Sure. Let me get your buddy Pace for you, kids, and we'll get going in a jiffy."

All the way out across the field to fetch the horse, she fought to concentrate on the job at hand. She tried to go over the exercises she'd have the kids do, but her brain refused to cooperate. Her mind turned on her, flashing scenes from last night like a strobe light before her eyes. Erik, his skin so pale, his strong, corded neck, his powerful wrists, his voice, the feel of his mouth on her everywhere.

What was he doing now? Was he planning a new climb? Had he gone out to breakfast? Was he with friends?

She had no idea. They had come together in a world of their own, completely isolated, insulated from the rest of their lives, and she knew nothing about Erik, about his existence apart from her.

It occurred to her that she knew exactly what Tony

was doing. She knew him inside and out, his likes and dislikes in food and clothes and movies and books. She could predict his behavior.

But Erik—he was a cipher, a mystery. Unknowable but for the passion he exhibited. Oh yes, the passion for *her*. She didn't question that, and a kind of wonder suffused her. *Why her?* When he could have his pick of dozens of gorgeous young women, why had Erik Amundsson chosen *her?*

She walked through the still-brown sage and rabbit brush to get Pace, her mind betraying her with memories of the night before. Her skin felt supersensitive, and a warm ache began between her legs. *No,* she told herself, *not now.* But it was there, lurking, waiting, and every moment of weakness allowed it to spread its yearning heat.

It seemed to her as if that delicious pain inside her would take over her whole body if she let down her guard, that it would swell and throb until she was encompassed by it, and then it would enlarge, covering her with acute sensation, until everything she touched or smelled or ate would be part of her, connected to her core. Open to every sensation as if she were newborn, the world around her fresh as well.

She caught Pace, a gentle bay gelding, who'd been trained for equine therapy. She buckled the halter over his head and scratched behind his ears and murmured a greeting to him, began to lead him to the barn. And all the time, her mind churned with questions: Did Erik like horses? Did he know about the Greene Ranch? What did he do in his spare time? How about his family? Did he have siblings?

My God, she knew nothing about him.

She brushed Pace off, tacked him up with a special saddle that was deeper and had more hand-holds than a normal one while Terry and Sean waited impatiently. They both loved to ride; they would have come all winter if Meredith let them; Saturdays at the ranch were the high points of their lives.

For kids, equine therapy was simply fun. They had no concept of the actual process itself, no idea of the way a horse's movement mimicked the movement of the human pelvis when walking. They just loved to ride.

Sean had taken his first steps after a therapy session; Terry had spoken her first word after one. Meredith was incredibly rewarded by her patients' improvement, and she adored the kids.

But today she was distracted.

She put the children through their routines, walked next to Pace, a hand on the rider's leg, as she directed the child in sets of exercises. "Sit up straight, Terry, that's it. Arms out, now down, now up again. And let's turn to one side, that's a girl, now backward. Oh, yes, Pace is a good boy, isn't he? And the other side. Well done, Terry. And twist to the right. And the left. Arms out. Good girl."

Pace walked around the ring calmly and steadily, giving the kids constant sensory feedback, forcing them to improve their balance, motivating them to reach beyond their limits.

She worked with Terry and Sean; she complimented them, hugged them, spoke to their parents, made plans for the following Saturday, fed Pace his ration of grain, and delivered him back to his home field. And all the time, the questions still posed themselves in her head.

Where was Erik now? What was he doing? Was he thinking about her? Was he as consumed with her as she was with him? Would he call her today? Had he already phoned and left a message on her machine? Would she let herself into her town house and find her message light blinking?

Her father came into the barn as she was finishing up cleaning the tack.

"Hi there, Merry." He'd always called her that. For a time, when she'd been younger, she'd refused to respond to the nickname, but she'd given up in later years.

"Hi, Dad."

"Did the therapy go well today?"

"Um, sure, just fine." They were polite to each other, always polite, but there was a distance between them. A carefully structured distance built up over two decades. A structure of guilt on her father's side and resentment on hers. A wall too high, too thick to cross except in banality and vaguely discerned duty.

"Can you stay for dinner?" Neil asked.

"Uh, gosh, I can't. I've got to get back."

"I see."

"Sorry. Maybe next week, okay?"

"I just spoke to Ann on the phone. She's going to try to drive up with the kids in a couple weeks."

"Hey, that's great. Let me know. Gosh, we haven't seen her and the kids since Christmas, have we?"

"No, we haven't."

She put the saddle back on its stand and rubbed her hands on her jeans. She felt her shoulders hunching with tension and tried to relax them.

"Well, good to see you, Merry," her dad said, and she sensed the disappointment in his voice, another disappointment in the long string she'd delivered to him. Did she feel the familiar satisfaction at her power to wound him? *How ugly,* she thought.

She drove back to Aspen that afternoon in a state of heart-pounding anticipation, the way she'd felt as a small child on Christmas morning when she'd awakened to the possibilities of marvels to come, of wonderful gifts and joy and happiness.

She drove along Highway 82, past El Jebel and Basalt, past ranches and posh new developments, past Old Snowmass with its general store and gas station. She didn't see the way the road followed the river valley or the mountains that rose on either side of her, brownish gray and bare on the southern exposures, still snow-covered on the north.

She noted none of this, not even the willow trees leafing out in pale chartreuse along the riverbanks. She was impatient to get home, to rush across her living room to the answering machine that sat on a small table near the stairs, to the blinking light, to Erik's voice.

She had so many things to ask him. She'd start with the little ones first: likes and dislikes in food and TV and then questions about climbing and where he was going next and his family. Yes, parents and brothers and sisters. And where he came from in Norway. All the details that made up a human being. They'd lie in bed together, and his hands would stroke her bare skin or just rest on her hip or belly or knee, and they'd exchange information. She wanted to know all about him with a voracious appetite.

And then . . . later, when it felt right, she'd ask him again about Bridget, about what had really happened, about his other climbs and Mount Aconcagua and how it felt to be so close to death and how he could face it time after time after time.

She craved knowledge of every facet of Erik Amundsson, as if she could hold him inside her brain as her body had held his flesh inside hers.

Possession. Fierce, obsessive ownership. *Yes.*

And she would tell him everything about herself, bare it all, the good and the bad. She'd tell him about her chocolate habit, and how she laughed loudest at her own jokes. She'd even tell him about her mother's death, about having to grow up so quickly, about raising Ann practically all by herself and her polite despising of her father, the ugliness she exhibited but was unable to control. Then Erik would own her, too, every cell and molecule.

She turned off the highway at Woody Creek and followed the winding road to her town house complex.

She pushed open her door and rushed across the room, precisely, exactly as she'd imagined all day.

She knew there would be a message from Erik. She knew it. How could there not be?

She reached the table, the answering machine sitting on it with impersonal but supreme dominion. Her heart was pounding. She could hear Erik's voice, tinny but unmistakably his. Saying . . . *asking* her to do something with him tonight. Our maybe not asking her to do anything except get together. Together . . .

The light on her machine was not blinking. She drew back and squeezed her eyes shut and looked again. The red light stared back at her with a baleful eye.

No, she thought, *impossible.*

But there was no message from Erik, and she did not realize then the suffering she would endure.

SIX

By seven that night, she had practically worn a path in the carpet of her living room. When the phone finally rang, she snatched the receiver up so quickly, she dropped it on the floor then thought, *What if it's broken, what if . . . ?*

It was not Erik on the line.

"Jesus," her high school friend Darlene said, "I think I just went deaf. Meredith, are you there?"

"Yes, oh wow, sorry, sorry, I . . . Oh, never mind. What's up?" Disappointment bludgeoned her.

"I haven't seen you for weeks, just thought I'd call. What have you been doing?"

"Oh, you know, just busy."

"Want to catch a movie?"

"A movie?"

"You know, those pictures on a big screen?"

"Tonight?"

"Of course. The Isis has nine o'clock shows. But if you're hung up . . ."

She made a split-second decision. "Sure. Yes, I'd love to. Want me to pick you up?"

"Great, yeah, I'll be out front at say, quarter to nine.
Should be plenty of time to make the show. I'm still
on Eighth Street, you know."

"I know where you live. See you at quarter to."

The minute she was out the door, pangs of anxiety
assaulted her. What if he called? What if he called and
she wasn't home, and then he gave up and never called
again?

She ate too much greasy popcorn and then topped
off the binge with an entire family-sized Hershey bar.
By the time the movie let out, she was sick to her
stomach.

"You look green, Greene," Darlene said when Meredith dropped her at home.

"Ha, ha."

"No, seriously, you do look kind of done in. You
feel okay?"

"I feel great," Meredith said. *Another lie?* "Let's do
a movie again soon. Okay? I hardly ever see you anymore."

"I'd love to. Now that I'm between men, I've got
nothing but time. And maybe we could go camping
when it warms up enough."

"Yes, like in mid-June. But I'd love to, really. We'll
plan on it."

She drove home, still nauseous, her nerves scratching under her skin. She just knew he had called. And
maybe this was good, really, she decided, because she
didn't want him to think she was staying home waiting
for him. Or was that the little insecure girl in her talking? Why shouldn't he know exactly how she felt?

Oh, God, this was driving her nuts.

There was no message from Erik; nor was there one
on Sunday or Monday.

She should have been too busy to notice. Off-season
was upon the resort town, and everyone who hadn't
already headed south to warmer climes was getting
ready to leave. Hair and nail appointments were impossible to book. And, she had learned, her own sched-
ule was full as well. For a lot of her clients, getting
their heads straight after the long, stressful winter was
as important as a manicure before racing outta here, as
the locals all said.

Nevertheless, on Monday, the minutes ticked by
with agonizing slowness.

And no call from *him.*

She was ready to lock the office at five when the
phone rang for the tenth time that day. *This* had to be
Erik. It had to be. "My name is McCord, John Mc-
Cord," the male voice said. "I was hoping to get an
appointment."

She scheduled him for the next day, on her lunch
hour, because every other time slot was filled. He'd
said he was depressed, and the one thing that was too
dangerous to put off was depression.

Tuesday morning, after another night of tossing and
turning and punching her pillow, she saw three patients
before John McCord arrived at noon and sat in her
outer office, doing the requisite paperwork.

"I'll be back in a minute," she told him, and he
smiled and nodded.

In the inner sanctum of her office, she sat and let
out a breath, straightened her shoulders, and ran her
hands through her hair. She had to pull herself together. Three practically sleepless nights, and she was

barely able to function, much less treat her patients properly. This wasn't fair to them. It wasn't fair to *her,* damn it.

Though most of Meredith's patients were women or children, she had treated a number of men over the years. She admitted to herself she'd much rather deal with females; in her experience, it could be difficult for men to discuss their emotions. She likened the process to peeling away layers, as on an onion, until she and the patient reached the core. With women, the process was simply easier.

Now, get your act together and concentrate, she told herself when she led him into her office and showed him the overstuffed chair across from hers.

John McCord was a man of slightly above-average height, attractive in an atypical way. His face was not quite symmetrical, as if his generous nose had been broken once, and his short brown hair ran down to a devil's point in the center of his forehead. All in all, his was an arresting face, no one feature standing out, but together they created a comfortable harmony of line and plane.

She looked at the form he'd filled out. Thirty-eight years old. And he was depressed.

"May I call you John?" she began.

"Sure," he said.

"And I'm Meredith."

"All right, Meredith."

She smiled. "Before we begin, can I ask where you got my name from?"

"Yellow Pages."

"Okay," she said, setting the information down on a notepad.

She rarely took notes during a session, as frequently the client became edgy if not alarmed, as if she were scribbling *crazy* or something. Usually she jotted down details when the patient was gone. After the last two days, though, she found herself having to depend on her notes more and more often during the sessions.

Not good.

And she thought, *Goddamn that Erik Amundsson.*

"Can we talk about your depression, John?" she started in.

"Why not?"

"Are you familiar with the terms *clinical depression* and *situational depression?*"

He shrugged.

They spent the hour deciding that he was suffering from situational depression due to a recent divorce. She had to take more notes than she would have preferred. He sat in his casual brown cords, a blue denim shirt, and navy V-neck sweater, slouched, hands in pockets, and she scribbled pertinent details such as: "Born New Jersey, 4 years Georgetown U., married 16 years, ex-wife Renee, son Jack 14, depressed over loss of family, moved Aspen Feb., does business over Internet, lonely? Suicidal—no."

But all the while he spoke, half of her attention was on the red eye of her answering machine that sat on a shelf behind John McCord, an unblinking red eye. No new messages.

She didn't need Erik Amundsson. He'd played with her, and he was done now, probably onto bigger and better conquests. *Screw it,* she thought. *Screw him.* She should thank her lucky stars he hadn't called. He was an egotistical, arrogant bastard.

She wanted to cry.

"... Jack is doing okay now," her patient was saying. "He was angry at first when we got divorced, but he's better."

"John," she said, tearing her gaze from the answering machine, focusing on his face, "why did you get divorced?"

Later, she would marvel that his reply went straight past her consciousness, but at the time, all she saw over his shoulder was the red eye, which began to wink at her.

It blinked, and John said, "Because I quit drinking."

When the hour was over, he reached through the V-neck of his sweater and pulled out a checkbook from a pocket in his shirt. "Seventy-five, you said on the phone?"

"Yes, please."

And then, in moments, he was gone, the door closing with a snick behind him, and she could rush to the machine and press the Play button.

"This is Maddy Lane," came the recorded voice. "Can we change my appointment to Thursday this week? Let me know. 555-4025."

Disappointment, as bitter as bile, rose in her stomach. For a time, she thought she might vomit, but it passed, and then she simply felt drained.

She drove home that afternoon, disgusted. She was the one who needed therapy. She couldn't trust herself, and that was scary. Then, abruptly, she was afraid of what she'd do if Erik did call, afraid she'd lose herself again.

When she got home, she thought she ought to eat

something. She opened the fridge and searched, but there was nothing that appealed to her. She was losing weight, suffering insomnia, barely able to do her job, yet all she could dwell on was Erik. Had he left town, gone climbing? Perhaps in South America or the Himalayas, where it was the season now. Maybe he'd even told her that, but she'd been too wrapped up in her needs, too focused on his touch to register anything but sensation.

She slammed the refrigerator door. *Damn him.* She was deluding herself. He got what he wanted from her: a fuck. He was a self-absorbed bastard, and she only had herself to blame for the sorry affair. He was cut from the same mold as her father, she realized in a lucid moment. How could she have been so blind?

God, she hurt.

She was starting a load of laundry when she heard a rap on her door. It was Tony. He'd seen her car out front, he knew she was home, and he wanted to talk.

Tony . . . Her love for him seemed distant, existing in another life. She'd tell him it was over, really, completely over. No more dates or kisses or jealousy. They could be friends, that sickly, damning relegation to a lower status. But it would have to do. Even if she never laid eyes on Erik Amundsson again, she and Tony were finished.

She opened the door.

At first she couldn't find her voice; it was clogged in her chest as blood surged from her heart. Her brain could barely fit itself around his presence.

When she finally spoke, what she said shocked her. "How dare you show up like this . . . you bastard!"

Then he was inside, kicking the door closed behind him, moving toward her.

"Don't you dare touch—" she got out before her back was against the wall and his mouth covered hers. His mouth, his hands, his entire body pressing into her until she trembled with elation, sagged into his arms, and was lost.

They made love fiercely. He lifted her with his hands, so strong, and she wrapped her legs around him while he drove into her. She screamed once, an alien voice forced from her throat while she stood outside herself and watched and listened, thinking, *This can't be me.*

Her orgasm came a second after his, shaking her, and it seemed to last forever, endless mountainous waves washing over her, crashing like a hurricane tide.

"Oh my God," she gasped.

"Yes," Erik said. That was all: *Yes.*

He released her, and she slid down his length, her knees weak when she stood.

"I needed you," he said, bending his head and kissing her forehead. His hands held her waist.

"You didn't call," she breathed.

"No."

She leaned into him, her fingers digging into his shoulders, her head buried in his chest.

"I had to leave town. A personal thing," he explained.

"Where? Where did you go?" She couldn't stop the interrogation. It wasn't any of her business, but she couldn't stop asking.

"Curious."

"Yes, I am. You made me feel like . . . like a whore, a one-night stand."

He tipped her head up. "You are not a whore. You are my Meredith."

"I am? What does that mean?"

"So many questions. You don't need to ask. You know what we mean to each other. Your body knows."

"Where were you?" she had to ask again.

"I was in Boulder."

"Oh."

"I missed you."

"Why didn't you call? Don't tell me there aren't any phones in Boulder."

"Don't you know what they say about us Scandinavians?"

"What?"

"We don't talk when it's not necessary."

He hiked his shoulders and let them drop. Obviously, no apology would be forthcoming.

She put her arms around his neck. "I can't do this. I'm not used to this. It makes me feel . . ."

"What does it make you feel?"

"I don't know. Obsessed, owned, out of control."

"Perhaps that's an accurate assessment. Is that bad?"

"I don't know."

They stood there, in her living room, half dressed, clothes hastily thrown aside. She should have been ashamed or self-conscious or angry, but none of that mattered now. He was there, his skin against hers, his hands on her. Nothing else mattered.

"You bastard," she whispered, but there was no sting in the epithet.

He smiled, one of the few times, and lifted her with

his hands still around her waist and bent his head to kiss one nipple where her sweater had been pulled aside. "Let's eat," he said. "I'm starving."

They sat at her kitchen counter on the barstools. All she had were crackers and cheese and a bottle of wine she found in the fridge. But the simple fare tasted like ambrosia. The acts of chewing, swallowing, slicing cheese took on a radiant sensuality. Texture and flavor burst on her tongue. The wine was tart and sweet and cool, sliding down her throat like honeyed perfume.

He held her hand while they ate, played with her fingers, wiped a crumb from the corner of her mouth once. The thousand questions that had flooded her mind slipped away like ghosts.

She forced herself to ask him once more, "What did you have to do in Boulder?"

"Personal business. Not any concern of yours, nothing serious."

That was no answer at all, yet she accepted it.

She turned on a light when it grew dark. He watched her, his eyes hooded, his head following her every movement. She felt beautiful under his scrutiny, graceful and sexy. She also felt brash and ready for anything. The total relinquishing of inhibitions lent her a kind of courage she'd never known. She closed the blinds on her front window, checked that the door was locked, stood in the center of her living room, and took off all of her clothes. Her skin glowed with heat, and she felt dizzy with desire.

"Come here," Erik said, and she went to him. He kissed her slowly and methodically and lifted his head and said one word: "Upstairs."

At the top of the steps, he swung her into his arms

and carried her into her bedroom, not hesitating at the other doors, as if he knew already, knew all there was to know about her.

He did things to her she'd never had done to her before. Her freedom was total, enlightening. Sometimes she experienced pain, but it was fleeting, only leading to heightened sensations, strange new feelings of pleasure that she'd never have believed.

She smelled herself on him, on his mouth when he kissed her, and his scent was on her. They were one being, she thought once, as he moved inside her.

Afterward, they lay in the dark, tangled in the sheets, the comforter dragging on the floor. Breathing evenly, quietly, hands entwined.

"Do you ever get tired?"

"Compared to climbing," he said, "this is easy."

"Easy."

She turned toward him and ran her hands over his skin, feeling for the puckered ridge of scar tissue she'd felt on his shoulder.

"What's this?"

He laughed lightly. "A climbing accident."

"What happened?"

"Hell, I don't remember."

"Tell me."

"I can't remember. It was years ago. I think I fell and hit something sharp."

"Are you careful?"

"Always."

"And this?" Her fingers traced a scar on the inside of his wrist.

"Broke it."

"Where? How?"

"I fell."

"Erik . . ."

"Well, that's what happened. I think it was on the Flatirons near Boulder. I needed a plate and screws."

She ran her fingers up and down the scar, then took his left hand between hers, saying, "And this?"

"You know about that already."

"I do?"

"Bridget must have told you."

Bridget. A bucket of cold water in the midst of a warm, scented bath. How could he speak of Bridget so casually?

"Tell me," she said. *Not Bridget, but me.*

"I got frostbite on Aconcagua. Those two fingers had to be removed."

"It hurt?"

"Hurt like hell."

"Does it bother you, I mean, not having them?"

"Does it bother *you*, Meredith?"

"No, no . . . I . . ."

"You what?"

"Nothing."

She moved her leg across his, flung her arm across his chest. One day she'd ask him about his relationship with Bridget. One day. But not now. The time was wrong. This night was for her, for them. She had plenty of time. Sooner or later, she'd know all there was to know about Erik Amundsson. It would be her odyssey of discovery, and she'd revel in the journey.

"And this?" she asked, fingering another scar on his thigh.

"Meredith . . ."

"Tell me," she said again.

"I stopped someone who was falling, and the spikes of his crampon got me there."

"Did you save his life?"

"Maybe. Probably."

She breathed in his scent, stroked the raised flesh of a scar. "How many people have you saved?"

"A few. Anyone who climbs long enough has saved lives."

"So modest," she said dryly.

He laughed, that light, careless abdication of feeling, and he didn't answer her but crushed her lips with his so that the liquid honey of his mouth was on her tongue. And his mutilated hand stroked her cheek.

SEVEN

The studded snow tires on the Jeep crunched on the patches of ice where the road lay in permanent shadow. She glanced at Erik, and her heart gave a sudden electric jolt in her breast, as it always did when she observed him.

There was something thrilling about the strength of his arms and the mastery of his hands on the steering wheel, something strong and eternal in his profile that was silhouetted against the growing darkness. She likened him to a statue that stood watch over the land. In Erik's case, he could have been carved in marble, placed atop a windswept cliff overlooking the North Sea, his sharp blue eyes seeing beyond the horizon.

"How far up Castle Creek does Chad's sister live?" she asked, breaking his comfortable silence.

"Past the turnoff to the Little Annie's Road."

"Expensive area."

He shrugged. "Kathy's ex-husband got the bank account, she got the house and mortgage."

"Oh. And you said she works for the prince, for Kemil?"

"Yes."

"Is that how you and Chad met the prince, through Kathy?"

"So many questions."

"Oh yes, I'm full of questions. I'm trying to get to know you." She smiled in the growing darkness. "Other than in the bedroom, that is."

She heard him laugh, and the sound fell on her ears like melodic notes.

"Erik, really, is that how you met Kemil?"

"Actually, we met him many years ago on a climb. He was with another outfit." He shook his head. "He didn't know any better at the time."

"So you lured him away from this other outfit?"

"Yes. He wanted the best."

"How does Kathy fit in?"

"She needed a job."

"And Kemil needed a girl Friday?"

"Kathy is a lot more than a girl Friday. She's a CPA, a very organized person. They were a perfect fit."

Meredith felt a stab of jealousy. The way he talked about Kathy . . . "Why did she need a job all of a sudden?"

"She was divorced. And then her daughter got leukemia. It was a very bad time for her."

"Oh, how terrible. Is her daughter, I mean, is she okay now?"

"Yes, she is in remission."

"Thank God."

"Kathy is a very strong woman, very determined. She did what she had to do."

He spoke of Kathy with respect, almost protectively. What exactly *was* their relationship?

"You like Kathy a lot."

He turned to her for a moment and smiled, mocking her a little. "Yes, I like Kathy. She's a friend, a good friend." His eyes switched back to the road. "I think you two will get along very well."

"You mean because I'm also determined and organized?"

"Yes," was all he said.

She couldn't help wondering what else he thought about her. Did he think she was pretty, intelligent? Did he know how much of her control she'd given up for him? Or was it all about sex? She wondered if she would ever get past that cryptic shell of his.

She knew she could barely function without him. When he laughed, she was filled with joy. When he withdrew into himself, her soul was leaden. He'd come along out of the blue, and she was complete now, as if she'd been half a person before. He had taught her how to love. Not just make love, but how to give herself fully. With Erik there was no shyness, no inhibitions. And yet she still didn't know the first thing about him. They'd been together every day, well, every night, for three weeks, and he was as much a stranger as he'd been the first time.

"You realize," she said as they passed the Little Annie's Road, "I don't even know if you ski. Do you ski, Erik? Or is it all climbing?"

"I'm better at climbing."

"Um. *I* ski. I even take Sno-Cat trips every year right here in Little Annie's bowls." She gestured up to their left. "I'm not half bad."

"You were born here in the valley," he said. "I assumed you ski."

"What else do you assume about me?"

"You always bring a couch with you."

"A what?"

"A couch. You're always analyzing people."

"Only with you," she fired back good-naturedly. "You're an enigma."

"Not at all," he remarked. "What you see is what you get."

The valley six miles outside of Aspen began to narrow. On both sides of Castle Creek, the mountains rose steeply, their slopes dotted with tall, skinny pines and stands of aspens. Overhead, the wedge of sky was turning inky black, velvety, and the stars were so brilliant they cast light on the ribbon of road.

She peered through the Jeep's window. "I'll never get tired of the mountains, you know that?"

"Yes, I know that about you."

"Um. But you know I won't climb them. Hike, sure, I'm a great hiker. But nothing steep."

He was quiet.

"Well?" she prompted, unable to keep her thoughts from straying to Bridget. "Did you know that about me?"

He shrugged.

"So don't bother trying to talk me into it," she ventured.

Then he laughed, but the sound was humorless. "Don't worry, Meredith, even if you wanted to climb, I would never allow it," he said, and again he fell into a stony silence.

She thought about his words the rest of the way to Kathy Fry's house. He would never allow her to climb. Because of Bridget? Was he admitting, in an indirect manner, that he was responsible for the girl's death?

But she didn't want to go there. Not yet, she thought, and she put the unsettling notion aside. Someday, the truth about the incident would come to light. Someday, she would understand. But not now. Not when her emotions were so new and raw and fragile and so very wonderful.

Kathy Fry's house sat nestled in the spruce trees on the far bank of Castle Creek. They had to cross a private one-lane wooden bridge to get there, and then Meredith could see two other branches of the drive disappearing into the woods. More mega homes at the end of the lane, no doubt.

"Nice place," she said when he pulled into a spot next to Chad Newhouse's pickup truck.

"Yes, it is."

"And where does Chad live?"

"Right here, actually," Erik said, climbing out of the Jeep. "He rents the guesthouse." He nodded toward a cabin behind the main house.

"How convenient."

"It works for them. Chad helps out around the grounds and pays rent, Kathy get some income, and Brit and Timmy have their uncle around."

"Brit and—?"

"Kathy's kids. You'll meet them tonight."

Kathy was one of the few people Erik had mentioned over the last few weeks. And her brother Chad, of course, Erik's ever-present shadow, whom she'd met several times. She was actually getting used to Chad calling at all hours, disturbing them, often catching them in the throes of passion whether at Erik's place or hers. But this was a first, being invited to dinner at

Kathy's, and she wondered how much, if anything, Erik had told Chad's sister about her. Would she live up to the superwoman's expectations? Did she really care what Kathy thought?

Yes, she answered wordlessly as they walked toward the entrance. She cared because Erik thought so highly of Chad's sister. Then she wondered again: Just how close were they?

Meredith had treated people for social anxiety disorder from time to time, so she was familiar with the symptoms, although she herself was never nervous in social situations. But, curiously, the idea of meeting Kathy face-to-face made her heart surge with trepidation. She realized how ridiculous that was. She also realized why she was tense. By gaining Kathy Fry's approval, she felt she would be raised in Erik's esteem. She disliked herself for her neediness, but she had to acknowledge the validity of the feeling.

Kathy was nothing at all as she had imagined. Although she clearly resembled Chad in appearance, she was not in the least intense or judgmental. She greeted Meredith and Erik at the door in worn blue jeans and a red cotton turtleneck that had seen better days, then banged a palm on her forehead and said. "Goddamn, the casserole," and sped off to the kitchen, dragging Meredith with her.

"I am such a klutz in the kitchen," she muttered, yanking open the oven door, fanning the steamy smoke away with a stained potholder. "I know it's ruined. I just know it. And I wanted to impress you. Some first impression." She opened a window over the kitchen sink and kept on fanning the air.

"I'm sure it's fine," Meredith offered, wondering at

Erik's description of Kathy as organized, and wishing she hadn't gotten so darn dressed up in a skirt and blazer. She was about to say something when a pair of teenage girls came loping into the room and interrupted them.

"Oh, God, Mom, did you burn dinner again?" The girls giggled.

"Oh shush, Brit, and introduce yourself and your friend Leslie to Miss Greene," Kathy said, sniffing the casserole now.

Then Chad poked his head into the kitchen. "Hi, Meredith," he said. "I should have warned you about this household. Brit, did you meet Erik's friend? And where is Timmy, anyway?"

Kathy shook her head. "Andy's mother was supposed to drop him here after baseball. My God, am I going to hate summer break. And it hasn't even started yet. I need an entire computer program just to keep track of the kids and their activities. Do you have children, Meredith?"

"No."

"Well, don't. Just ask Brit here."

"Oh, Mom," Brit said, "you are so dumb sometimes."

Kathy sighed. "Aren't I, though? Now show Meredith the house while I try to salvage dinner. Oh, Meredith, the beer's in the fridge and there's soda. If you want a real drink, Brit will show you where the booze is. I'll get my act together in a minute, and we'll all sit down in the living room and chat, okay?"

"Fine by me," Meredith said. "But would you like some help?"

"Oh, don't worry, I'll catch you for cleanup after dinner."

"It's a deal."

While Erik and Chad sat in the living room, Brit and her school friend Leslie showed Meredith the house. It was a beautiful place, perhaps ten rooms, built mostly of log and stone and glass. Amazingly, there was a small indoor stone pond separating the living room and the rest of the house, which you had to walk around on flagstone to get to the bedrooms and baths. Plants flourished in the warm, humid air around the pond.

"Wow," Meredith said, "now this is different."

"Dad built it," Brit said. "He's a contractor."

"Does he live in Aspen?"

"No way. He split town owing a bunch of bills and moved to Idaho. We like never see him. Even when I was sick, all I got was a card."

"That's so bogus," Leslie said.

"No, sh—I mean, yeah, real creepy," Brit put in.

She and her friend led Meredith through the house, and all the while, Brit told her about her recovery from leukemia. Meredith enjoyed listening to the girls. It was always refreshing to hear such honesty and openness. But then, in her experience, children were usually far more in touch with reality and their emotions than adults were.

"Uncle Chad really helped Mom then. Dad had only been gone a year when I first got diagnosed with leukemia, and Uncle Chad did everything. He even gave up this real neat climb and all, and he got Mom the job with the prince, too."

Both girls giggled and repeated "the prince" while rolling their eyes.

Meredith wanted to ask if Erik had also helped out, but she was certain these two sharp thirteen-year-olds would see right through her.

Instead, she asked, "And how old is your brother, Tim, isn't it?"

"Timmy's my twin," Brit announced. "We're fraternal twins, thank God."

"Why thank God?"

It was Leslie who chimed in. "He is so nerdy."

Meredith laughed, but her mind was on Brit and Timmy—twins. Erik hadn't told her that. Another missing detail in an endless stream of missing details. Silly. But as close as he was to this family, shouldn't he have mentioned it? And where *had* he been during Brit's illness, when Chad had given up this "neat" climb? Had Erik stayed in Aspen and pitched in? Had he gone to the hospital with Chad to visit Brit? Brought toys to the sick child?

Dinner was noisy and eaten in front of the fireplace on laps and the glass coffee table in the living room, a casual family affair. Meredith noticed that she and Kathy did most of the talking, with Erik and Chad listening quietly or occasionally commenting on a subject with an, "Uh-huh" or "Um." They only became animated when Timmy, who'd finally arrived at eight, asked about their next climb. Still, it was the more outgoing and intense Chad who did most of the conversing.

She was discovering that Erik had a larger-than-life presence, despite his lack of verbosity. His presence was aloof but keen. She knew he could be in a roomful of people, never utter a word, and still be the one person everybody recalled.

After dinner, she and Kathy and the girls had the dishes done quickly. She realized she'd been hoping for a more time-consuming cleanup in order to broach the subject of Erik. She was sure Kathy would understand. But the moment alone with Chad's sister looked to be lost.

"Okay, all done," Kathy said, wiping her hands on a dishtowel. "Coffee? I've got decaf or the leaded stuff, if you can take it at this hour."

"Decaf," Meredith said. "But let me make it. I haven't done anything to help."

"Oh, don't worry about it." Kathy tucked her shoulder-length dark hair behind her ears and smiled. "There will be lots of time to help in the kitchen when summer comes."

"Oh?"

"Sure. Come June, the boys will circle their wagons for the climb."

"I'm afraid I don't—"

"Oh, right. What I mean is, they'll be together constantly getting ready for the McKinley climb in July. Mostly, they'll prep up at Kemil's, but they'll be here a lot, too. You'll be so sick of it." Kathy cocked her head. "You don't climb, do you? I mean, Erik never said. Well, you can imagine. He's what you call very private."

Meredith saw a crack in a previously closed door. She seized the opportunity. "Heavens no. Hike, yes. Climb, no. But I did meet Erik through climbing in a roundabout way. Through one of my patients. Maybe you remember her, Bridget Lawrence?"

Kathy pursed her lips and nodded.

"Anyway, that's how we met, really. A tragedy."

"Yes, it was. She was so young, too. Damn. And I remember one night here, oh, it must have been in July or August last year, but Bridget was so excited. She told me she was going to do South Maroon in the fall. . . . Oh, hell, I should have discouraged her, I guess. We all should have. It's just that she wasn't the first one, and nothing had ever happened before."

Suddenly Kathy stopped and let out a whistling breath. "I am *such* a bigmouth. I'm so sorry, Meredith, what a stupid thing to say."

"It's all right, really."

"No it is not. It was completely thoughtless. Listen, you should know this, and I seriously doubt *he'll* tell you, but his women, they were just ships passing in the night. Not Bridget, well, not exactly, because Erik saw her for nearly three months, I think it was. But the others. Mostly weekend flings. It's different with you. Honestly."

She didn't know what to say. She couldn't tell Kathy she didn't really care. Kathy would spot the lie in an instant. Nor could she tell her the truth, that she was as obsessed with Erik as Bridget had been. Maybe even more.

"You're upset," Kathy said.

"No, really, I'm not. I understand he has a past. We all do. And after all, I've only been seeing him for less than a month. Who knows where we're headed, right?" Then Meredith lightened the mood. "One place I know we aren't headed is up a mountain together."

"Boy, do I hear that," Kathy said, placing a hand on her forearm.

"Okay," Meredith said, flashing a smile, "now where is the coffee?"

She chewed Erik out before they were even past the Little Annie's Road. "I wish you had told me Timmy and Brit were twins. And you certainly should have told me dinner was casual. I mean, I'm in a skirt and blazer, and Kathy and the rest of you—"

Surprising her, he jerked the steering wheel, brought the Jeep to a stop on the side of Castle Creek Road, and turned to her. "I think we should remedy that," he said.

"Remedy what?"

"This."

In moments, her skirt was tossed on the backseat, and he was tugging her arms out of the blazer, his hands rough and warm on her skin as he pushed her turtleneck up.

"Erik, God, no, not here," she protested. Then he forced her bra up and his mouth was on her breast, his free hand making its way down beneath her panty hose.

"Are you crazy? What if someone stops and . . . ?" But words failed when his hand took her, probed her until she cried out and pressed his head fiercely against her breasts, his beard prickling her in a thousand tender places.

He stopped her from putting her skirt on, saying nothing, only draping a discarded parka from the back floorboards over her nakedness.

He started the Jeep. Drove quickly to town—because his place was miles closer than hers.

They sneaked like thieves up the side garage steps and into his apartment, Erik stoic-faced, Meredith laughing with shame and delight.

On the floor, in the very spot he'd first taken her, he laid her down and stripped her. She knew he was in his masterful mood. She knew he wanted her to struggle and murmur no, over and over. They both knew it was a game.

"No, Erik, no," she whispered when he traced her belly button with his tongue, and then, "No, don't," a small cry of protest when his head moved lower still.

She thrashed against him. But she was only struggling now for the ecstasy of release.

EIGHT

Prince Kemil al Assad arrived back in Aspen from his London flat on June 10, and the real work began, the organizing of the McKinley expedition.

A month ago, she would have been bored silly, bombarded by so much information on mountain climbing. But now, because this was Erik's life, she took an interest and even found herself developing a certain fascination for the subject.

Summit Expeditions, Erik and Chad's employer, was one of a few select outfits that had a concession from the National Park Service to guide climbs on Mount McKinley, at 20,320 feet the tallest mountain in North America. Meredith learned that the mountain had a native name—Denali—and some people called it that, but Summit Expeditions used the older name, McKinley, named after the twenty-fifth president of the United States. The owner of the company, Randy Meyer, booked climbs all over the world and, depending on the season, sent his guides where they were needed.

Summer was McKinley season. The statistics were

dry: Many people would attempt the climb this year, perhaps 1,200. Fifty percent would summit. One in 200 would die trying.

McKinley was farther north than all the other tall peaks in the world. It had the highest base-to-summit elevation of any mountain on earth, 18,000 feet from base to summit. Everest only rose 12,000 feet, in contrast.

The weather was unpredictable, the peak so huge it created its own miniclimate. Storms on McKinley were colder, wetter, and lasted longer than anywhere else.

Meredith absorbed this information as if by osmosis. Erik gave her some of the statistics, and she asked him questions, but the atmosphere around the climbers was so thick with knowledge that she absorbed it without any effort on her part.

She became familiar with climbing equipment. Erik showed each piece to her, named it, and explained how it was used. Carabiners, crampons, ice axes, flukes, ice screws, ropes, snowshoes, harnesses. His hands touched each item with undisguised reverence, a caress. That small metal circlet, that set of spikes, that sharp-tipped ice ax, could save his life.

She often thought that he held the tools of his profession with as much care as he held her, and she reluctantly wondered which he would choose under duress.

She saw her patients during the day, and after that, there was Erik and the other climbers.

Besides Kemil, two men and a woman, all Aspenites, were going on the expedition. They were relatively experienced and had passed the required five-day test climb on Washington State's Mount Rainier the previous summer to qualify for McKinley.

By mid-June, the team members were shifting into high gear, preparing for the expedition, and when Kathy's house was unavailable, Kemil kindly offered his home as the gathering spot.

"Are you sure I should come along?" Meredith asked as they drove up the Red Mountain Road in the summer twilight.

"I'm sure."

"But I'm not going on the climb. I'm not even a climber. I'll be in the way."

"Meredith." He had a way of saying her name that stopped words in her throat and made her quiver inside.

"But—"

"You're with me."

"Will Kathy still be there?"

"Of course not. She finishes work at four and goes home."

He drove into the prince's driveway and parked next to several other vehicles.

"They're here, I guess," she said, a little nervous.

"Climbers have to be on time."

Kemil met them at the door, the darkly handsome man she'd seen at the end-of-the-ski-season party weeks ago. His English was British accented, his teeth brilliantly white against his black mustache and perfectly trimmed goatee.

"You are Meredith," he said. "Of course. Kathy has told me so much about you. Welcome." He took her hand, covering it with both of his. "I welcome you to my home."

"I'm so glad to finally meet you," she said. *Kathy,*

of course. But a small disappointment welled up in her. Erik had not told Kemil about her; Kathy had.

"Come, come." He gestured them through the living room that she remembered, down some steps, into a cavernous room filled with levels: broad, shallow tiers. A media room, she realized, a private theater.

But tonight it was filled with equipment, piles of brightly colored nylon, tents, down parkas, sleeping bags, coiled ropes, fleece outerwear. Glinting stacks of metal tools, duffel bags, cooking stoves, plastic containers, maps.

Chad was already there. Also a woman and two men, the other climbers. They looked up from their work sorting and counting and packing, and greeted Erik. "Hey, man." "Hi, Erik." "About time." Glad to see him, the welcoming of a comrade-in-arms, a compatriot in an alien land, a true believer.

"This is Meredith," Kemil said.

"Hello, Meredith," Chad said, a bit mocking, and she realized, as she had several times before, that he was jealous of her.

The others said hello, and she smiled and replied and tried not to feel too out of place. Superfluous.

And yet, her singular status of being there yet not being a part of the climb allowed her a certain perspective, an objectivity. She studied the tableau with a professional eye as she sat quietly off to the side.

Erik, the center. They revolved around him as if he were the sun; they deferred to him, needing his approval. He possessed natural leadership, unspoken but obvious. She felt a burst of pride in her breast. He was the strongest, the smartest, the bravest, and he had chosen *her.*

Chad, the sidekick. Intense, competent, charming in his way, but definitely subservient.

Daniel Froberg, boyish-looking, no more than twenty-five, she judged. Blond and strong and gung ho. He was a ski patrolman on Aspen Mountain, Erik had told her.

Dan's best friend, Kevin Moore, athletic, lean and hawk nosed. Sober, intent on doing everything right, a bit anal, whereas Dan seemed more haphazard, easy-going.

Jessie Robertson, Dan's fiancée, a tall girl, not beautiful but wholesome-looking, with that self-confident, outdoorsy appearance of sports-minded Aspen women. Flat-chested, flat-bellied, narrow-hipped, long dark blond hair in a ponytail.

There was a lot of talk Meredith didn't understand, terms she didn't recognize. She listened and she watched, and she began to comprehend the closeness of the climbers, the shared knowledge, the passion.

They spoke of blue ice up to sixty degrees in steepness, step-kicking, rotten rock called schist, ice gullies, whiteouts, and cornices. Glaciers and headwalls, front-pointing down a slope, postholing in fresh snow, crevices, and avalanches. And more mundane concerns: the van that would pick them up in Anchorage, food, airplane service into base camp on the Kahiltna Glacier, timing, shortwave radios set for Channel 19, batteries. The risks: exhaustion and falling and frostbite and hypothermia and hypoxia or oxygen deprivation.

They spoke of these things lightly, bandying about coarse jokes and stories and anecdotes. They'd climbed together before, the men in South America with Chad and Erik, Jessie last summer on Mount Rainier, and then all of them as a group on several of the four-teeners, peaks over 14,000 feet tall, in Colorado.

"No, wait," Dan said, "I've got a better one. Remember the time we were stuck in a storm on Coto-paxi? In hammocks glued to the side of a headwall? And Kevin here decides he has to take a piss." He rolled his eyes, and everyone laughed. Kevin punched him in the biceps, and they both fake boxed, jabbing at each other, scuffling with fancy footwork.

"Come on," Jessie said, "you guys." Then, more soberly, "Erik, I'm really serious. Aren't we better acclimated then lowlanders? I mean, we live at eight thousand feet."

"Yes," he replied, "you have an advantage, but sometimes that doesn't count for much."

"It must count for something."

"Given perfect conditions, no problems, no bad weather, there'd be an advantage. But altitude is strange. Sometimes the best-acclimated person hits a wall at, say, fifteen thousand feet, or eighteen thousand. You never know."

Kemil said, "You remember that fellow we did Everest with, Erik? In '98. The one who bragged?"

"I remember."

"He climbed like mad for days and then, one day, at Camp Four, he simply quit. Had a slight case of pulmonary edema. He barely made it down." Kemil shook his head. "Each climber has his own wall."

Meredith listened and tried to imagine what it was like at those heights. The cold, the altitude draining your strength. The possibility that each step could be your last. She remembered very well the carnage of the terrible spring on Everest in '96, when so many had died in a sudden storm. Two of the best, most experienced guides had lost their lives and one, a New Zealander—it had been broadcast all over the world—had spoken to his pregnant wife on a radio telephone as he lay dying, unable to descend.

That could happen to Erik. If it didn't happen on this trip, it could on the next or the one after that. How did he bear it? How could *she* bear it? She looked at him, and her heart squeezed with fear.

Kemil had arranged for a topographical map of Mount McKinley to be shown on his huge screen, so they could study the route.

Chad doused the lights, and they all sat in chairs on the raised steps staring at the giant black-and-white map.

"Who's going to narrate?" Kemil asked.

"I will," Chad offered.

Erik sat silently next to Meredith, his stillness pulled around him like a shroud.

"Now, you all know there are a lot of routes up McKinley. The commercial climbs use one route, though. It's the easiest. Not the shortest, but technically the easiest. The West Buttress Route. Fondly called the Butt. Okay, here it is." He pointed with the shaft of an ice ax at the bottom of the map. "The Kahiltna Glacier, Base Camp, seven thousand two hundred feet. They'll try to fly us all in on the same day, but you never know when a storm will blow in and leave some of us marooned in Talkeetna."

"Can you get to Base Camp any other way?" someone asked.

"Nope," Chad said, "one way in, one way out. So, we set up here. It's always a madhouse, groups going up, groups coming down, people waiting to get flown out. I picture one night here, unless the weather's bad." He pointed again. "Five and a half miles up the glacier, Ski Hill Camp. Lots of crevasses here, so we'll be very careful. Then up Ski Hill to the camp at eleven thousand feet. This one is windy as hell. Avalanches and ice falls all around. Okay, then it's two and three-quarters miles up to Fourteen Medical, that's sort of a small village of tents. The Park Service has a medical tent there for rescue and emergencies."

Chad cleared his throat. "Then, guys, it gets steep. There are fixed ropes from here up the headwall. Ridge Camp's at the top. Sixteen-two. Very exposed. Then the three-quarters of a mile to High Camp. The view's great here, but watch where you put your feet."

"How long to High Camp?" Dan asked.

"Ah, hell, two weeks, three, depending on weather and how quickly you all get conditioned."

"Okay."

"And then summit day, a five-mile round-trip back to High Camp. We start real early in the morning. Luckily, it's light out up there, because it could take all day."

"Piece of cake," Dan said, as the lights went on.

"Right," Chad replied, laughing.

"It's a very tough climb," Erik said, breaking his silence. "Don't underestimate it."

No one spoke for a second. The enormity of what they proposed to do hit them all. And it had been Erik who'd reminded them.

After that, Kemil directed them into the dining room, where an array of food had been set out, warm pita bread stuffed with meat and vegetables, eggplant dip, a whole tray of baklava for dessert. No cook was in evidence, no servants, no one.

She wondered who had prepared and laid out this feast. The prince's wives, those three fabled but unseen women? Did they wear veils? What did they do all day? Did they envy or despise brash American women?

Did Kemil love them equally?

The group ate, quieter, more subdued than it had been. Was it Erik's warning that silenced them, or was it this ghostly repast?

She wanted to be gone; she wanted to be alone with Erik, to touch him and love him and ask him about the people he would take to Alaska. She couldn't really judge them until she heard his opinion.

They left Kemil's house, walking out into the cool, star-studded night, with the lights of Aspen laid out below them in a diamond-bright grid. The moment the car door shut them off from the world, she put her head on his shoulder, her hand on his thigh.

"That was interesting," she said, "but I didn't really belong there."

"You belong with me."

"They put up with me only because of you, Erik."

"Perhaps."

"Tell me about them, now that I've met them. Can they climb McKinley? Do you trust them?"

"They're all good, yes, very good. Young and tough. Daniel is a bull, amazingly conditioned, Kevin is determined. Jessie, well, she has a drive in her. Very strong. But she's the weak link. *If* there's a weak link. But I believe they can all summit, or I wouldn't take them."

"Um." She wanted to believe in his judgments. She longed to believe he was always right when it came to mountaineering. He was, after all, a climbing god. Omniscient. The deaths years ago on Aconcagua ... Bridget's death ... Accidents, out of Erik's control. He, of all the climbers on the face of the earth, knew what he was doing. She knew that now. Yes, she knew it.

He drove down Red Mountain and headed out the Woody Creek Road to her place. She couldn't wait till they arrived; the warm throbbing began in her belly as she thought about what they'd do, how she'd feel. She was Erik's minion, only alive in his arms. Otherwise, she was a pale copy of a person, insignificant, barely there.

It occurred to her then, in a moment of objectivity, that she had reached a point in which her lover's opinion was her reality, so that she agreed with his take on people, on life, on herself. He created and he reflected her identity; without him, the mirror was dark. Her common sense told her this could not be true. She'd been a complete person before meeting this man, and she was that same person, wasn't she?

But he overshadowed her, and common sense was unavailable to her.

She knew she would never again press him about Bridget's accident. Questioning him was a dangerous undertaking at best. And really, he had explained it to her. "What else is there to say?" he would reply to her queries, anyway, and then he would kiss her into acquiescence.

He came in with her that night, and they shed their clothes on the way up the stairs, not even bothering to turn the lights on. She responded to him as she always did, with reckless delight, as if she were a machine he could start with the flip of a switch. Yet despite their sexual intimacy and his openness when it came to discussing climbing, he remained a conundrum. She still knew practically nothing about his Norwegian family. She still knew nothing about his innermost desires and fears or if he suffered even an iota of guilt over Bridget's death.

Two evenings ago, they'd stopped at the local market, and in the vegetable isle a lovely brunette had approached him and kissed him on the lips. He had touched the woman's shoulder as if he knew her too well, then she'd gone about her shopping.

"Who was that?" Meredith had asked.

"An old friend." He had shrugged.

His ability to keep his past and much of his present life apart from her was frustrating. He didn't even want to know about her history, it seemed. He had no interest in her profession. No interest in equine therapy or the ranch or her sister Ann in Denver or her strained relationship with her father. He'd shut her down cold when she'd opened the painful subject of her mother's death.

She yearned for him to dig inside her, to know how proud she was when one of her equine therapy kids made even the smallest progress, or if a patient at her office had a breakthrough. She needed to share her ups and downs with the man who had set her physical body free. Why couldn't they share their minds, their souls with each other?

She would. She would do that for him. But Erik . . . He only lived in the moment.

Then, as the Alaska climb neared, she began to notice small changes in the way he made love. His mounting tension, if that was what it was, caused him sometimes to grip her more tightly, so tightly once that she had bruises on her hips in the morning. He had even tried to enter her from behind, but she'd drawn the line there. He had gotten angry. Rolled away. Of course, minutes later he'd sighed, pulled her to him, and said, "Someday I'll teach you to enjoy it," and made more conventional love to her.

Tonight, still on the stairs where they shed their clothes, he again tried to enter from behind, but she wiggled away, heard herself say, "No, Erik, please," and couldn't believe she was asking that he *please* not hurt her. Where was her will, her determination, her sense of *self*?

Later, in bed, she lay holding him inside her as fiercely as she could, knowing he was leaving soon. He'd always be going somewhere or coming back from somewhere. He would never belong to her wholly, while she belonged to him, utterly and without reservation.

He fell asleep, but she lay there, entwined in his limbs, a bar of moonlight silvering his skin, their sweat mingling, his manhood lying slack and surfeited against her thigh, and she rested her hand on his chest to feel the beat of his heart and the rise and fall of his breathing. She knew who she was now, but when he rose in the morning and left her, who would she be then?

By the last week of June, the expedition was nearly ready. All the plans were made, food ordered, duffel bags packed, transportation organized. Prince Kemil had generously offered his private jet to fly the group to Anchorage. Erik and Chad had left for several climbs: one to Grand Teton in Wyoming, one to Washington State's Mount Rainier, three short climbs on a couple of local peaks. And each time Meredith waited, barely breathing, unable to concentrate until he returned. He laughed at her fears. He laughed, and then he swung her into his arms and took her to bed.

There had been more evenings at Kemil's, and several at Kathy's, but sometimes Meredith begged off. She didn't want to be a groupie. But it was hard, turning Erik down. He seemed to want her with him every moment he was home.

"No, Erik, not tonight. I've got some work to do," she told him once.

"Do it another time."

"You don't need me there. I don't get the inside jokes."

"I need you there. Do you doubt me?"

"No, but—"

"Come, Meredith."

"No, no, really. Go without me." God, it was hard to say, but she knew, somewhere deep inside, a tiny light, nearly submerged, that she had to be apart from him sometimes.

She finally called her sister Ann one evening when Erik was at Kathy's with the other climbers.

"Meredith?"

"Hi, Annie."

"Well, long time no see or hear, you bum."

"I've been busy."

"It's been weeks. And you forgot Amanda's birthday, and you never answered any of the messages I left."

"I'm sorry. Oh, poor Amanda. Tell her I'll send her something right away."

"Well, what's up?"

"I've met someone," she said.

"Oh my God," Ann breathed. "Who? Tell me about him. Oh, Meredith!"

"His name is Erik Amundsson, and he's a famous mountain climber. He's incredible, Ann."

"Oh, really? And you're in love?"

"I think so." She paused, then, "Yes."

"What about Tony?"

"That's been over for a long time."

"I can't believe it. You even sound different."

"I am different."

"He's handsome?"

"Gorgeous."

"Bring him down to Denver to meet us. Has Dad met him yet?"

"No."

"Why not?"

"Because."

"Damn it, Meredith, when are you going to forgive your own father?"

"Probably never," Meredith said lightly.

"But can *we* meet him?"

"Sure. Sometime. He's always off on climbs. He's going to McKinley in July, and he'll be gone for weeks."

"Poor baby."

"He's so wonderful, Ann."

"Of course he is. Otherwise, you wouldn't love him."

It was so easy for Ann, Meredith thought after she'd hung up. But then it had always been easier for Ann, because Meredith had made sure of that.

On the last meeting at Kemil's before the expedition was to leave for Alaska, she consented to go. It was more of a social occasion, Erik promised.

The evening started out fine. Jessie Robertson even warmed to her, asked her about the Greene Ranch and told her she knew one of Meredith's equine therapy patients, said what a wonderful program it was.

Meredith beamed with pride. She hoped Erik had heard, but when she turned to see where he was, she witnessed an uncomfortable scene.

Just beyond the media room, standing near the double teak doors to the living room, Erik, Chad, and Kemil were head to head in what seemed to be an argument.

Jessie shrugged and went back to her checklist and a conversation with her fiancé Dan, but Meredith studied the three men just beyond the doors. Chad and Kemil seemed to be in each other's faces, Kemil with folded arms, on the defensive, Chad gesturing angrily with his hands. She could overhear a couple of words.

". . . sure as shit wait till after the climb." Chad said.

Then Kemil: "Do not doubt my determination."

And finally Erik, as if mediating: "Okay, okay, it's settled. We must focus on the climb. The climb is too important. Enough of this bullshit for now."

The altercation was over in a moment, and no one seemed to give it a second thought. Meredith chalked the incident up to heightened testosterone and a lot of tension. After all, in a little over a week, they'd leave for Alaska. She realized her nerves were growing more raw by the day, too.

They ate dinner, the outgoing ski patrolman Dan cracking his usual jokes, his fiancée Jessie shaking her head at him, the more intense Kevin fretting about flights and storms and equipment, Chad back to reassuring everyone they were prepared.

Erik was quiet. And Kemil entertained Meredith with descriptions of his Saudi family's breeding stables located outside Riyadh.

When dinner was over, the gear checked and rechecked and stacked in the rear of one of Kemil's Suburbans, everyone said good night and headed to their cars. Erik opened the door to the Jeep for her, saying nothing, then shut it hard when she was in. He climbed in behind the wheel, leaned forward, and turned the key in the ignition, then sat back for a moment, waiting for the engine of the old Jeep to run evenly. She kept quiet about the argument and his part in it, but she wondered. There were always questions batting around in her head, hundreds of them, like flocks of birds wheeling first this way, then that. But few ever reached her lips, because he got so impatient when she persisted.

He put the vehicle in gear and pulled out of Kemil's driveway, the car's headlights piercing the summer twilight, swinging as he turned, sweeping across stone walls and trees and a dark SUV that was parked on the road.

Erik muttered something, curse words that must have been in Norwegian, then flicked his bright lights at the SUV and gave it the finger.

She was surprised; he *never* showed that kind of emotion, never let anger get the better of him. Maybe the tension between Chad and Kemil had upset him more than he wanted to admit.

"What was that all about?" she asked.

"Nothing. Nobody."

"Come on, Erik, it must have been somebody. Do you know whose car that was?"

He stared straight ahead, driving. "It was nobody. Some jerk. Those goddamn stinking rich and their politics."

"You mean Kemil? What politics? Do you mean—?"

"Meredith."

She fell silent.

"Meredith, it's not your problem, it's not my problem. I care nothing about politics."

"What politics—?" she began.

"Nothing. Stop asking questions." He reached out a hand without taking his eyes off the road and touched her breast, then his fingers trailed down to her crotch. Fire followed, and she drew in a sharp breath.

"That's better," he said.

She tried again after they'd made love on the floor of her living room, not even getting as far as the stairs. She forced herself to ask, trying to recapture some of herself, her curiosity, her independence.

"Erik," she said, her head on his shoulder, their fingers wound together, resting on his hip, the sharp hipbone that she'd jokingly taken to calling his lethal weapon.

"Um."

"Erik . . ." This was so hard. "You never answer my

questions. I know it irritates you, but how can we . . . how can we have a relationship when you won't confide in me?"

"Meredith," he sighed.

"No, no." She pulled her hand from his and rose on an elbow, staring down into the shadowed pools of his eyes. "I mean it. You never tell me anything. I don't know much about you. That thing tonight, the car outside Kemil's. You know who it was, I know you do, but you won't—"

He put a finger to her lips. "Words, words. I don't deal with words. I'm a hopeless case. I'm not a psychologist, Meredith. I don't analyze everything and everyone the way you do."

"I don't mean you have to analyze. But, Erik, sometimes . . . I don't know . . . I feel like you're a stranger."

"You know me inside and out. We belong together."

"Please?" She hated to beg. "Try to understand. I need to know certain things about you."

"Ask away."

"Oh, not now. Not like that."

He lifted his head and kissed her lightly. "I'm sorry. I'm bad at that stuff. You're not the first who's told me so. I'll try to be better, I swear to you." Then he rolled her over on top of him, spanning her waist with his hands, holding her there tightly against him. "You know I love you?" he asked.

"Yes," she breathed.

"That's all then, that's enough."

She was going to disagree, to tell him she had to know him. But he rolled her over again, his weight crushing her, then he rested his weight on his elbows and drew her close, tasting the sweet nectar of her mouth, sucking and licking and teasing until she bucked under his hand, and then he entered her and impaled her, and once again she was climbing that peak, higher and higher, sweating, reaching for it, climbing . . .

At dawn she awoke, shivering. They were still on the floor of her living room, only Erik's shirt drawn over them. And she realized that he hadn't answered any of her questions; he had dodged the bullet again with his mouth, his hands, and his perfectly tuned body.

NINE

She spotted an empty corner table in the upstairs Bistro at Explore Booksellers and set her armful of books and magazines down alongside her sandwich. She had over an hour till her next patient was due at the office.

Ignoring her sandwich for a moment, she opened the first book and flipped to the index. There he was, Amundsson, Erik, page 140. She noted that the book had been copyrighted back in 1985, some years before Erik had reached world-renowned status among climbers. Turning to the page, she scanned several paragraphs in which his name was mentioned. There was even a photograph, a beardless Erik in full climbing gear, a shockingly blue sky behind him, a banner of snow blowing off a far peak. He looked so young, so very young.

She picked up another book, no Amundsson in this one, but it appeared interesting, nevertheless, about Sherpas and Katmandu and the Himalayas. Places Erik had been, exotic places she'd probably never see.

She wanted to know everything about his world; she had a compulsion to learn about it. She supposed that

was only another aspect of her need for control. On
the other hand, she wondered sometimes if she were
searching for answers that he would not supply. Or
maybe she expected corroboration of her worst doubts
and fears about him.

Whatever her reasons, she kept buying volumes
about mountain climbing, or going to the library, im-
mersing herself in the subject.

She knew that Erik lived in a world she would never
fully comprehend. She could no more control that part
of his life than he could control her need to treat her
patients or work with the kids at the ranch. Not that
he *wanted* to enter that corner of her existence. In that
respect, he was so different from her—the yin to her
yang. Weren't opposing personalities supposed to
make for a balanced relationship?

Okay, she'd keep that in mind, she was thinking,
when a voice cut into her consciousness.

"Meredith Greene?"

She looked up, startled.

"Hey, it is you," a man said. "What a coincidence."

It took her a second before she recognized him.

"John McCord. I came to your office a while back."

"Oh, sure, John." She shook his proffered hand.
"Nice to see you again."

He'd been carrying a sandwich and a cup of coffee,
which he sat on the table. He was halfway in the chair
before he asked, "Mind if I join you?"

"Well . . . why not?"

He craned his neck and looked at her books. *"Solo
Faces,"* he read, taking a bite of sandwich. *"Alaska
Ascents, Aconcagua: A Climbing Guide.* Heavy read-
ing. You climb, Meredith?"

She laughed and put a finger to her chest. "Me? Good God, no."

"Um." He swallowed, took a sip of coffee, put the mug down. "It's a fascinating subject. I supposed you must treat a few climbers, right?"

She tilted her head. "Not really. Though if you live in this town long enough, you're bound to run into some."

"Weren't there a couple of locals who damn near died on Everest a few years back? Lot of people did die, as I recall."

"Yes. Too many. And yes, there were three Aspenites on the climb. They all made it down. Still . . ."

"Takes more guts than I've got," he said, and she noted the ease of his demeanor, the openness, the keen interest in his blue eyes.

As before, when he'd been in her office, she decided that he was a good-looking man. Sturdy build, competent carriage, his features imperfectly balanced but attractive.

She felt his charm, and she thought, *He's so different from Erik, so open and . . . nice.* Being with a man who wasn't so intense was restful.

Funny, in her office she'd barely noticed that Irish charm. Then she remembered; she'd been waiting for Erik's call, waiting and waiting and suffering.

"Know someone going on a climb?" He wiped his mouth with the napkin, balled it, and tossed it on the empty plate.

"Oh," she said, wondering why she didn't tell him the truth, "I always know someone going up some mountain."

"You'd have to be nuts to risk your life like that, if

you ask me. Of course, nuts is probably not a word you like to use too often." One side of his mouth lifted in a smile.

She grinned back and found herself enjoying the moment, a shared warmth in her belly, a small pleasure. "Oh, sure, I say things like that all the time."

"Not politically correct, I guess."

"Not about that."

"So we agree," he said drolly, "people who climb are nuts."

She laughed. And then she caught herself, and she realized she hadn't felt so lighthearted in a long time.

She sat back in her chair and studied him as he thumbed through one of the magazines. For all his charm, there was something in those blue eyes, an alertness, something plugged in and sharp, and for a moment, she wondered.

"I'm sorry," she said after a time, "but I can't recall offhand, what is it you do in Aspen?"

His gaze lifted. "Sales. I'm in sales. Nowadays, with computers and wireless communication, you can live just about anywhere."

"Um," she said, and then she glanced at her watch. "Oh, gosh, I've got to run."

"So soon?"

"Duty calls."

"Well, it's been a pleasure bumping into you like this."

She rose and straightened her navy blue linen blazer, then collected the books to put back on their respective shelves.

"Well," she said, and then she had to know. "John, mind if I ask you something?"

"Sure, go ahead."

"Most of my patients come back for at least a second visit. I was just curious . . ."

"Why I never came back?"

"Yes."

"Maybe you cured me."

"I doubt that."

He grinned.

"So why *did* you come to my office?"

"Maybe I just wanted to meet you?" he said teasingly.

She hefted the books and rolled her eyes. "I think I just heard a bunch of blarney," she said, and she turned to go.

"Say," came his voice. "Would you like to go to dinner some evening? Or maybe a movie?"

"Thank you, but no," she said, turning away again.

"So you're still seeing Amundsson," he said.

"What?"

"The climber." He nodded at her armful of books. "Erik Amundsson."

"How did you—?"

"Hey," he said, "I may be new to Aspen, but it's still a small town."

"Oh," was all she could think to reply, and she finally made her way to the mountaineering section in the bookstore, all the while aware of his gaze following her.

She was hurrying down Main Street, secretly smiling from the flattering encounter, when a notion struck her. There was Tony, who still occasionally called. And there was, of course, Erik, who dominated her existence. Now there was John McCord, who'd just come on to her and whom she couldn't help liking. Was it possible her pre-Erik life had been that controlled, that chaste? Perhaps something in her had been awakened, a sexual awareness that had always been beneath the surface. Tony must have recognized it. And now John. But she owed the awakening to Erik.

She unlocked the door to her office, sat her purse in her desk drawer, and smiled.

Erik and Chad drove out of town the next morning for a three-day climb in Rocky Mountain National Park. They were guiding a group from Denver and would meet them at the base of Longs Peak.

She was leaving for work, just opening her car door, when she saw Tony come out of his place two units down.

Tony.

Even though they lived so close, she really had not run into him in weeks. She felt bad about that, guilty. She started her car and realized she'd ignored all their mutual friends, ignored an entire part of her past life since that first night with Erik. Should she call Tony from work? Say hi? They'd been friends, well, lovers, for a long time, and she'd never actually put the relationship to rest.

Halfway into Aspen, her mind rejected the idea. Maybe she'd done a poor job of breaking up with him, but it was over. Better to let sleeping dogs lie. But by the time she parked behind her office building, she was thinking, *Chicken, he was your friend for a long time.* She needed to get over the guilt, which was, if nothing else, a demanding mistress.

Professionally, she knew there was guilt over death

and crushing guilt over divorce; guilt from placing a parent in a nursing home; guilt over quality time not spent with children; guilt over business deals, friendships, sexual relationships, even over the use of the word *no*.

She was no stranger to the condition. She'd suffered guilt over the death of her mother. Should she have stood up for her mother when she had not wanted to make that drive to Denver? And there was her guilt that her little sister had deserved a better role model than Meredith. Now she was going to suffer every time she bumped into Tony.

Yes. She'd phone him.

She reached his secretary and left a message, and he returned her call within the hour.

"Meredith, my God, I thought you'd dropped off the face of the earth."

"No such luck," she said lightly.

"What's up?"

"I thought you might want to come over for dinner tonight."

"Excuse me?"

"I just thought—"

"So where's lover-boy?"

"Tony."

"Well, where is he? Christ, I see his Jeep parked outside your place just about every night."

She was aware that her fingers were squeezing the receiver so hard they hurt. Maybe calling him had been a bad move. "He's out of town."

"And you're lonely already? Is that it?"

"For God's sake, Tony, I just wanted to get together over a pizza or something and talk," she said tightly.

"Sorry. Damn, there I go, acting like an ass."

"If you don't want to—"

"Sure I want to. We're friends, aren't we? At least that's what you said we were."

"Yes, we are."

"Okay, sevenish?"

"That's fine. I'm looking forward to it, Tony, honestly."

"Just don't analyze me," he said. "Okay?"

"It's a deal." She bought a self-rising frozen pizza at the store on her way home, the kind with everything, the way Tony liked it. And she thought, as she preheated the oven and unwrapped it, that she didn't know Erik's preference in pizza. He'd eat anything, it seemed. Food wasn't important to him except as fuel.

Tony arrived at seven-fifteen, straight from work, carrying an expensive bottle of cabernet. He wore an oatmeal linen sport coat over a short-sleeved silk shirt in creamy white. And Meredith remembered how attractive she'd thought he was when she'd first seen him.

"Hi," he said, giving her a kiss on the cheek, holding both her hands. "Sorry I was such a jerk on the phone."

The situation was so ordinary; they had shared pizza or Chinese takeout or ribs so often. In her place or in his. And they'd been easy together, comfortable.

But now, when she'd experienced the intensity of loving Erik, she knew her relationship with Tony had been a poor facsimile of love.

"You know, I'm not exactly sure how to act around you anymore," Tony said, sitting on a barstool, his usual place, leaning his elbows on the counter.

"It's a little awkward, isn't it?"

"I'm the same, but you're not, Meredith."

He's right, she thought, but she smiled and said, "It's still me, Tony."

He cocked his head and eyed her, and she felt his gaze crawling over her. "Not quite," he said.

She felt herself flush and turned her back on him, busying herself with making a salad.

They ate at the counter, and he kept refilling her glass with wine every time she took a sip. He also drank three glasses while she was still working on her first.

"Good pizza," he said. "Thanks."

"Good wine."

"That, too."

She got up to put the dishes in the sink, and he laid a hand on her arm, holding her still.

"What'd you want to talk about?" he asked, a slightly reckless glint in his eye.

"Nothing special. Just what you've been doing, you know, work, the usual stuff."

"You don't want to talk about Erik the Great?"

She drew back. "No, not really."

"You sure fell for him like a ton of bricks."

"Tony, I didn't ask you over to talk about Erik." She disengaged herself and walked to the sink to deposit the dishes.

"Maybe we're not quite friends, Meredith. What do you think? I mean, what's your *professional* opinion?"

"I'm not getting into that. Do you want to change the subject?"

"Not especially."

He got off his stool and came up behind her. Too close.

"Tony, please."

"Please what?"

"Now you really are acting like an ass."

She could feel his breath on her neck, warm and winy.

"Stop it right now," she said.

He stepped back, and she pivoted to face him. This was turning ugly. She never should have asked him over. *Stupid. Stupid.*

"Where'd the big hero go this time?" Tony asked.

"He and Chad Newhouse are guiding a group up Longs Peak."

"Um. I don't suppose . . ." Tony grinned. "I don't suppose you'd like to, ah, you know, for old times' sake?"

At first she wasn't sure she'd heard him correctly. "What did you say?"

"You heard me."

"Oh, my God, Tony," she breathed, "you can't mean that."

"Why not?"

"Because . . . because you can't possibly think I'd do that. You can't . . ."

"Oh, come off it, Meredith," he sneered, "if you let Amundsson, I figure you'll let anyone."

"What the hell are you *talking* about?" Fury flamed up her neck.

"You know exactly what I mean."

"The hell I do!"

"You're just another one of Amundsson's conquests. You're no different than any new summit he sets his sights on. And I'll tell you something else. Once he's there, he doesn't hang out for long. Hell, no, he climbs down and starts looking for the next challenge."

"You don't know what you're talking about!" she began, but he turned his back on her, lifted his hand in a dismissive wave, and started off toward her front door.

Rage and disbelief held her rooted for a moment, until she moved with a jerk toward him.

"Good night, Meredith," he said sarcastically.

"You can call me when you're ready to apologize," she shot back, but he paid her no mind, opening her door and sauntering off toward his own unit.

That son of a bitch, she was thinking, hugging herself in the doorway, when she saw a car out of the corner of her eye, a dark SUV with tinted windows parked across the main road, its headlights on, motor running. It looked like the same vehicle that had been parked outside Kemil's the other night, the car Erik had given the finger to.

Then she caught herself. How ridiculous. There were hundreds of dark SUVs in the valley—thousands of them. This couldn't possibly be the same car.

The vehicle pulled away then and disappeared down the long, curving descent of Woody Creek Road that eventually crossed the river.

Ridiculous, she thought again, why would anyone have been watching her?

She shook herself mentally as she went back inside. *First obsession with a man and now paranoia,* she thought, and she closed her door, her mind once more on Tony and the spiteful things he'd said.

Well, Tony was wrong, she decided. He was just a jealous asshole.

•   •   •

On Saturday, Meredith loaded her riding gear into her car and slammed the hatchback, turning to stare at Tony's town house.

She was still pissed. She'd fumed half the night.

But by the time she finished with the kids' therapy sessions that afternoon, she finally felt revived. There was something so uplifting, so special about the children and the horses and the scents in the barn, in the paddocks, in the wide fields where the tall grass brushed against her blue jeans and the clouds scudded by overhead in that sapphire Colorado sky. She didn't know what she'd do if her dad ever sold the place. She guessed she'd have to get rich and buy a ranch of her own.

She put Pace back in his field and waved to the kids and their parents as they drove away down the ranch road that ran alongside a hayfield.

The sessions had gone wonderfully today. Jodie Smith had even taken a step on her own toward her wheelchair when Meredith had helped her down from the saddle. No one had spoken a word. They'd just watched in mute amazement. And then finally someone had breathed, "Holy cow," and then everyone was talking and exclaiming.

She left Pace in the field with his equine buddies and walked back toward the gate, smiling. *A bad night last night, okay,* she thought, *but a great day today.*

Her father found her when she was changing out of her paddock boots, knocking mud off and tossing them into the back of her car.

"Oh, hey, Merry," he called out, "hold up a sec."

A cloud drifted over her sunny mood. *What now?*

He strode up to her, dusting his weathered hands on his worn jeans. "How'd the kids do?"

"Great. Jodie took a step by herself after dismounting. It wasn't a big step, and it wasn't steady, but—"

"That's good, yes, very good." He looked distracted.

"So?" She stared at him.

"Oh, I . . . I," he began, "just thought I'd say hello."

She smiled falsely. "Hello, then."

"Um," Neil said, and he started to stride away but abruptly halted. He turned back toward her. "I was wondering . . ."

She waited.

"Well, Soren down the road, you know Soren, bought the old McPherson place?"

"Uh-huh."

"Anyway, he said something about you seeing this man, this Amundsson character, and I just wanted to, well . . ."

"Go on," she said tightly.

Neil sighed. "Ah, hell, Merry. I mean, isn't Amundsson the same man who took your patient on that climb and got her killed?"

She felt her face freeze.

"What I'm saying is, should you be in a relationship with a man who caused you so much damn heartache?"

He might as well have slapped her. She stood back and narrowed her eyes and the words flew out. "Of all people, *Dad*, you should know about being responsible for the death of a loved one. Right?"

Neil looked as if he'd been punched. "Merry, *Meredith*," he began, "I didn't mean to—"

"Oh, the hell you didn't," she ground out, and she slammed the hatch and got in her car and drove away.

My God, she thought, shaking with anger. First Tony and now her father, and Erik wasn't here. And even if he had been, would he be any support to her now? Would he even listen to her problems?

No, her brain echoed back.

TEN

Still upset, she phoned Sandra Cohen that night. A friend and a colleague, Sandra was a psychotherapist, and in one of her increasingly rare moments of insight, Meredith knew she needed to talk to someone both objective and sympathetic. There was no one else, no one impartial she could speak to about her inner turmoil, certainly not her father or even her sister or any of her friends, whom she'd neglected for months now.

She was isolated, and suddenly she was afraid.

Sandra was older than Meredith, in her forties, a petite woman with prematurely gray hair. She'd been Meredith's mentor when she was starting her practice, and Meredith regarded her with the highest respect.

On Monday afternoon, she drove to Sandra's office, which was located in the woman's home in Aspen's Eastwood subdivision, on the road that lead over Independence Pass. It was a glorious summer day, warm and dry, the sky robin's egg blue shading to sapphire at the edges. Independence Pass rose in deep green ranks, twenty miles distant, and white billowing clouds massed above its heights. Postcard pretty. But the beauty did not touch her as it normally would have. She was unsettled and distracted.

Sandra hugged her and said, "Let's call this a professional consult. I'll listen, and we'll decide where to go from there, okay?"

"Thanks, Sandra, I really mean it."

She sat across from her mentor in the familiar office. She'd come to Sandra last winter when she had been having so much trouble with her feelings about Tony, about their proposed engagement. Sandra had helped her then; she prayed that Sandra could help her now, too.

"I've met a man," she began. "I think I love him, no, I know I love him, and I believe he loves me."

My God, she thought, she sounded exactly like Bridget Lawrence at their first session. She took a deep breath. "But I feel, I don't know, he's so different than most men, a mountain climber, a famous one, actually. Like no man I've ever known before. He's so powerful, I don't mean physically, well, he's that, too, but mentally, emotionally. When I'm with him, it's as if I have no mind of my own."

"I can't believe that, Meredith. You have a very strong self-image."

"I know, I know, but . . . Sandra, I'm afraid. He's got a kind of control over me, and I don't understand it."

"Sexual control, emotional control, physical control?"

She looked down at her hands clasped in her lap. She felt as if she were vibrating inside, like a tuning fork. "All of the above. The sex, well, I was always a prude, but he . . . I respond, you know? I lose myself."

"That's not always bad."

"No, maybe not. Sandra, you know about my control issues. Well, I have no control in this relationship."

"Do you feel this lack of control is destructive?"

That was the point, wasn't it? "I'm not sure. I don't know whether it's liberating or just the opposite." She looked up. "I don't know him. I've been with him for almost three months now, practically every night. We're intimate. I love him, but I don't *know* him. He won't answer questions; he laughs them off." She drew in a quavering breath. "And lately, I've come to realize, he doesn't ask me questions, he doesn't care about my past or what I do or my family. . . . It's always the present, and sex, and how we feel together."

"Do you think this will change when you get over the first flush of physical attraction?"

"I don't know." She leaned forward. "There's a situation I want to ask him about. You remember I told you about Bridget Lawrence and how she died? This is the man she was with. And, Sandra, I've tried asking him what happened up there. He won't answer. He just says it was an accident, end of story. I don't even know how he felt about Bridget dying. And there are other climbs he's been on where people have lost their lives, but I won't bother you with the details. He's a hero, a real leader, he saved lives, too, and guided climbers all over the world, but . . ."

"But . . . ?"

"People have died on climbs with him," she finally whispered.

"Meredith, climbing is an extremely dangerous undertaking. All guides have lost clients."

"Yes, but . . ." She squirmed in the chair, crossing

her legs, uncrossing them, folding her arms across her chest. "I'm so afraid. Am I the only one who can see it? Is he careless or foolhardy? Does he risk people's lives? Is he . . ." She paused and swallowed, her throat constricted. "Is he . . . is he like my father?"

"Ah," Sandra said.

"Yes," Meredith breathed. "I'm scared, terrified. They say women unconsciously look for a man like their father. Is this what I've done?"

"Your father is not a mountain climber. His profession isn't dangerous. I'm not sure you're drawing a valid parallel there."

"Neither of them," Meredith took a breath, "neither of them will take responsibility. It's as if they . . . they don't *care*."

"People, especially men, have very strong defenses. Are you mistaking a natural defense mechanism for not caring?"

"I don't know."

"I get the feeling that this man you love, well, you're not sure you trust him. Is that right?"

"Yes," she murmured.

"A difficult situation. You love him, but you don't trust him. And he isn't forthcoming, so you feel you can't communicate."

"Oh God." Tears pricked behind her eyelids. "It sounds so awful, so stupid."

"You do feel that he loves you, though."

"Yes."

"But you don't trust your own perceptions? Am I stating it correctly?"

"Yes, I don't trust myself anymore. I feel . . . I feel

like I'm dangling from a limb, and if I let go, there'll be no one to catch me."

"You don't feel secure about this man catching you?"

"Erik," she said. "You may as well know his name. Erik Amundsson."

"Yes, I realized that's who it was." Sandra looked at her. "But you don't feel secure. . . ."

"No, I guess I don't. When we're together, everything is fine. I'm happy, wonderfully happy. But when I'm alone, I look back, and I realize he's taken over my life."

"That may change after you've been together longer."

She shook her head. "I'm afraid it won't."

"Could you take some time away from him, see how you feel with a little distance between you?"

"He's going on a climb soon. To Mount McKinley. He'll be gone a month."

"That may be a very fortuitous thing."

"I'm scared to death he'll get hurt . . . or killed. Or he'll lose someone else on the climb. God, I know everyone who's going with him. If anything happened . . ."

"Difficult . . . hm."

"He loves climbing. He won't ever stop, I know that. And I just have to stay behind and worry."

"I'm sure that, too, will change with time. You're projecting into the future, Meredith. You know, certainly, you know that intensity of emotion can never last."

"I know it intellectually, but that doesn't help." She still felt that unnerving quiver inside. "What should I do, Sandra? Should I just break up with him?" She put her face in her hands. "But I can't. I love him. I'm nothing without him."

"Meredith, look at me," Sandra said. "That's better. Now, you know I can't tell you what to do. No one can do that. And if I did," she smiled slightly, "you wouldn't do it, anyway. Okay, this is what I see. You've lost your most precious possession, your control. It's made you very uncomfortable. You don't trust Erik completely, but that may be your problem, not his. He's going away soon. You have time to think, to tell yourself you aren't lost. You're still there. Your brain, your feelings. No one can take those away from you. You tell yourself that every day, several times a day. 'I'm all here, I'm the same person. No one can take me over.' "

"Cognitive behavior," Meredith sighed.

"It works."

"Am I crazy?" Meredith asked beseechingly.

"Crazy in love."

"Is that all it is?"

"No, no, you're dealing with other issues. This man, Erik, he may have his own issues. They'll come out eventually. Try to talk to him, ask those questions you say he won't answer. But don't be confrontational. Keep trying, a little here, a little there. See how things develop."

"What if he . . . ? What if he . . . sometimes . . . he almost frightens me."

"Is he physically abusive?" Sandra asked pointedly.

"No . . . I mean, well, no, not really." She shifted in her chair. Was she telling the whole truth? Hadn't he left bruises on her?

Sandra leaned forward. "I draw the line at physical abuse, Meredith. And you have to do so as well. There is no good outcome to a relationship like that."

"I know. Oh, of course I know. He's not abusive, my God, I couldn't, I . . . wouldn't . . ."

"All right then."

"Can I call you if I have problems? I feel so fragile, I can't trust my judgment."

"Of course you can. And if you want to come in later this week . . ."

"Let me see. I'm not sure. I have to work some things out myself."

"I'm here for you."

"Thanks, Sandra, thanks so much."

She returned to her own office for her last patient of the day, forcing herself into the role of therapist, switching her mind-set 180 degrees. She was getting better at this, learning to put her own problems aside to focus on her patients. She owed them her complete attention and her complete sympathy.

Nancy Randall needed help; she'd been seeing Meredith for years and was finally coming to terms with her husband's alcoholism. Halfway into the session, she sighed and blew her nose in a tissue. "I don't know. The minute I showed Frank the separation papers, he said that was it, he'd get help, and he swore he'd stop drinking for good this time. God, he even got all choked up. I just don't know what to think or do. I . . . I love Frank. I'll always love the man he was when we were first married. Even after the kids were born, he still had control. But then . . ." Nancy pulled another tissue out of the box on the table next to her chair.

Meredith waited.

"I just don't know. I realize I've been coming to you for three years. I've tried so hard to get my head together and to do the right thing. The kids aren't really a factor now that Lisa is in college. It's just Frank and me. And both Pete and Lisa support me in this. Still . . . What if Frank really could quit drinking this time? I mean, what if my finally going to a lawyer last week does the trick?"

"What do *you* want to do, Nancy? Do you want to give Frank another chance?"

"I . . . I don't know. I guess in my heart I realize he'll probably fail this time, too. But what if I'm wrong? What if I throw him out, and I'm wrong?"

She listened, knowing Nancy wasn't really asking for an answer.

"I think if I give Frank another chance, I might be falling back into the role of enabler. I know that, but . . . Sorry, I'm using your whole box of Kleenex."

"I have more." She smiled.

"Anyway, the awful truth is, I'm fifty-three years old, and I don't want to be alone the rest of my life. At least with Frank I have someone. I know he drives me crazy, and I can't stand it when he drinks, but still . . ."

"Why do you think you have to be alone, Nancy?"

The woman's eyes widened and abruptly she laughed. "Are you serious? In *this* town? Where everyone is thirty-something and gorgeous?"

"I'm quite serious. You're intelligent, you're a very attractive woman. Not every man wants a young model type. Don't sell yourself so short."

Then Meredith said, "Let's back up a minute and

discuss the possibility that you might still be enabling Frank to drink if you give him another chance."

"Then you think I shouldn't give him a shot at quitting?"

"That isn't what I said. I want to know how you feel about it. Do *you* think you would be enabling Frank?"

While Nancy struggled with the question, Meredith thought: *Am I like her? Am I sticking to a man I know is bad for me because I'm terrified of being alone?*

"Listen," she finally told her patient, "you don't have to decide all by yourself. Ask your family. If you aren't comfortable discussing this with your children, you can talk to your sister. Didn't you say you have a sister?"

"Okay," Nancy sniffed.

"Or friends. Talk about it. But think of this: By forcing Frank to face what he could lose, do you think it's possible you'll be giving him the best shot he's ever had at getting sober?"

Nancy lowered her eyes. "It's so hard. Oh, God, I hope I can go through with this. Maybe I should see you again this week?"

"See how it works out tonight. If you need me, you know I'll fit you in."

She closed the door behind Nancy and took a deep breath. She could usually see so clearly what direction her patients needed to take, and she could urge them, sympathize with them, ambush their denial, show them their alternatives. Yet she was helpless with her own problems. Useless, weak.

No, she thought, *I'm all here, I'm the same person. No one can take me over.* That was better.

Erik would be home tonight. She felt the excitement take hold, the yearning, the need to have him close, to smell his scent and feel his hands on her. He'd gone to Rocky Mountain National Park, and he said he'd be back by seven or eight. Only a few more hours.

She'd go home and take a bath, wash her hair, shave her legs, dab on that perfume he liked. Be all ready for him when he arrived, sweaty and tired and euphoric from the climb.

But first, she stopped at the library to return a couple of books on climbing that they hadn't had at the book-store. She dropped them off at the desk, said hi to one of the librarians she knew, then made her way to the section on mountaineering. By now she knew it well, had read dozens of the books. *Into Thin Air*, about the Everest climb of '96. *Annapurna: A Woman's Place*, covering an all-female climb in 1978, on which two of the women had died.

Books with titles like *High Exposure: An Enduring Passion for Everest and Unforgiving Places,* and *Tibet's Secret Mountain: The Triumph of Sepu Kangri.* She'd become familiar with the names of famous climbers past and present: Chris Bonington and Dougal Haston and John Harlin, who'd died young on the North Face of the Eiger, Mallory and Irving and Sir Edmund Hillary. David Breashears and the crazy climber from Aspen, Fritz Stammberger, who left for a solo ascent on Tirich Mir in the Hindu Kush and disappeared, never to be seen or heard from again. Herman Buhl, who walked around with snowballs in his fists to prepare for climbs, and Harvey Carter, who started *Climbing* magazine.

Royal Robbins and Reinhold Messner, perhaps the most accomplished and famous climber of modern times, Rob Hall and Scott Fischer, who died on Everest in '96, Anatoli Boukreev, a Russian veteran who was either hero or irresponsible cad, depending on one's view, who had died on Annapurna at thirty-nine.

So many young men dead, was all she could think.

She also located an article in an old magazine about the Aconcagua climb on which Erik had lost his fingers and copied it from microfilm to take home with her. She felt guilty doing this behind his back, as it were, but she couldn't ask him; he'd laugh it off, refuse to answer, tell her it didn't matter anymore. But it *did* matter—to her.

She took her bath, pulled on a pair of sweats and a green T-shirt that flattered her eyes. "They're like emeralds," Erik had told her, "so beautiful, so rare." And she ate leftover lasagna she'd bought at the store days ago. Then she curled up on her green couch, the library books piled on the coffee table, and pulled out the Aconcagua article from between the pages of one of the books.

The article was dated ten years ago, a month after the three people had died on the tragic climb. She scanned the material she already knew, that Mount Aconcagua was in western Argentina, near the Chilean border. It was the highest peak in the Western Hemisphere at 22,841 feet and was visible from Santiago, Chile's capital.

It was a deceptive mountain, some of the climbing routes merely hikes to the summit, but this was the reason that Aconcagua had one of the highest death rates in the world. The climb was considered technically easy, and too many mountaineers underestimated its weather and elevation.

She knew all that already from previous reading. She

also knew what Erik thought of Aconcagua. "It's treacherous," he said, "like a woman who is disloyal." And that was all. But the author of this article—she glanced at the byline, Glen Darnauer, and found it unfamiliar—went on.

Aconcagua provides the worst kind of conditions, rotten ice and rock. It is demoralizing, chipping away at a climber's mind and strength until he is weak, his judgment impaired. Men can be destroyed as they trudge hour after hour, day after day, through slippery shale and crumbling rock, over moraine and glaciers honeycombed with crevasses.

At the top there is wind crust and crotch-deep snow, and often you can't see the summit because of swirling spindrift.

This is the background of the 1990 attempt. Erik Amundsson and Chad Newhouse were the guides out of Aspen, Colorado's Summit Expeditions. An experienced team. The eight climbers with them, however, were neophytes. Young, wealthy, and out for adventure, they set out in the South American summer, our winter, to climb this infamous peak.

The facts are plain. At 19,000 feet, a storm hit, and they were pinned down away from their camp. Two days passed, and finally rescuers reached the party. Three were dead of the cold and altitude, the guides were alive, suffering from frostbite, as were five of the climbers. Erik Amundsson emerged as a hero, having saved the five survivors by giving them his own sleeping

*bag and parka, digging a snow cave and build-
ing a fire and actually carrying Joseph Frankel
to the snow cave on his back when Frankel collapsed, then returning to locate the disoriented
Tom Bolander and three others, leading them to
safety.*

*A hero some say. Yet there was something else
going on here, a nasty undercurrent that professional climbers don't like to admit. Questions
about judgment. Did Summit Expeditions know
its clients well enough? Had they been tested on
lesser peaks? Had Amundsson, the leader, paid
heed to weather reports? Other teams on Aconcagua that day had stayed in their camps. Had
Amundsson and Newhouse gone too fast, pushed
their clients mercilessly, weakened them so that
they could not withstand the storm? Was this all
undertaken with the perhaps untenable goal of
summiting, regardless of cost?*

One more question: Was this good business?

Oh dear God, Meredith thought, and a chill ran
down her spine. Could this man have been right? No,
of course not. And even he admitted Erik was a hero.
He was just trying to stir up trouble, make his story
interesting, an armchair critic after the fact.

Then she heard the door open, and the familiar
sound of Erik's footsteps.

She rose, combed her fingers through her hair,
dropped the article on the couch, and went to him.

"How was it?" she asked.

"Good. It was good. Everyone kept up." He put his
arms around her, rested his chin on the top of her head.

"I thought of you on the summit. I thought you'd like the view."

She leaned into him, drawing in the scent of sweat and fresh air and satisfaction. "I'd love the view." She tilted her face up. "I'll hire a helicopter and see it."

He didn't reply, dipping his head and kissing her hard, and all her nerve endings shivered in delight.

"Tired?" she finally asked.

"A little."

"Hungry?"

"No, we stopped in Leadville on the way home and ate at that Mexican place."

"Can you stay tonight?"

"Yes, I can stay."

He released her and moved to the couch, dropping into it. Idly, he picked up the article she'd been reading.

"Oh," she said, reaching for the photocopies, somehow knowing he should not see them.

"What in hell is this?" he asked, his voice low and dangerous, his body suddenly tense.

"Nothing, it's nothing. An article. I've been reading about climbing, you know that. I . . ."

He rose, towering over her, his face paling with anger. "You've been reading this, this bastard, Darnauer, this liar?"

"I was just—"

His big hands grasped the papers and ripped them in half; he threw the pieces down, and they fluttered like wounded birds to the floor. "That's fucking history!" he yelled.

She was afraid for a split second, shrinking at his display of rage. But then she grew irate herself at the injustice of his overreaction and she drew herself up, and out of her mouth came words that surprised her. "I was reading a goddamn article! What are you so mad about? Because that guy, that Darnauer was *right?* Is that why?"

Erik glared at her, his blue eyes wintry, crystallized ice. "No, Meredith," he finally grated out, "he is *not* right. He wasn't even there. He's not even a real climber. He's a nobody."

"I can read what I want, Erik. I'm a big girl. I don't need you to censor my reading. I can make up my own mind, for God's sake."

"You don't know enough to read that crap." He made an angry gesture at the scattered paper on the floor.

She began to pace, her heart pounding in her chest, so angry. He was unfair. "How can I trust you? How can I? Every time I ask you something, you duck the question. You never tell me anything. I'm an adult, goddamn it, and I deserve your respect. Oh Christ, you're just like my father, you won't talk, you won't take responsibility, you're in so much denial—"

"Meredith," he said. That voice, the one that soothed her and resonated deep inside.

"No, don't do that!" She cut the air with her hand.

"Come here."

"No . . . no." She stopped and looked at him. "Don't try to turn me off. You started this. What happened on your climb? Are you pissed off at something, and you're taking it out on me? Did you and Chad have an argument? Is it Kemil? Talk to me, Erik. Come on, where's that famous courage of yours?"

He came to her, and she stood up to him, chest to

chest, her eyes sparking defiance, suffused with the freedom of pure, burning fury. "Well?" she demanded.

He put his hands on her waist, drew her closer. "Um, so angry. My Valkyrie."

She trembled, trying to hold onto her anger. "No," she said.

"Oh yes."

"Erik . . ."

He kissed her, he stroked her back, kneaded her buttocks, pressed his hardness into her stomach. "Yes," he whispered against her lips.

"No." Faintly, a breath.

His hands were pulling up her T-shirt, pushing down her sweatpants, his beard tickling her face, her neck, the tender spot beneath her ear. "Yesss . . ."

"Oh God." She sagged in his arms, surrendering shamelessly, the bright flame of righteous indignation doused, her rage transmuted to passion, one heat melding into another.

Afterward, in her bed, Erik asleep beside her, she sobbed, burying her head in her pillow, hiding her anguish. She was too weak to cling to the limb anymore, her hands were slipping, her grip failing, her body heavy, so terribly heavy, and she lost her hold and there was no one to catch her and she was falling, falling.

ELEVEN

At six A.M. on the Fourth of July, two dynamite blasts on Smuggler Mountain rocked Aspen awake.

Dogs howled, tourists leaped out of hotel beds, frightened and confused, and the deputy sheriff rolled his eyes, jammed his Stetson on his head, and started out of the office. This year he'd find the goddamn perpetrators.

The explosion woke Meredith, but Erik was already up, packing the last few items, checking his equipment. They'd spent the night in his apartment over the garage, neat now that his gear was stowed.

"What time is it?" she mumbled.

"Early," he said.

"That noise . . ." She turned over and rubbed her eyes.

"Those crazy guys set off dynamite again." He came and sat on the edge of the bed, wearing only a white T-shirt and a pair of low-cut briefs.

"Um," she murmured as he ran his hand down her neck, trailing his fingers to her navel.

He lifted the blanket and slid beneath it, his long,

hard body against hers. Warm, so warm, even though he'd been walking around in his underwear. He was always warm. Probably even on the highest peak in a raging blizzard, Erik would be warm.

His hands woke her fully, familiar and skillful, and she responded as always. She remembered as he was entering her—such an odd time to recall, she would think later—that he was leaving that morning. So very soon he'd be gone, and the notion made her respond even more passionately than usual, crying out under him, then straddling him, her head thrown back, climbing her own peak, panting and working and ascending until she was there, on the summit, riding the waves of sensation, then over the top and slowly, descending, coming to earth lying on Erik, out of breath, stuck to him with sweat.

"I'll have to leave for climbs more often," he said, tickling her ribs with a finger.

"No," she breathed.

"But it makes it better, doesn't it?"

"What makes it better?"

"The going, the parting, not knowing when is the return."

"No," she said, but she thought she might be lying.

She drove him to the Pitkin County Airport to meet the others at nine. Kemil's plane would leave from Aspen Fixed Base Operations, the terminal for private aircraft. The building was close to the public terminal, a cozy log and stone and glass edifice that could have been placed on a lot on Red Mountain without raising eyebrows.

Erik had only one duffel bag, all the large items previously packed and loaded into Kemil's Suburban.

Kathy had given Chad a ride, and stayed for the leave-taking.

There was a special aura around the climbers. It manifested itself in the way they greeted one another, the way they interacted with those not going to Mc-Kinley. A heightened tension, a turning inward, a quietness. Even the voluble Dan said little. And yet their eyes were bright with excitement, their bodies sparking with accumulated energy. Adventures lay ahead. Risk and challenge would enrich their lives. They were the chosen ones, apart and above ordinary folk.

She tried to smile, but she felt left out, already lonely, even though Erik stood only a few feet away. She was beginning to tremble. She'd just overheard Kemil say something about a climber missing on Mc-Kinley, a storm . . . How many climbs could Erik make until he, too, was lost?

He stood there in the charming, tastefully designed FBO terminal, and she watched Erik, watched her lover, the man she'd been more intimate with than anyone else in her life, and he was still a stranger.

A thousand questions filled her head, wheeled around like a frightened flock of birds, but she couldn't ask one of them. He wouldn't answer, or maybe he couldn't. He was, perhaps, unknowable.

God, that hurt.

Kathy had finally said her good-byes and left, but Meredith couldn't seem to move. And Erik, whose attention was on his climbing buddies, his focus completely changed now, paid her no mind.

He finally came over to her and took her hand. "Come," he said, "I want to talk to you."

Her heart surged. One word, one lousy word, and she blossomed.

He took her aside, near the windows that separated them from the dozens of privately owned jets parked outside. "You look so sad," he said.

"I am sad."

"Don't be."

"Okay, if you say so."

"I loved you this morning, you loved me. We won't forget."

"No."

He smiled and brushed her lips with his, then he reached into the pocket of his jeans, his shoulder hunching up so he could slide his hand in, and pulled out a small velvet box. She peered down at it, then up at him, puzzled. He put the box in her hand, closing both of his over it.

"What?" she asked stupidly.

"Open it."

She snapped up the lid; inside was a gold ring. Simple, exquisite, a gold band holding a solitaire diamond. She lifted her eyes again, wide, wondering.

"Marry me," he said.

She was stunned; the floor shifted under her feet, and for a moment she was dizzy. She stared at him, her lips parted, and she would always remember the room, the hot yellow sun spilling through the window, laying a bright square on the floor, the other voices, the drone of a plane taking off, a loudspeaker squawking somewhere. And Erik, in a plaid shirt, his ice-blue eyes pinioning her, the gray hairs in his beard shining silver in the sunlight streaming through the glass. His hand, missing two fingers, warm on hers.

"Why me?"

"Because I love you. Because you're so centered, so grounded and so goddamn wonderful. My Meredith."

"Marry you?" she breathed.

He laughed. "You sound so surprised."

"I . . . I am."

She held the box with the ring still in it, afraid somehow to touch it or take it out of its velvet slot. She would be doing something irrevocable then.

"Well?"

She had to say something, he was waiting. "It's so soon, too soon. Shouldn't we think about it?"

"*I'm* sure, Meredith."

"But . . . but this is so, I mean, such a shock. I . . ."

"You what?"

"I . . . maybe we should . . . wait a little while."

"Do you love me?"

"Yes."

"Well, there we are."

Out of the corner of her eye, she could see the prince's copilot gathering the group for boarding. So suddenly, so amazing—he'd proposed to her. And she wondered whether he had picked this very time and place to spring his surprise so that she could not gain control and bombard him with her endless questions.

"So, I have to go now," he was saying.

She took the silver chain from around her neck, and with trembling fingers she strung the ring on it and looped the chain back on. "I'll keep it here," she said, holding her hand on the ring, "until you get back."

"I'll see you then, my love."

She smiled, a mournful, shaky smile. "Just don't do

anything stupid on that mountain of yours. Don't . . . die on me."

In answer, he drew her into his arms and kissed her breath away, then he shouldered his duffel bag and walked through the door onto the black tarmac, out into the sunlight of the warm July day.

She would always remember his erect, strong back, the heavy bag balanced easily on his shoulder, the way his long legs ate up the distance to the delicate, shining Learjet. She would remember that he never looked back.

Ordinarily, Meredith would not go into Aspen on the Fourth—too much traffic, too many people, too much carnival atmosphere—but after cleaning her house and doing the laundry and tending her neglected flower boxes, she was still too tense to stay home.

She phoned her old schoolmate. "Darlene? It's Meredith," she said to the machine that answered. "This is probably dumb, but are you free tonight? You want to watch the fireworks together? Give me a call."

An hour later, Darlene phoned back. "I'm free as a bird. I was going to watch the fireworks from my balcony. Me and a bottle of Merlot."

"That sounds healthy."

"Yeah, well, what's a single girl to do?"

They met at eight P.M. at the base of Aspen Mountain in front of the Ajax Tavern. Over wine and oysters on the deck of the restaurant, Darlene managed to wheedle from Meredith the fact that she had been practically living with Erik Amundsson since the end of the ski season. Of course by now, Meredith realized, everyone in town knew about the affair. Still, she kept the proposal to herself, her necklace and the ring safely tucked between her breasts.

She and her friend caught up on gossip and griped about the traffic, the hordes of tourists invading their little jewel of a town, and had a bottle of wine between them before the fireworks display began.

Meredith had hoped the cheerful atmosphere and the company of a close friend would allow her to forget Erik's absence. And she was enjoying the evening. Still, every time Darlene turned away to chat with someone, Meredith couldn't help thinking about Erik, feeling the ring against her skin, wondering if they'd gotten into Anchorage safely. Were they already in Talkeetna?

She should have stayed home, she thought over and over, clicked on to tallpeaks.com, the web site that Dan would use to broadcast over the Internet. Had Dan gone on-line yet? Filed his first report? Maybe he'd even put photos up, photos of the climbing party in Talkeetna, photos of Erik.

"Hey, Greene, the fireworks crew is getting ready." Darlene pointed to the top of the summer road that switchbacked up the face of Little Nell, the base of the mountain.

A sudden *boom,* followed by a rapid succession of explosions, shook the night, and howls and whistles rose from every square inch of town.

Meredith and Darlene stood and leaned against the wooden rail of the deck, necks craned upward, as brilliant bloom after bloom of color burst in the sky over the mountain. Some of the blossoms refused to extinguish and fell to rooftops, even to the deck in showers of sparks. Everyone cheered more loudly.

She wished suddenly, with all her heart, that Erik was there to share this with her. *Why* had he gone off to some mountain a million miles away and left her alone?

"God, this is great, isn't it, Greene?"

"Beautiful," Meredith got out.

After the fireworks, the town really went crazy, every bar and disco filled to overflowing, the holiday crowds spilling onto the downtown streets and malls.

Meredith and Darlene walked for a time, taking in the sights.

"It's like Disneyland, isn't it?" Darlene shook her head.

Meredith put on the sweater she'd brought along and hugged herself. "It's a zoo, all right."

They stopped to listen to a guitarist and a fiddler and then watched a tireless clown blow up balloons for the weary-eyed kids. A mime, his entire body painted in marble, cleverly dressed as a Greek statue, delighted a group with his infrequent moves into different poses.

"Local talent," Darlene muttered.

It was then that Meredith spotted John McCord on the far side of the audience. He and another man were also watching the mime. For a moment, she considered walking around the cluster of people and saying hello, maybe introducing Darlene, but she dismissed the idea. No sense encouraging John.

John finally spotted her. He waved a casual hello. She nodded. Then he and his friend wandered on.

She and Darlene also moved along, running into two men with whom they had gone to school. One of them was a sweetheart, a realtor, shy; the other was a ski instructor—in the summer he golfed. He'd always been a rich, arrogant jerk.

"So," Buddy the jerk said, "I guess Amundsson must have left for Alaska, right, Meredith?"

God, she thought, *everyone really does know.* And she realized they all must think the same as Tony: She was another Amundsson conquest.

She almost showed Buddy the ring. Almost stuck it under his nose and said, "See? I'm the one." But of course she didn't. And how would she explain not wearing it on her finger?

Why hadn't she said yes?

"You're still an ass, you know that, Buddy?" Darlene said.

"It's okay," Meredith put in. "Erik left this morning, in fact."

"And you're already out on the town," Buddy observed.

"Just watching the fireworks." Meredith shrugged. She wasn't about to let him get under her skin.

She and Darlene walked to Wagner Park, where the downvalley buses were loading.

"Sure you don't want to wander around some more? It's only ten-thirty," Darlene said.

"I'm sure. You know Dan, Daniel Froberg, the ski patrolman?"

"Yes?"

"Well, he's on the climb in Alaska, and he's a real computer freak. He's broadcasting it over the web, and I thought, well . . ."

"I get it," Darlene interrupted. "You can't wait to get home and check out the web site."

"Guess I'm busted."

"Hey, if it were me, *I'd* do the same. Amundsson," she said, pondering. "He's quite a catch, Meredith. I'm very proud of you."

"A catch," Meredith repeated. "I'll have to think about that."

She was home by eleven. She immediately dashed upstairs and turned on her PC, clicking onto the web. She'd already bookmarked tallpeaks.com.

While the web site downloaded, she threw on her pajamas and plumped down in her squeaking old office chair in front of the computer, which she kept in the spare bedroom upstairs. Automatically, her fingers fondled the ring, felt its smoothness, its coolness. When had Erik bought it? When had he made the decision to ask her to marry him?

Tallpeaks.com was slow to download, and then she had to locate the icon for the McKinley climb and click on that. Then she waited again, wishing she had DSL—expensive but lightning quick compared to her cheaper local Internet provider.

When had Erik decided to ask her?

Her mind raced, recalling every moment they'd been together. Maybe he'd decided on the climb last week. She should have asked him.

Mrs. Erik Amundsson. Meredith Amundsson. My God.

She was frightened to death. She was thrilled. She watched a series of photographs load onto the screen, and her heart pounded. The very concept of his profession terrified her. She had known that from the start. Was that why she'd hesitated to say yes? Because of the very real fact that one day he might not come back to her?

Or maybe it was the parallel she'd drawn in her mind between Erik and her father. She was so afraid Erik was a mirror image of the man who'd insisted her mother drive to Denver in that treacherous storm. So like her father—locked up inside, unable and unwilling to face reality, perhaps untrustworthy.

Was that why she'd hesitated?

Or maybe she didn't love him enough. Maybe her feelings were only sexual desire. After all, he had a reputation with women. . . . *Was* she just another conquest?

No. No. He asked her to marry him. *Her.* He must love her.

She blinked away her fog and saw that Dan's dispatch was fully downloaded. It read:

We landed in Anchorage early this afternoon. The fireworks display was scheduled for the half-light between 1 and 3 A.M. tomorrow morning, and we would have liked to see that, but our trusty van was waiting to drive us the three hours to the village of Talkeetna. I say trusty advisedly, because the van appeared quite dilapidated. However, Erik and Chad assured us it would get us there. It did.

We will spend a couple of days in Talkeetna, then fly in to the Kahiltna Glacier.

Prince Kemil al Assad, Kemil to his friends, and our two guides Chad Newhouse and Eric Amundsson from Summit Expeditions have climbed McKinley before, but me and my other climbing buddies have not been to Alaska. We doubt we'll sleep tonight. As I type this, the

*sun is circling the horizon. It's quite a sight. The
sky is cloudless and lit by the glare of the sun
and it's 11 at night. Strange, exotic.*

*We can see McKinley, miles away. It looms
out of its surroundings, a huge, glistening white
pyramid. We'll be there soon, God (and the Talkeetna Air Service) willing.*

*The Native Americans call the peak Denali,
meaning "the great one" in Athalbascan. It's
been said there is magic to the Indian name.*

*Talkeetna is tiny, a rustic village catering to
tourists and climbers. We are staying in one of
the small hotels, along with lots of other climbers.*

*Fingers crossed for continuing good weather,
Dan Froberg.*

Meredith smiled. *Denali.* She hoped it was good
magic.

She started to scroll down through the photographs.
The first two were of Talkeetna, apparently a small,
rustic conglomeration of log cabin–style buildings. She
spotted a country store, an outfitters, and a grocery
store with gas pumps in front. Down home Alaska.

How many times had Erik been there? Did he know
the locals by name, the Indians, the Denali National
Park rangers? Probably. After all, everyone knew him.
He was world famous, and he'd asked her to be his
wife.

She suddenly missed him with shocking desperation.
So what if he was bottled up inside, in denial over the
two climbing accidents? So what? She'd help him heal.
Together they would both heal their wounds.

She should have said yes. Yes, she loved him and wanted to marry him, and they should have set a date. No big affair. Just them. Just her and her soul mate and the cosmos. He'd like that.

Her hand was trembling a little as she scrolled down further on the screen. A blurry photo of the park beyond town. One of McKinley in the background.

Then there was the group, all but Dan, of course, who was behind his digital camera.

There was Kemil, grinning like a white-toothed fox. And Chad, looking annoyed. Probably tense and ready to climb just about anything. And Jessie and Kevin, smiling along with Kemil.

But it was Erik who held her attention. He stood half a foot above the others, on the right side of the picture. His expression was neutral, his feelings, whatever they were, carefully masked. He was wearing jeans and the same plaid shirt he'd had on that morning at the airport—suddenly seeming a lifetime ago. And he was also now wearing a bright blue fleece vest that was the exact color of his eyes.

She remembered that vest. It was the same one he'd bunched beneath her hips that first night on the floor of his living room.

She was abruptly overwhelmed by desire, the images of that intimate joining flashing behind her eyes. Thousands of miles away, and a mere photo of the man in the blue vest had the power to cause her belly to coil in need. Why hadn't she said yes?

TWELVE

She called Kathy the next morning before leaving for the office. She was jumpy and full of strange forebodings, and she hoped Chad's sister could set her mind at rest.

"Lunch?" Kathy said. "Sure, but I have to pick up the kids from soccer. Can we be done by one?"

"Absolutely."

"Where?"

"How about the Main Street Bakery? We'll sit outside and watch the cars go by."

"Okay. Noon?"

"See you then."

She had two patients that morning. Susie Watts, who was working on bulimia, and Jennifer Damato, a girl of eleven, who suffered from social anxiety. Meredith was thankful she had her work to keep her busy; otherwise, she knew, she'd be worrying about Erik, imagining all sorts of things, even though he was still in Talkeetna.

But she was finished with her clients by eleven-thirty, and she began to get jittery again.

Kathy was a few minutes late, hurrying into the Bakery in khaki hiking shorts and a white T-shirt and sandals, her dark hair pulled back haphazardly in a ponytail, wisps escaping.

"Oh my God," she breathed. "What a morning."

"The kids?"

"Yes, the kids, and about a dozen other things. Phew, let's get some lunch. I need to sit down and relax."

They stood at the counter and ordered sandwiches on freshly baked bread, then carried them outside to sit at a table under an umbrella.

"Have you heard from Erik?" Kathy asked, making it surprisingly easy to open the subject.

"Well, no, he said he probably wouldn't call. He said he has to focus on the mountain."

"The rat. That sounds so typical of him."

"Um. But I can follow the climb on the Internet."

"Oh, that's right. Dan was going to send dispatches, wasn't he?"

"He sent one yesterday. From Talkeetna. With pictures."

"So they got there."

"They got there."

Kathy seemed distracted, tense. The kids, maybe? Or Chad in Alaska?

Meredith's sandwich was wonderful, smoked ham and Swiss cheese with all the fixings on fresh sourdough. She took a couple bites, but the ring pressed against her skin like a brand. No one knew, not a soul, except for her and Erik.

"Kathy," she began, "I . . ."

Kathy cocked her head, her mouth full.

"Erik asked me to marry him."

Her friend's eyes widened. She chewed and swallowed. "Wow."

"Yeah, wow." She pulled the ring out from the V of her blouse. "He gave me this. Right before he left, in the airport."

"Oh my goodness, how fantastic! Oh, Meredith. Are you happy? Are you delirious?"

"I'm happy, God, yes."

"Well, why isn't that ring on your finger? Hey, show it to the world. You nabbed the Ice Man."

"Oh, Kathy . . ."

"He never asked anyone to marry him before, Meredith. That's huge."

"I guess, well, it's so fast. We haven't known each other very long, and I . . . I suppose I'm not completely sure."

"It's because he's a climber, isn't it? Hey, it's hard to be married to a guy who goes off to try to kill himself regularly."

Meredith flinched.

"It's true. But if you love him, and he loves you, well, there are plenty of married climbers."

"And plenty of climbers' widows," Meredith added.

"Some. But wouldn't it be worth it?"

"I guess that's what I have to decide, don't I?"

"Does Chad know?"

"I'm not sure. Probably not. Still, don't say anything. Not yet."

Kathy leaned forward across the table and put her hand on Meredith's arm. "It's perfectly natural to have doubts. He's in a damn dangerous profession. And the women . . . Sure, there've been some, but he never wanted to *marry* anyone before. He loves you, Meredith."

"Yes, I believe that."

"I'm so happy for you."

But Kathy was preoccupied, leaving part of her sandwich unfinished, listening with half an ear and allowing long, uncomfortable silences to fall between them.

"Are you worried about Chad?" Meredith finally asked. "It must be awful every time he goes on a climb. I don't know how you can bear it."

"Oh, hell, it's not that."

"Maybe you're more worried then you'll allow yourself to admit. You know, denial is a protective device."

Kathy smiled. "I keep forgetting you're a shrink."

"I'm not a shrink, I'm a psychologist."

Kathy waved a dismissive hand. "Same thing."

"I can tell you're uptight."

Kathy sighed and sagged back in her chair. "It shows that much?"

"Uh-huh."

"It's not Chad, it's not the climb. It's not even the kids, really. It's the job. The goddamn job."

"What's wrong?"

"The IRS. I hate them, I tell you . . ." She closed her eyes and gripped the table's edge. "They've called for a four-year audit of Kemil's returns. And I've got to put it together."

"Why on earth is the IRS after Kemil? He isn't even an American citizen."

"He has to file returns as a part-time resident. His finances are very complicated, as you can imagine. I do the U.S. end of things. God knows what goes on in Saudi Arabia."

"But why the audit?"

Kathy grimaced. "The government doesn't like some of Kemil's friends. You know, the Middle East and all those terrorists. You know how the government is."

"I do?"

"They're nuts, paranoid."

"But why would—?"

Kathy rose quickly, dug in her purse, and threw a ten-dollar bill on the table. "Listen, I've got to get the kids from soccer. I'm late." She bent down and kissed Meredith on the cheek. "Congratulations, and don't you worry about Chad and Erik. They'll be fine." Then she ran out to the street where her car was parked, giving Meredith a wave. As she pulled out into the Main Street traffic, Meredith stared after her, confused, wondering about Kathy's explanation—Middle East, terrorists, Kemil?

And then she saw a dark, perhaps black or charcoal SUV pull out a few cars behind Kathy's Cherokee. It had tinted windows.

She sat there at the table, surrounded by people eating lunch, chatting, laughing, the sun pouring down on an idyllic summer day, and she felt a small blockage in her chest that descended into her stomach and would not budge.

That night she settled in front of her computer and logged on to tallpeaks.com. There was another dispatch from Dan.

We're still in Talkeetna, learning about the eccentric Alaskans that live here. Our van driver

Tom was the first, a crusty old guy who swore at his vehicle to keep it running as he drove us to Talkeetna.

The village itself has a seasonal population of 200 to 600 people. It used to be a stop on the railroad for gold miners. Jessie took one look and called it a shopping mall, full of log cabins, restaurants, and gift shops. She also noted that prices are very high, which is why our expedition bought all its food in the Lower Forty-eight and had it shipped here.

Then there are the bush pilots. They're all crazy, according to Chad. They'll fly us to Base Camp on the Kahiltna Glacier, which we've learned is called the Kahiltna International.

There is a National Park Service ranger station here, a prominent log cabin, and we had to sign our expedition in. All of us climbers owe a lot to the NPS. McKinley is the only peak in the world patrolled by park rangers. They are the first ones to go up the mountain when climbing season starts in May. They install the fixed ropes we will use to ascend the headwalls. They check the anchors and the ropes daily.

The Park Service also runs a large medical tent at the camp called Fourteen Medical, for injured climbers. But we won't think about that right now.

We're all excited and raring to go. Tomorrow we'll fly to Base Camp. Jessie and Kevin and Kemil and Chad and Erik all say hello to loved ones at home. Dan.

And then there were the photographs. Jessie, hands on hips, looking at a huge pile of food supplies, dried packaged goods, bags of bagels, which would be distributed to each climber. Kevin standing in front of the ranger station. Chad and Erik and Kevin in front of the ranger station.

She read Dan's words over and over, and she scrolled down through the pictures so many times she knew every one by heart.

She envied Jessie, a girl so strong and confident that she could go on a climb with her fiancé. Jessie wore her ring proudly; the whole world knew she and Dan were going to marry, while Meredith skulked around, her ring hidden and her lover thousands of miles away.

She tried not to think that way. She and Jessie were different people. Erik loved her, even if she wasn't an intrepid mountaineer.

She shut down her computer finally and went to bed, but she lay there for a long time, her heart thudding. Erik and the climb and Kathy, with her peculiar story of the government after Kemil, Mideast terrorists, and the dark SUV all mixed up in her mind, and she couldn't sort them out. Kathy had said the government was paranoid, but Meredith was beginning to think she herself was the one suffering from delusions.

Come on, she told herself, and then, repeating the words, now grown familiar: *I'm all here, I'm the same person, no one can take me over.*

Just before she fell asleep, she found herself invoking the Native American mountain god Denali, asking him to keep Erik from harm. She never prayed, but she did that night, begging the primitive, ancient spirit to return her lover safely to her. And then she would tell him yes.

THIRTEEN

The following day rushed by in a blur. She saw her patients, ran errands, and raced home to click onto the Internet. She suspected Dan would not be able to post a dispatch every day; she also suspected disappointment would overwhelm her if he didn't.

She waited for tallpeaks.com to download. Waited on the edge of her creaking chair after she'd clicked on the link to Dan's site, and her heart pounded once furiously, then settled when she saw the new report.

"All right," she whispered, her eyes already devouring the words.

Here we are at Base Camp at 7,200 feet on the Kahiltna Glacier, 15½ miles from the summit.

The flight in was incredible, and if I don't go another step, it will have been worth it. We flew over tundra, and our pilot dipped low so we could see the moose and bear below. The tundra was rolling and green, but when we left that behind and arrived at the glacier, there was only snow and ice and rock. Monochromatic. But not boring.

I naively asked why the pilot called our route "One Shot Pass." He thought that was a riot and told me we had one shot at flying a direct route to Base Camp. We were all very quiet after that.

But we made it, the plane rising through clouds to view the three great peaks of the Alaska Range: Foraker, Hunter, and McKinley. It was a moving sight.

The plane landed on skis in powder snow and halted before a snowfield cluttered with tents. The Kahiltna Glacier is in a spectacular, steep-walled valley, with avalanches hissing off walls all around us.

The glacier is crisscrossed by crevasses. We've been told to be very careful not to wander too far from camp. It's a bit intimidating, but no one's been lost yet.

It took two trips of the Cessna to get our whole party in, but the weather is still good, so we lucked out. We've heard horror stories about parties where half of them reached Base Camp, but the other half was stuck back in Talkeetna when the weather turned bad very suddenly, which it does here routinely.

Even worse, Chad says, are the stories of climbers who summited, descended, and then had to wait up to a week to get flown out because of storms. Those people are really fed up, he says, really ready for a bath and a hot meal and a soft bed. I can imagine.

Base Camp is a carnival of activity. Now we

know why it's called the Kahiltna International.
Many climbers are here getting ready to go, as
we are. Other groups are setting out, and some
are returning and waiting to fly to Talkeetna.
There are Brits, a Japanese team, French, Ca-
nadians and, naturally, other Americans.

There are no animals here, the only wildlife
big black ravens that flap around and land to
peck at food scraps. This is, truly, a place where
humans were not meant to live.

Tomorrow we start our ascent. We're all
pretty nervous, but excited, too. Chad and Erik
are so blasé it's funny. Been there, done that is
their attitude.

Hello to all back home. We're healthy and in
good spirits. Dan.

Meredith lived their excitement. To be there, ready
to start up McKinley . . . She closed her eyes and tried
to imagine the setting. Erik had told her you could fly
into Base Camp, not as a climber but as a tourist, stay
a few hours or overnight, and fly out. It was the most
beautiful scenery, he'd said. Breathtaking, flying into
the valley. She'd love to do that someday, so that she
could at least share that much with him.

We used snowshoes today to make the 5½ mile
trip to camp at the base of Ski Hill, which we
will take on tomorrow. You wouldn't believe it,
but it was so hot we suffered a lot. And we were
dragging sleds containing our food and gear.

A rope called a prussik hangs from a locking
D carabiner on our harnesses to act as a brake

on the rope if we fall into a crevasse. It's hard to believe, but the snow beneath our feet is constantly shifting and moving downhill and a crevasse could open up under us at anytime. Erik and Chad trained us how to climb out. I hope we never need that training.

The sun was fierce, and it took its time setting as we descended (yes, the route goes down here for a ways) Heartbreak Hill, swinging wide onto the main part of Kahiltna Glacier to avoid large crevasses. We jumped over small ones.

Camp is at 7,800 feet. We used snow walls erected by earlier teams. We had to probe the entire campsite for crevasses and mark them with bamboo poles called wands.

Rule No. 1—Never leave camp boundaries unroped. That means we are roped together with harnesses that go around our waists and legs, and we are attached with carabiners, snap link affairs, at the center front of the harness. Two of us on a rope with a guide, 40 feet apart. Even when the going seems not in the least dangerous, we're roped together. Erik and Chad have impressed on us how vital this is. Erik is roped with Kemil and Kevin, Chad with Jessie and me.

It was a hard climb today, similar to a tough hike to a peak around Aspen. Morale is high.

Dinner consisted of Top Ramen soup and army rations, supposedly stew, but none of us would vouch for that.

It was hot today as we snowshoed, as I said, maybe 70 degrees, but when the sun sank, it got cold very fast, and we're all glad for the heavy

*down parkas we brought along. Jessie says we
look like Michelin men.*

Must get my beauty sleep. Dan.

There were photographs with this dispatch. A long,
rough glacier, the line of climbers toiling along it, their
backpacks making them look like hunched-over bee-
tles. Then a few from the camp: igloolike walls and
bright tents and the mountain rising in the background.

The climbers in puffy down parkas and sunglasses,
all of them smiling, Chad holding two fingers up behind Kevin's head. And Erik, a faint upturn of his lips.
He looked so very comfortable, at home. But then he
would.

They were at 7,800 feet, just below Aspen's altitude,
so no one would be feeling any effects of high altitude
yet. That would come, Meredith knew, perhaps later
for the Aspen group than lowlanders, but it would af-
fect them as they ascended.

She almost wished she could be there with them,
with Erik. Nestled close together in sleeping bags in a
tent. Roped to him as they trudged upward all day.
Silly, she thought. *A pipe dream.*

She went to the ranch on Saturday and worked with
her kids. She said little to her father, not even telling
him she was engaged to be married. Well, almost engaged, in a limbo of not quite engaged but promised.
She nearly told her sister Ann one night on the phone,
but something stopped her, a small impediment, a su-
perstitious fear of speaking the words out loud.

Mostly she talked to Kathy. Kathy knew all the people involved, understood, knew Erik perhaps better
than Meredith herself.

"Did you check the dispatches today?" Kathy asked her. "The twins have been following them on the Internet. They think it's way cool."

"Me, too."

Kathy laughed. "I hear the weather's good, and they're doing fine."

"Don't you worry?"

"Nah, Chad and Erik are the best."

"But things can happen."

"Sure, and you could get hit by a car tomorrow."

"Oh, Kathy."

Chad's sister never again mentioned being uptight about an audit of Kemil's income tax returns or the government paranoia of which she'd spoken. And Meredith hadn't seen the dark SUV again, either.

Amazing what stress could do to the imagination, she thought.

We ended up staying another day at the base of Ski Hill, because Jessie was feeling a little tired. Another team, who'd arrived the day before we did, took off on their way up. And a team of nine climbers and three guides came down and spent the night with us. Four of the climbers had not summited, due to tiredness or high-altitude symptoms. The ones who hadn't made it were a little dejected, but Chad cheered them up with some of his funny stories.

Today we did Ski Hill, a 1,000-foot gain in elevation. We stopped and camped at 9,700 feet, 2½ miles short of Ski Hill Camp, although some teams make it in one day. Erik is urging caution, telling us the story of the tortoise and the hare in Norwegian, which was pretty funny, even though he didn't laugh.

We've grown very close on this climb. I'd say, of us nonprofessionals, Kemil is the strongest climber, also the most experienced. Kevin is pretty good, too. Jessie is finding the climb harder than she expected, and it's bothering her a lot, being the only woman. Chad is great, smoothing all problems over, cooking up quite decent food from the awful dried packages. And Erik, well, he's simply indefatigable.

Tomorrow we'll get to the 11,000-foot camp at the base of Motorcycle Hill, named for the equally steep hills dirt bikers like to climb.

The weather has held, but the reports on the CB radio from Talkeetna are calling for an arctic front to move in. We may have to hunker down and wait it out.

Best to all back home. Dan.

The days dragged by slowly for Meredith. She missed Erik; she missed his closeness, his warmth, his body. She felt so alone. It occurred to her to phone Sandra Cohen again, but she wasn't ready. Frankly, she couldn't handle probing her feelings right now. She only had the mental energy to plod through each day until Erik returned safe and sound to her.

We reached the 11,000-foot camp today. As we heard, the camp is notoriously windy. I hope you can see in the photographs how bad the wind is here. We set up our tents with snow walls to protect them, but the wind still batters them. The

*sound of a tent wall snapping in the wind is like
a gunshot, and the wind is like a wild animal
clawing at us. You can hardly walk outside. And
that's nothing compared to the wind up higher.
When we get a break in the gale here, we can
still hear a wild, wailing roar from the top of the
mountain. I can't imagine how bad it is up there.*

*We may have to wait here until the weather
clears, because the next leg to Fourteen Medical
can only be attempted in good weather.*

*It's very cold, and we have to stay in our tents
most of the time to avoid frostbite. This kind of
forced inactivity is tedious but unavoidable.*

*Chad cooks up his "gourmet" meals, and we
brew cup after cup of tea loaded with sugar to
fight off dehydration, and we wait.*

Hoping for better weather. Dan.

The photographs showed white snow walls and
barely discernible tents. Some figures bundled in heavy
clothing, unidentifiable, stood with backs to the wind,
while a blizzard obscured everything.

There was one picture, taken inside a crowded tent,
all five climbers sitting shoulder to shoulder. Erik
looked as if he'd lost weight, his face thinner, his
cheekbones more hollow than she recalled.

She'd had no idea the endurance or determination
required to assault a mountain. The hardships they
were undergoing astonished her. And Erik *chose* to go
back and face this kind of grueling test again and
again.

Yet she was curiously jealous, too. Wishing she

were there, sharing with them, with *him*, the pain and effort and triumph.

The weather finally cleared enough for us to make the ascent to Fourteen Medical. We had to traverse Windy Corner, the climax of the climb up the lower flanks of McKinley. Some history: The famous climber and mapmaker Bradford Washburn named it Windy Corner during a 1951 expedition. The wind blew at 80 miles per hour for two days straight. BTW, Washburn pioneered the West Buttress Route we're doing now.

We climbed out of a layer of clouds, an unbelievable sight, bright blue sky above, cotton candy below. It reminded me of one of Washburn's quotes: "It's like looking out the windows of heaven."

We finally climbed like true mountaineers, with ice axes and crampons strapped to our boots. Our party is one in a crowd of climbers who'd been held back by the storm, so there was a veritable line of ants on the route up Motorcycle Hill.

We reached 13,200 feet, and then Chad and Erik and Kemil went back to our last camp to haul the rest of our gear up. My God, they're tough.

Tomorrow we'll go up to Fourteen Medical.

We made camp and huddled around our camp stoves, listening to the CB radio. It seems a climber from Tokyo is stranded at 17,000 feet with abdominal pains, unable to descend. They are sending the specially trained park rangers to

rescue him and bring him down to the doctors at
Fourteen Medical. Scary.
    Till tomorrow, Dan.

More photographs. Windy Corner, the wind blasting
at the climbers leaning as they walked, everyone bundled up, goggles, hats, gloves. She recognized no one
but Erik, and then only because he was taller than the
others.

Scenes of an immensity of blue sky, clouds amassed
below, the tops of peaks in the distance. Glorious.

She had lunch with Kathy again, and once she went
to Kathy's house for dinner. The affair was rather casual, a barbecue on the back patio, hot dogs and ham-
burgers and baked beans and salad Meredith brought.

After they ate, the twins disappeared into Kathy's
office to access tallpeaks.com and Dan's latest dispatch. Meredith could hear them talking in there, and
she wanted nothing more than to join them. She craved
the words, the pictures. They were her only link to
sanity.

"So how's the IRS audit going?" she asked.

"The what?"

"The audit of Kemil's returns."

"Oh, it's a headache. I've been getting together files
for days."

"It probably won't be as bad as you expect."

"Oh, yes it will. They're going to want to know
where every penny went," Kathy said bitterly, and
Meredith dropped the subject.

We made it to Fourteen Medical, a hard day. The
world narrows down to one job: Kick steps in

*with the front points of your crampons, breathe,
dig ice ax in above you, step up. Over and over
for hours. It's crazy, but after the storm, the sun
came out and it turned hot again, and we had to
stop often to hydrate.*

*We will remain here at 14,200 feet for several
days to acclimatize. Jessie is feeling the effects
of altitude and will be grateful for the rest.*

*This camp, on a large plateau, is an interna-
tional melting pot. It's very crowded, being the
staging area for the upper reaches of the mountain. Teams are coming and going or resting, as
we are. It's like a small town.*

*As we got into camp, some of the park rangers
were bringing down the climber with abdominal
pain. He'd recovered somewhat, but they sent
him down to the lower camp with a bottle of
oxygen. The prognosis was favorable.*

*We are exhausted from the tough climb today,
and it seems as if it should be bedtime, but the
sun shines down stubbornly on us.*

*Word has just come in that a climber has
fallen higher up and is hurt. The rangers gear
up to climb to him, the resident doctor is alerted.
We'll keep you posted on the outcome.*

Good night. Dan.

Fourteen thousand feet, Meredith thought. The highest peaks in Colorado were 14,000 feet tall. Looking
at peaks around Aspen, she couldn't imagine a veritable village of tents and people at that altitude. And
the party still had over 6,000 feet to go to the summit.
There were no dispatches for a couple of days, prob-

ably because they were all just sitting in camp, waiting,
gathering strength, getting used to the altitude. What
did they do all day? She'd have to ask Erik when he
got back. Did they carry reading material? Did they
play cards or just talk? She put aside her disappointment as best she could and tried to conjure up the camp
in her head. She'd seen Dan's photos, the plateau, the
tents, the big medical tent, the teams standing in front
of their own tents. Jessie looking drawn, Kemil smiling
whitely, his goatee as dapper as ever, Erik sober, and
Kevin frowning, a week's growth of beard on his
cheeks.

> *The injured climber was rescued by a team of
> park rangers, who got up to him very quickly
> then lowered him on a litter down the West But-
> tress ridgeline between 16,000 and 17,000 feet
> to the fixed ropes at the top of the headwall. Then
> he was lowered on another rope.*
>
> *The doctor here decided the injury was serious
> enough that the man had to be evacuated by he-
> licopter, a decision not to be taken lightly, be-
> cause flying at this altitude is very dangerous.*
>
> *But the Chinook helicopter came in, a huge,
> buglike shape, whose rotor wash obscured the
> whole camp when it landed.*
>
> *The patient was carried to the chopper, loaded
> aboard, and flown away. By now, he is in an
> Anchorage hospital. One more climber plucked
> from danger. We all cheered when the Chinook
> lifted off.*
>
> *And some of us may have been tempted to
> hitch a ride with it!*

Tomorrow, we will climb to 16,200-foot camp, also called Ridge Camp. We have to ascend the headwall, as mentioned, the steepest section of the West Buttress Route.

We're getting closer to the summit.

Well, we made it. We're at 16,200 feet. The camp here is very exposed. Tent platforms must be chopped out of the tilted ice and snow. Erik told us this camp has been the site of many dangerous situations when climbers were trapped here in bad weather. We're all hoping this doesn't happen to us.

The views are incredible. Clouds boil up below us, and the peaks of Foraker and Hunter appear to be ice islands floating on a white ocean. We can look up and see the clouds torn by the wind off of McKinley's high ridges in streamers of white. Today would not be a good day to summit.

Tomorrow, Erik and Chad will move some of our gear up to High Camp at 17,200 feet. They will bury it in the snow up there, so that we will be able to use it when we make our summit attempt. Then they will descend, and the following day, we'll all climb to High Camp.

Some not so good news—Kevin has developed a cough. Not a good sign. Erik has spoken to him about what will happen if it persists. I think it's merely temporary. Keep your fingers crossed.

Signing off, Dan.

The photographs were stunning. A cloud ocean, the peaks poking up the way he described them. McKin-

ley's peak, towering above, with tattered clouds
streaming off its summit.

The camp seemed precarious, and Meredith could
tell where the tent platforms had been hacked out.

She felt a pang of apprehension looking at the pictures. The people were so puny compared to the mountain, the weather, the snow and ice and rock. There had
already been two medical evacuations while she'd been
logging on. How many more would there be? It could
happen any moment: a fall, an avalanche, high-altitude
edema, frostbite, Kevin's cough, Jessie's exhaustion.

Men were truly not meant to go to those high places.
But then, men were not meant to fly through the air or
dive to the bottom of the sea. Yet they did. They did
it every day.

And the great majority of the time, nothing happened to them.

*This is a big day. We are at High Camp, 17,200
feet. The next stop, folks, is the summit. We've
built tall snow walls to protect our tents, and the
wind is howling. The weather report calls for another storm, but we should have time to summit
before it hits.*

*Kemil and I are in great shape. Kevin's still
battling the cough. He's a little tired but determined. Jessie, however, is complaining of a bad
headache. We're going to have to keep an eye
on her.*

*The climb up the ridge from 16,200 to High
Camp was unbelievable. It took eight hours, but
the scenery was worth it. Words cannot begin to
describe what it's like.*

*If the weather holds, we will rest here one day
and make our attempt on the summit. The winds
need to be low, the visibility good. One group,
all expert climbers, had to turn around on summit day, due to poor visibility and wind. They're
waiting here at High Camp with us.*

*This camp, by the way, is the highest, coldest,
windiest one. We could be stuck here for days.
We can see Fourteen Medical 3,000 feet below
us, but if the weather is bad, you simply can't
make it from here to there.*

*We aren't going to be able to carry the laptop
on our summit push, so you won't hear anything
from me until we get back. Don't worry, I'm taking the camera.*

*The day we try for the summit will be the hard-
est day yet. It's five miles round-trip, up through
Denali Pass and across a plateau dubbed the
Football Field. Then the Summit Ridge, which
goes the last 220 vertical feet. Of course, we
have to get back down to High Camp, so no one
can attempt the summit unless he's feeling pretty
strong. I think Kevin's cough is better.*

Wish us luck. Dan.

Why was she so nervous? she wondered. Everything
on the climb seemed to be fine. Perhaps Jessie was not
doing as well as the others, but Kevin's cough was
better, and Erik was safe and sound, doing the job he
loved.

She sat in her spare room on her old squeaky chair
and stared at the screen, at the words and the pictures.
Climbers on a white ridge, ragged snow contrails

blowing beyond them, toiling their way up, roped together and so bundled in down that they were sexless,
featureless, all individuality sucked out of them. And
she was here, warm and comfortable. There was no
reality to the photographs, yet she knew Erik and Chad,
Kemil, Dan, Kevin, and Jessie were undergoing the
hardships.

The day after tomorrow, they would try to summit.
Five miles round-trip. *If* the weather cooperated. She
wanted to believe the worst was over for the team, but
that just wasn't true. The worst lay ahead.

And she knew that at 17,000 feet, a person didn't
get stronger with rest. The lack of oxygen and the ex-
treme cold caused deterioration. Cuts didn't heal, ap-
petites vanished, coughs really didn't go away. The
longer a person stayed at that altitude, the more uncertain were their chances for summiting, for descending safely, for surviving.

Erik had climbed McKinley five times, Everest
twice, Annapurna and K2 and Aconcagua and God
knows how many other peaks. He'd be fine.

*A great disappointment. I'm sorry to have to re-
port that Kevin's cough has gotten much worse,
and Jessie is ill with altitude sickness. Neither of
them will be able to summit, and they'll both
need to descend as soon as possible. After a hard
discussion, it was decided that I would also stay
here in camp with Jessie and Kevin, while Erik,
Chad, and Kemil try for the summit tomorrow.*

*The weather is good right now, little wind,
clear skies, perfect visibility. A storm is on its
way, as I reported previously, but the three most*

*experienced of our team should have no trouble
reaching the summit and returning before it hits.*

*I will be reporting on their attempt tomorrow
from here in High Camp, as we're waiting for
rangers to arrive with medication and oxygen for
Kevin and Jessie.*

*The attempt to summit will start in the early-
morning hours, because it may take all day for
Erik, Chad, and Kemil to get there and back.
Eight hours is an absolute minimum for this task.*

*Another not so minor detail—the snow is soft-
ening in the warm daytime temperatures, as it
always does this time of year. The climbing season will end soon because the soft snow makes
crevasses more and more dangerous. It's likely
we'll all be descending at night when the cold
firms up the bridges of snow over the widening
cracks in the glacier.*

Talk to you tomorrow, Dan.

Oh my God, she thought, and she felt a chill. *Dan,
Jessie, and Kevin—left behind after all they'd endured.
And tomorrow Erik would be going for the summit.*
She'd watch the weather reports on TV tonight to see
if the forecast storm was closing in on Alaska.

But when he descended to High Camp tomorrow, or
perhaps turned back because of dangerous conditions,
the ordeal would be practically over. Did she mean her
ordeal or Erik's? She wasn't sure. Hers, probably, because he was in his element. She wondered how he felt
about leaving the three others behind, but she had no
real key to comprehending his feelings.

Summit day dawned cold and clear. We all got up at 4 A.M. to see our teammates off. We wished them luck and watched them file off, roped together, Erik in the lead, then Kemil, then Chad. They looked like Jessie's Michelin men, except for their ice axes and the other equipment that clanged and rattled, hanging from their harnesses. We'll be out of touch with them until they return to High Camp.

It was light out, the arctic sun smiling down benignly even though the temperature was close to zero degrees Fahrenheit.

It's three in the afternoon now, and we assume they made it to the summit or are on their way down already. We hope so, because the storm is blowing in sooner than expected. So far, the wind is gusting and the clouds are building, but it's not too bad yet. We figure they can see the front approaching as well as we can, so it's possible they turned back earlier and will walk into camp at any moment.

Signing off for now. Updates later. Dan.

She bit her lip. She should do something to keep her mind off the climb, the storm, Erik in trouble, lost, freezing. Catch up on her reading of the psych journals piled up on her coffee table, do laundry, iron, bake cookies. *Oh, God.*

She sat there, watching the screen till her eyes wouldn't focus, waiting and waiting. It was earlier there, she thought. How many hours earlier? Outside her window, darkness fell. Night had arrived, while there it was still afternoon, and the sun barely set in any case.

By eleven o'clock, she was both panicky and paralyzed. There had been no dispatches in hours. Nothing. Dan's last words remained on the screen.

Erik, where are you? she thought.

> *The storm blasted in. We're hunkered down here in our tents, waiting and hoping. Erik and Chad and Kemil are tough and experienced enough to get through this. They've most likely dug a snow cave to wait the storm out.*
>
> *It's pretty bad. The winds are so strong, you can barely stand up. We've spent the last few hours repairing our snow walls and brushing snow from our tents. We can't see very far because the visibility is terrible, but we can hear the booms of slopes avalanching around us, as the wind tears at cornices. The wind sounds like a roaring train.*
>
> *I'll send dispatches as long as I can, but we may lose contact because of the weather.*
>
> *Still no sign of our three friends. Dan.*

More hours crawled by. Meredith sat there, heart hammering, frozen in place. It was very late; she should go to bed, she thought once, but she didn't move.

Then, finally, her screen came to life.

> *There's a break in the storm. Thank God for the light here, because we can finally see up the mountain.*

We've been watching and waiting all after-
noon, and I can report now that we have spotted
a single figure making its way down the ridge
from Denali Pass.

It's too far to tell who it is, so all I can report
is that one person is walking down from the sum-
mit of Mount McKinley. We hope for the best but
fear the worst.

Send prayers. Dan.

Meredith would never clearly remember the next
hours. She did recall Kathy phoning her that morning,
and she talked to Kathy, she must have said something,
but she didn't know what it was.

At one point, she turned on the television set to
CNN, and there was something on about two climbers
missing on McKinley. No names were released, no
further information was to be had. She turned the set
off and paced her living room, still in the clothes
she'd had on since yesterday, pacing and trying not to
think, to conjecture, to fall so far into the depths of
fear she'd never climb out.

When the phone rang, she jumped out of her skin,
stared at it in a kind of horrified fascination, then
snatched it up.

"Meredith Greene?" a voice said.

"Yes," she tried, but nothing more came out.

"Miss Greene?"

"Uh, yes."

"This is Jim Bennett calling from Denver Channel
Nine. I wonder if you could comment on the climbers
lost in Alaska."

"What?"

"Your name was given to us by Summit Expeditions. I wonder if you could—"

"Do you know who it is?" she asked. "Do you?"

"We have no information as to the identity of the lost climbers, Miss Greene."

She put the receiver on the hook. Carefully, as if it were breakable. Her hand shook.

Again, later, the phone rang.

"Miss Meredith Greene? We would like a statement from you regarding the relationship of Prince Kemil al Assad to the guides of this expedition. Can you—?"

She hung up.

The phone rang and rang. It wouldn't stop, and she'd wait, the way you do when you have the hiccups, waiting to see if they were over or if there would be another . . . then another.

Eventually, she unplugged the phone from the jack.

Her mind raced, but it never budged from its anchor of the most exquisite apprehension. She started cleaning her town house, doing the dishes she'd left in the sink last night, scrubbing her counters, scouring the sink and cabinet doors, mopping the floor. She got the vacuum out and did the carpets, upstairs and down. Dusted shelves, cleaned toilets with mindless ferocity, until she was exhausted.

But still her thoughts dashed themselves like frantic waves against a harsh shore.

Late that afternoon, she curled up in on the couch, Erik's ring clutched in her hand. She prayed selfishly that it was Chad and Kemil who were missing.

FOURTEEN

Nine hours later, a few minutes before midnight, she was jolted awake from an exhausted stupor. She rose to her feet from where she'd been lying on the couch still fully dressed. Someone was knocking at her door.

Kathy, she knew it was Kathy. Her phone was unplugged, and Chad's sister had driven over with news. Then she froze. What if Erik had not been the survivor?

No, no, he had to have made it out, she told herself fiercely. He was the strongest, the most experienced. But then that would mean Chad . . . How could she be pulling so desperately for Erik and have forgotten about Chad? And Kemil? How could she be so selfish?

It took all her courage to walk to the door and open it. Then it was a minute before she realized it wasn't Kathy standing there in the outside light.

"What?" she breathed.

John McCord nodded at her. "May I come in?" he said. That was all. As if his appearance were perfectly natural.

She kept her hand on the doorknob and stared at

him, trying to fit her thoughts around his presence.

"May I come in?" he repeated, and in the dim light, she watched him reach inside the brown leather jacket he was wearing and pull out a thin black wallet, which he flipped open and showed to her.

"John, what on earth . . . ?" She looked briefly at the ID, then her attention moved up to his face. "I don't understand."

"I'm with the State Department," he said. "This is official business."

State Department? Hadn't he told her . . . ? "Is this about . . . Erik? I mean . . ."

He edged inside and glanced around. She was still holding open the door, rooted to the spot. *State Department*, she thought again, confused.

"Look," he said, "I have to ask you to come with me into town. There are some people who'd like to talk to you. You can refuse, of course, in which case I'll be back with a warrant."

She couldn't think. All she could do was stare in bewilderment at him. He wasn't even the man she knew, the handsome, easy-in-his-skin John. This man was expressionless, cool, his entire demeanor businesslike.

A chill crawled along her spine.

"Listen, Meredith," he said, turning to her, "I advise you to come with me now and talk to these people. This is for your own good."

"What . . . what people?" she stammered.

"A couple men with the National Security Agency. They're investigators. Now, do you need a sweater? Your purse?"

Somehow, she found a sweater to throw on over her

wrinkled green tank top and tan jeans. She picked up
her purse automatically. Her mind was reeling. The
next thing she knew, he was leading her to a car parked
in the lot behind hers, a dark SUV, with dark-tinted
windows. The chill spread throughout her body.

"I don't understand," she said, shaking her head,
halting. "Is this about Erik? Do you know something?"

He pulled open the passenger door, said only,
"Please, get in," then urged her gently but firmly up
into the passenger seat and closed the door.

When he was behind the steering wheel, she tried
again. "Goddamn it, is this about McKinley?"

He told her what sounded like mumbo jumbo about
not been at liberty to discuss anything with her at this
point, then he drove off.

She was unaware of the five-mile ride into town. Car
lights from late-night workers and bar hoppers heading
downvalley blinded her, but she stared straight into
them. Her skull felt as if a tornado was whirling inside
it, and she couldn't grasp and hold a single thought.

Then they were parking, and for a moment she was
able to focus. The Sheriff's Department. They were
behind the old brick courthouse on Main Street, parking at the basement entrance to the Sheriff's Department.

When she stepped to the pavement, John holding the
passenger door, a scene flashed unbidden through her
mind: Sheriff Hatfield informing her it was not Erik
who'd made it down. How John McCord or the State
Department fit into the scenario never once occurred
to her. Not yet.

He led her down concrete steps and through a narrow door. She'd never been here, and she looked

around, not curious, not truly cognizant, her heart beating in her ears. Narrow hallways. Lots of doors. A few uniformed policemen milling around. Everyone noticed her and the tall, stern-faced man in the leather jacket who held her elbow, guiding her. But she saw only the sheriff, heard in her mind his words: *Erik did not make it down the mountain.*

She looked up and was aware of a rectangular room, perhaps twenty by thirty feet. Large. And there was a long, rectangular table at its center. Eight or ten chairs around it.

John pulled out one of the chairs, asked her to sit.

"Look," she breathed, still standing, "I don't understand. What's going on? Why have you brought me here? If it's Erik, for God's sake just tell me."

"Please sit down, Meredith," he said. He took her purse out of her hands and set it on the table. "My advice to you is to cooperate. Answer the questions put to you as truthfully as you can, and afterward, I'll drive you home."

She was about to demand once again he tell her what in hell was going on, when the door opened and closed behind her, and she swiveled, seeing two unsmiling men carrying file folders move around to stand across the table from her.

"Sit down please, Miss Greene," one of them said. He indicated a chair.

The other man made eye contact with John but remained silent. He pulled out a chair, sat, opening his file, taking a pen out of a shirt pocket.

She sucked in a breath, told herself to calm down, to focus, and she finally sat. "I . . . I want to see your identification," she got out, shocked at the determination in her voice.

They each produced an ID declaring the bearer to be an employee of the NSA. She made a point of studying them, though why, she had no idea. She only knew she felt threatened and intimidated, lied to. Yes, she realized, for some reason John McCord had lied to her all along. He'd said . . . he'd said he was in sales or something like that. New to town. Divorced. Depressed. He could run his business from anyplace with modern telecommunications.

State Department.

She suddenly felt as if she'd been struck. He'd deceived her.

Heat rose from her neck to her cheeks and into her brain, where it began to sizzle. He'd betrayed her trust. He had sat in her office and told her those bullshit stories. He'd approached her at the bookstore, smiled at her, shared a meal, flirted with her. And he'd known about Erik, she remembered abruptly, asked if she was still seeing Erik Amundsson, something like that.

State Department.

She felt as if he'd taken something precious from her, taken it without asking.

She looked down at the IDs the two men were showing her, then back to their faces. "What is this about?" she said, her voice shrill, foreign to her ears.

John, she realized then, was now standing behind her. She could just make him out in the periphery of her vision, leaning against a wall, jacket still on, arms folded across his chest. *The bastard.*

She looked at the other two men. "Is this about Erik? I want to know . . . I demand you—"

"Miss Greene, we'll ask the questions," one of them cut in. He was young, twenty-nine or thirty years old, very sharp looking, spiffy razor haircut, extremely unfriendly appearance despite the casual dress of a pastel plaid summer shirt and blue jeans. The other man was older. Maybe fifty. He wore a white shirt and suit jacket, no tie, trousers. He had a good face, was gray and balding with pleasant features, but his brown eyes were flat, incapable of surprise, the eyes of a man in any police force or army in the last 4,000 years.

"*You'll* ask the questions," she repeated, looking from one to the other, trying not to turn around toward John. As if he'd help. As if she'd ask him. "Well then, should I call a lawyer or something? I mean, if no one will tell me—"

"Is there a reason you need a lawyer, Miss Greene?" the older one retorted.

"Of course not," she said, but then she corrected herself. "How should I know? No one will tell me—"

But again, she was expertly cut off.

They shunted away every question she asked for the next fifteen minutes, until her head was spinning. Every time she glanced inadvertently toward John, he seemed to have moved farther out of her vision. He was there, though, directly behind her. She could feel the weight of his scrutiny through her sweater.

They'd begun their interview by asking her the most ordinary, meaningless, endless, *stupid* questions.

"Where were you born, Miss Greene?"

"Aspen Valley Hospital." Erik, she thought, desperate, feeling as if she might vomit. This was about Erik, she was positive. But why? Was he alive? *Was* he?

"Your sister lives in Denver?"

"Yes, yes, Denver. What the hell does that have to do with anything?"

"And your father, Neil, was born in Rifle, Colorado?"

"No. Not Rifle. He was born in Glenwood Springs."

"But raised in Rifle?"

"Yes, sure. *Yes*," she cried.

Her mind turned to the dark SUV—a Blazer, she thought—John's car. The same one she'd seen at Kemil's, the one Erik had also spotted. "Politics," Erik had said. He didn't give a damn about politics. *Kemil's politics?* she wondered. *Was this ridiculous grilling in the middle of the night about Kemil?*

The SUV. She'd seen that car outside her place, too. The night Tony had come over and again, pulling out from the curb behind Kathy. And she had told herself she was merely paranoid.

"Kathy Fry? How long have you and Mrs. Fry been acquainted?"

"What has this got to do with Kathy? With anything?"

"Miss Greene," the younger agent said, "it's in your best interest to cooperate here. If not—"

"If not *what?*"

"Mrs. Fry," the older one said, his tone even, almost friendly, "you met her when?"

She put her pounding head in her hands, felt her hair falling in strings over her fingers. "I don't know. I don't know. A few months ago. This past spring, I guess."

"And Chad Newhouse, Mrs. Fry's brother?"

"About the same time. In April."

"Wasn't it the second week of April?"

"Yes, sure, maybe. I don't know."

"You met Chad Newhouse at a party at Prince Kemil al Assad's?"

"Yes. No. No, not then. Later."

"But you met Erik Amundsson at that party on April eighth, isn't that correct?"

"How do you . . . ?" She looked up, startled.

"Please answer the questions, Miss Greene."

"If you say it was April eighth, then it must have been."

"No need to assume that tone, Miss Greene," the young one said. He went directly on. "Did you know of, or had you met the prince on a previous occasion?"

She shook her head, suddenly bone weary.

"So your friend Anthony Waterman, I believe you know him as Tony, never introduced you to the prince before the evening of April eighth?"

How did they know about Tony? About any of this?

"You were engaged in a sexual relationship with Tony Waterman prior to that evening?"

She drew in a quick breath.

The older one pressed on without missing a beat. "But that night, the night of April eighth, you spent in the company of Erik Amundsson."

"That is none of your—"

"Did you ever spend an entire night at Prince Kemil al Assad's Aspen home?"

"No. This is insane. Why are you asking me—?"

"Then you have never had sexual relations with Prince Kemil al Assad?"

"*What?* Good God, no!"

"Or Chad Newhouse?"

"Stop it!" she cried. "Why are you . . . ? This can't

have anything to do with the war on terrorism. You can't possibly think I would have anything to do with terrorists."

"But you did have sexual relations with one of the prince's closest friends, Erik Amundsson, for the past four and a half months? Isn't that true?"

She bit her lip in horror and moaned, "Please, please stop this." Then she pleaded, "Just tell me if Erik is alive. I don't know what you want from me or why and I don't give a damn. Just tell me if there's been word about Erik. . . . Please, please just . . ."

She heard John's voice as if from a great distance at first and then closer, directly behind her. "That's enough."

Then the younger one: "We're not through. Not by a long shot."

John: "It's over."

The older one, his brown eyes sparking to life: "Look, McCord, you don't have the authority to—"

"*And,*" John cut in curtly, "neither do you. I'm ending this right now."

Through a blur, she saw the exchange of steely glares, the vying for authority.

"A few more questions," the older one finally said, "and then Miss Greene can—"

"It's ended," John said again, his tone brooking no argument.

She wanted to break down and cry, sob till there was nothing left. But she wouldn't. Not in front of these men. Not in front of John. Especially not him.

They exchanged a few more heated words, but they went over her head. She didn't care. She was now positive from their questions that this all had to do with

Kemil—with Kemil and his politics and the IRS and his friends, here and in the Mideast. But why wouldn't someone tell her who had walked down that ridge? One man . . . only one man had walked out.

The two NSA men finally stood and put their pens in pockets and folded up their files.

The young one said to John, "You're making a mistake here."

And the older one: "You should know how this works, McCord. Christ."

But all John said was, "I'll talk to you in the morning," and he moved into her vision and pulled out the chair next to hers. He sat. She heard the door open and close and mercifully, her tormentors were gone. A headache crashed behind her temples.

"Goddamn it," she whispered.

"They're through."

"Yes, I know. I can see that. How could they? How could you . . . ?" She turned to face him. Gone was the neutral mask he'd worn at her door. His features were soft again, his eyes moving from hers to her hands, clasped whitely in front of her.

"Answer me," she said. "How could you do this to me? And don't tell me another lie."

He regarded her silently, and then said, "It's my job."

"Deceit is your job?"

"When I deal with issues of national security, yes, that is my job. Call it undercover work. Call it deceit. After September eleventh, it's a necessary evil."

"A necessary evil," she repeated, chilled.

"Would it help to know I feel like shit about this?"

"No."

"Then I won't say it."

"Fine. Don't. I only want to know if there's news from McKinley. If you know anything, anything at all . . . John, you have to tell me. I'm begging you to tell me."

"There is news," he said quietly.

Her heart stopped beating.

"There was an accident on Denali Pass," he said in a sober voice.

Still, her heart would not pump.

"Chad Newhouse is safe." He paused. "I'm afraid Prince Kemil was killed in a fall."

"Oh, dear God," she breathed. "And Erik? What about Erik?" She looked beseechingly at him, her heart suddenly lurching against her ribs.

Slowly, he shook his head. "They haven't found Amundsson." His voice was so low she could barely comprehend him. "The early reports from the rescue team state that even if Erik survived a fall, he could not have survived the night. I'm sorry, Meredith."

Sorry, he'd said, he was *sorry*.

FIFTEEN

The sense of time and space deserted her. John took control of her physical self, and she mindlessly allowed him to help her up, tuck her purse under her arm, and guide her out of the interrogation room. His hand at the small of her back, he steered her as if she were on strings, down the hall and up the cold, concrete steps. He urged her into the passenger seat of his SUV and closed the door. She was aware of a secure chunking sound.

She felt herself take a sharp breath and wondered how she could have let this man lead her, manipulate her as if she were demented, but the notion was fleeting and without merit.

He reversed out of the parking space, his hand resting on the back of her seat while he pivoted, and his fingers brushed her thigh for a heartbeat until he moved his hand to the steering wheel.

Main Street was empty; the three traffic lights were blinking yellow. She registered that it must be very early in the morning. She was shivering, she thought. *Is it that cold out?*

"Can you turn up the heat?" *Turn up the heat.* Odd how the body required maintenance even in the most dire situations.

Hugging herself, she fixed her attention on his profile. Words formed in her throat, bypassing her brain. "No one, I mean Chad, that is, actually *saw* Erik fall?" She was unaware that she had asked him the exact same question only moments before.

"The report I read was not specific in that area." John turned onto the lower Woody Creek Road, his attention apparently focused on the stands of aspen hugging the riverbank, where deer would be gathering in the quickening of dawn.

"Chad couldn't have seen," she said, as much to herself as John. "He must not have witnessed the accident. I mean, if he had, then he would have been able to tell the rescue team where to look for Erik."

"That's a safe assumption."

"But the report . . . When exactly did you read it?"

"Right before I drove out to your place. I'd say around eleven-thirty last night."

"You should have told me immediately. It was cruel to let me wait."

"Yes, it was. But like I told you, I was under orders."

"Right. State Department orders. Or is it the NSA?"

"I am sorry, Meredith. There isn't anything more I can say."

In the dim light she saw his skin tighten across his features. "What good does it do to say you're sorry?" she said. "*After* the facts."

"None. I'm sorry I said I'm sorry."

"Are you being sarcastic now?"

"Not in the least."

"I should hate you for this." She let out a sigh. "But I don't have any hate in me right now. I . . . I don't know what I feel."

"I understand."

"No, you don't. You can't."

Silence.

"So you said the report from McKinley was faxed to you here?"

"I didn't actually say, but that's right."

"And it stated, for sure, that only Kemil's body was recovered?"

"Yes."

"Oh, God." She stared out the window. Kemil dead. Erik missing, missing for nearly twenty-four hours. If he survived the fall, he couldn't have survived the night. That's what John had said. The *report* said. But they didn't know Erik. He was not an ordinary human being. If anyone could have made it, Erik could. She knew it. She *knew* it.

"Why were you watching *me*, anyway? I mean, this is all about Kemil, I assume. Why follow *me* around?"

He pulled into a slot next to her car, slid the gearshift into Park, and killed the engine. "We're keeping an eye on all of the prince's associates."

"I'm hardly an associate."

"You spent a lot of time in his company."

"*Erik* spent the time in Kemil's company. Erik and Chad and Dan and Kevin and . . . But no doubt you were watching them, too."

He made a noncommittal sound.

"And that's why you started watching me. I went

home with Erik. Oh, let's see," she said, "it was April eighth."

"You're tired," he said, opening his door. "I think you should get some rest,"

"I'll never rest until I know. Not until I know about Erik. Not until they . . . find him."

"All right. I understand."

"You don't understand."

He followed her inside her town house, and she didn't say a thing. She didn't care. She stood in the middle of the curiously unfamiliar living room, lost and aching and afraid, and John's presence meant nothing. No one could hurt her now. No one could help. Nothing would matter until she knew for sure about Erik.

He couldn't have died. Not climbing.

John's voice scratched across her thoughts. "I'm going to have to stay for a while."

She turned and focused on him. She shook her head. "No. I don't want you here."

"Look." He leaned his back against her dividing counter, folded his arms, and gazed at her with calm and tolerant acceptance. "I don't think you understand the media blitz that's about to begin. And believe me, you'll be a focal point. Why not let me do my job?"

"A media blitz? Because of Kemil?"

"Kemil, of course. And Erik Amundsson as well. Remember, this is Aspen. They'll hound you right along with everyone else who even heard of the prince. It's going to get ugly."

"You said, do your job." She sagged onto the couch and felt the tears press hotly against the back of her eyes. *Not yet,* she thought, *don't break down yet.*

"Well, now that you've followed me and interrogated me, what job would that be, John?"

"Let's say it's to protect you."

"From the media?"

"That, and from any foreign queries that might come your way."

"You've lost me."

"I'm sure the Saudi al Assad family will want to talk to you, Meredith."

"Oh, great. And all because of that stuff Kathy mentioned, I suppose."

"What did Kathy mention?"

She shook her head. "I don't know. Something nebulous about Kemil's income tax returns and Mideast affairs. Or maybe Erik told me that. I don't know."

"Um."

She looked quizzically at him. "What awful thing did Kemil do, anyway, that has the government so interested?"

He regarded her soberly for a minute, then seemed to come to a decision. "Kemil has . . . had an associate in the Middle East who is known to have a relationship with a particular terrorist organization."

"Kemil is a friend of a friend to some terrorists? But he's on our side."

"It goes a little deeper."

"Oh? How deep? I suppose Erik and Chad were friends of this friend, too." Near hysteria, she laughed.

"I obviously can't go into matters of national security, but I can tell you that both Erik Amundsson and Chad Newhouse were guests of this associate of Kemil."

"Come on."

"I'm afraid it's fact. In Lahore, Pakistan, last year before a climb on a mountain called Nanga Parbat."

"You *are* joking."

"This is no joke."

"Just because Erik and Chad stayed at someone's place before a climb does not mean they're involved in terrorism. How absurd." She paused. By the look on his face, she knew he didn't agree. "You can't believe that. Erik and Chad, all they cared about was climbing."

He studied her with a closed expression.

"And Erik, he hated politics. It was so meaningless to him. You don't know. You don't have a clue what you're talking about. This whole thing . . . it's insane." She glanced at him. "Don't look at me like that," she said.

"Like what, Meredith?"

"So . . . so skeptically. Kathy was right. This is government paranoia."

"Kathy Fry said that?"

"Yes. And after tonight, I'm inclined to agree."

"Uh-huh," he said. Then, "Why don't you try to get some sleep?" He checked his watch. "It's almost seven A.M. Like I said, I'll take care of the phone."

"Only the Internet line is plugged in."

"I think I can handle that."

She didn't want him there. She didn't want anyone there. She needed to think, to sort out in her mind what had happened on the mountain. She needed to picture Erik, to embrace the knowledge that he was the best, the toughest—he was a survivor. And she needed to cry. If she didn't release the flood soon, she'd burst.

"All right," she finally said. "Stay. Man the phone.

Do whatever it is you do, John. I probably couldn't
stop you, anyway."

"I'm here to help you," he said quietly.

"Sure."

"Look. Kemil is dead. The media will be on his acquaintances and his business dealings, his whole life,
like flies on stink. Accusations will surface, and between the press and his Saudi family, no one who knew
him is going to get a break. You're not immune. I can
and I will do everything in my power to protect you
from the fallout."

"Should I thank you?"

"Just get some sleep."

She finally moved. Her muscles were tight, and her
mouth was dry. Her nerves were grating beneath the
surface of her skin, and her heart was pumping. De-
hydrated and exhausted, she knew, but she didn't give
a damn. Slowly, gripping the handrail, she pulled herself up the steps. Out of the corner of her eye, she saw
the screen saver on her computer, and she remembered
she was still on the Internet, awaiting news from the
web site. What a laugh.

She took a hot shower and tried to tell herself that
really, there was still no concrete news. All right,
Kemil was dead, and certainly his loss was a horrible
tragedy. But Chad was okay. Chad had walked out.
Had Erik . . . ? It must be significant that they hadn't
found him. Maybe he'd dug a snow cave. Maybe
he . . .

If she actually fell asleep, and there was news, would
John wake her?

Of course he would. She wasn't buying for a second
his announcement that his role now was to protect her.

He and his superiors would keep on watching her till they were convinced she knew nothing about Kemil and terrorism. But surely, John would have no reason to keep information concerning Erik from her.

She towel-dried her hair and padded into her bedroom, closed the door, and stared at the bed. She could see him there, see herself beside him, his blond head on the pillow on the left, his silver-sprinkled beard against the sage-colored pillowcase, one arm flung across her hip.

She'd washed the sheets after Erik left. Why had she washed them? Shouldn't she have known there was a possibility he would not return?

Her bed felt cold and empty, despite the bright, hot day that had dawned. She didn't want to be in bed. She didn't want to sleep. If she slept, she'd dream.

The sob finally broke free from her throat, and the tears came. She tossed her head from side to side and clutched her stomach, wrapping her arms around her waist, as if she could hold in the misery. *He isn't dead,* she told herself. *He is missing.* There was hope.

"Goddamn it," she breathed. Wouldn't she know if he were dead?

She opened her eyes at noon and was astounded to realize she'd fallen asleep.

Then the despair returned. And behind it, the hope. Her emotions welled inside her, receded, and welled again.

Dressed in jeans and a blue V-neck T-shirt, she finally walked down the familiar staircase, her hand on the rail, and she noticed how cool, how smooth it was. All her senses were overly acute, as if she could smell the air, feel its vibrations, and somehow receive a message from Erik, word from another dimension that he was all right.

It was afternoon, she thought. He'd been missing for an entire day. Was the rescue team still looking for him? They must have been. They wouldn't give up this quickly. She didn't know if the passage of hours was good or bad at this point. He hadn't been found; surely that meant there was hope he'd survived.

Or maybe the passage of time was bad.

John was in her kitchen. His leather jacket was gone, and he was wearing a white cotton shirt with rolled-up sleeves. He'd made coffee. It smelled strong. Or were her senses still too acute?

He noticed her and nodded at the coffeepot. "It's fresh. A little strong, but . . ."

"Yes, I'll take a cup."

"Cream? Sugar?"

"Yes, the works, please." She sat on a stool, her head heavy and achy. "Has there been any word, any word at all? I didn't hear the phone."

"I turned the volume down."

"Then there have been calls?"

"Quite a few."

She took a ragged breath. "Erik? Has there been . . . ?"

"Nothing yet. Here." He handed her a mug. "I hope it's not too sweet."

"I never let anyone in my kitchen," she said dully.

"I would have asked, but I was afraid I'd wake you."

"You don't have to ask. It's funny, but I don't seem to care right now."

"Shock."

She held the mug and looked up at him, trying to

muster the distaste she'd experienced last night. He'd befriended and betrayed her. A Judas. She should throw him out. But then, who would fend off the media? It was, perhaps, better to let him stay, to work at her anger—anything to keep her mind from picturing Erik alive or . . . No. She wouldn't go there. "I suppose it is shock. I should have realized I'm not thinking straight," she said.

"That's understandable."

She drank for a minute. "You said there were phone calls?"

"Oh yeah. There were the local papers, even a Denver one. A TV station. They're just getting geared up. And your father called. He wants you to get in touch. Oh, and your sister and a lady named Darlene."

"Um."

"A few of your patients left messages. I wrote them down. They're all pulling for you."

She smiled weakly. "So it was more than a few calls."

"You could say that."

"I have to phone my patients. My God, I can't . . . I just can't. I'll have to . . ."

"I can help you with that."

"I have a list on my computer," she said, distracted. "I'll have to . . ." Her voice trailed off.

"We'll take care of it." Calm, reassuring, an air of incurable goodwill.

"I can't believe I slept."

"You were exhausted."

"Thanks to you and your friends, yes, I was. I still am."

"I won't say I'm sorry again."

"Good. I don't want to forgive you. I can't believe there hasn't been word from McKinley. Nothing on TV? Did you even try the TV?"

"I tried."

"God. I mean, shouldn't they have found *something* by now?" Even as she spoke she knew how futile her words were. If she'd learned nothing else in her reading, she'd learned that often the remains of climbers were never recovered. But they had found Kemil. Did that mean there really was a thread of hope? What did it *mean?*

She had dealt with the crushing pain of death before, when her mother had been killed. And she knew from her patients that the terrible hurt behaved much like birth pangs, but in reverse. The worst came just after the loss. Pain gripped you suddenly and fiercely and with merciless frequency. But then, within a few hours, the pains grew farther apart and the intensity of them diminished.

None of this had struck her yet, because without news, without concrete news, she simply couldn't give up hope. She wouldn't mourn. But then why was she feeling such despair?

The phone rang, and her heart lurched. But it was one of the television stations in Grand Junction. She heard John say, "Miss Greene is not giving interviews. No, don't bother calling back, the answer will be the same." He hung up.

"They really are piranhas, aren't they?" she said.

"Sharks, vultures, piranhas, whatever."

The phone rang again. "God," she said, but it was Ann calling back.

"You're awake. How could you sleep?" Ann said.

"Oh, that was an awful thing to say. You're exhausted. Do you want me to drive up? I could—"

"No, I'm okay, really."

"Who's that who keeps answering the phone?"

"A . . ." She almost said *friend*. "A man from the State Department."

"What?"

"Oh, God, it's a long story. Let's just say the government is worried about fallout from Kemil's death."

"Fallout? But how are you involved?"

"I'm not. I only knew him through Erik. But the press doesn't care." Meredith exchanged a look with John. She hadn't said too much, had she? But really, what did she care? What could he do, arrest her?

"And there hasn't been any word about Erik? Nothing?"

"Not a thing. They're still searching, though."

"Hey, he's a survivor, right? You've got to cling to that, Merry. Okay?"

"Okay."

"Have you spoken to Dad? He called here. He's really upset."

"Oh?"

"About *you*."

"No, I haven't called him."

"Will you?"

"Maybe. All right, later."

"And you don't want me to drive you up, you're sure?"

"I'm fine."

"Maybe on the weekend, then. I'll bring the cherubs, but we'll all stay at the ranch. By then . . . Well, Erik will be home safe and sound. Right?"

"Absolutely."

"Call me if you need me."

"I will."

"Promise?"

"Promise."

The minute she hung up, the phone rang again. John frowned and picked it up. She knew at once it was for him. "Okay, I see," he said, then he listened. She saw his frown deepen. "Give that to me again?"

She was on her feet. "John? What is it? What—?"

He held up a hand. "And the report was filed by who?" He listened. "So it's preliminary."

"John," she cried.

He shot her a look. "All right. As soon as there's anything else . . . Yeah, this number or my cell phone. Okay. Right." He hung up.

"For God's sake, tell me! What's happening? Have they found . . . ? Oh no, tell me they haven't . . ."

He was steadying her suddenly, his hands on her shoulders. "They haven't found Erik. Okay? Did you hear me?"

"I . . . They haven't?"

"No. He's still missing."

"Oh. Oh, thank God," she breathed, and she stepped backward, away from him. "Then . . . What was that about?" She waited, but he was regarding her, his expression cautious. "John?"

He shrugged. "It will come out soon enough, anyway, I guess."

"What?"

"The report. It's only a preliminary report," he said, "but there's been a development."

"What development?"

"The report is from the lab at Alaska State Police headquarters. Apparently . . ." he said, but he hesitated.

"Apparently *what?*"

He paused for another moment, then said, "The safety rope found hooked to Prince Kemil's harness appears to have been cut."

It took her a second. "Cut? You mean, like cut with a knife?"

He nodded.

"I don't understand. If Kemil's rope was cut, then . . ."

"Then his death may not have been an accident," John finished for her.

She half collapsed on the stool and shook her head, unable at first to digest what he'd said. She felt as if someone had put a vise on her head and was tightening it. Finally, she looked up. "But that just doesn't make any sense. It's wrong. Someone made a mistake."

He raised a brow.

"Of course that's it. Someone in the police lab screwed up. Why . . . those guys, Kemil and Chad and Erik, they were the best of friends. A cut rope? How ridiculous! Even *you* can't believe that's right."

Abruptly, she shook her head and laughed, but it was anger and disbelief popping to the surface. "A cut rope. It's no wonder they haven't found Erik. They're nothing but a bunch of backwoods incompetents. You *have* to realize that."

But when she glanced at his face, there was nothing there but doubt—not doubt about the rope but doubt in her judgment.

She laughed again, and she knew, she was positive in a minute she'd wake and realize this was nothing more than a horrible nightmare.

SIXTEEN

Sometimes it felt as if she had lived years in the last thirty-six hours. She wondered if it would be better to know the worst outcome, to know he was dead, gone, existed no longer. Or was the faint and exhausting possibility of hope better?

Today, a day and a half after Chad had walked down the ridge into High Camp, the thought of Erik dead didn't seize her quite as savagely. She knew from her studies that the mind did this whether you gave it permission or not; it acclimated itself, started getting used to the idea, going on with life. Each hour became easier. A little easier.

But there were moments when a picture would form behind her eyes—Erik sitting there on her couch or eating at the counter, Erik in her bed, in the shower—and the pain sliced with renewed ferocity.

That long afternoon John stayed with her, planning to sleep on the living room couch, using the downstairs powder room. He tirelessly screened all her calls, answering only certain ones, and then his response was simply "No comment." He used his cell phone to speak to his office in Washington and the NSA investigators, who were still in Aspen, waiting for Chad to return.

"I wish I could talk to Chad," she said that evening. "I *need* to talk to him. I don't suppose you know when he's getting back?"

Earlier, John had gone into town to pick up his belongings, and he'd done some grocery shopping. He'd left her phone on the machine and told her not to answer any calls from strangers. Now he sat at the kitchen counter eating a sandwich and a bowl of soup.

"Chad's getting back in the morning, I believe."

"But you don't know for sure?"

"I could find out."

"I suppose those same men will want to talk to him," she mused aloud. "Those NSA men."

John kept eating.

"Of course they will. Then there's that absurd business about Kemil's rope. I've given it a lot of thought, and—"

"Don't."

"Don't what?"

"Don't waste your time thinking about it."

"Why?"

"Because the report was preliminary, and even if the rope was cut, Chad Newhouse will be the only one who can explain what went on."

"Still . . ."

"Meredith, forget it."

"Easy for you to say."

"Hey—"

"I wonder," she cut in, "if those jerks are going to ask Chad if *he* slept with Kemil, too."

He took a bite of sandwich, ignoring her.

"And what about Kathy? Is she in trouble? Are they hounding her like they hounded me? Do they really think we're all somehow involved with terrorists? They couldn't, could they?"

"I can't answer those questions."

"Can't or won't?"

He lifted his shoulders, let them drop.

"Oh, for God's sake," she said.

"You really should eat something," John said. "This takeout isn't bad."

"I don't have any appetite."

"You should try anyway."

He finished, rose, and took his bowl, spoon, and plate to the kitchen sink, washed them, stacked them neatly in the dish rack.

"You could put them in the dishwasher, you know," she said to his back.

"This is just as easy."

She couldn't bear it anymore, the waiting, the not knowing, the wondering and hoping.

"Am I allowed to use the phone?"

"Sure, it's your house."

She dialed Kathy's number. Maybe there was some news, a tidbit, something. But all she got was Kathy's machine, then, as she was leaving her message, someone picked up.

"Kathy?"

"Who is this?" came a stranger's voice.

"Meredith Greene. Who are *you?* Where's Kathy?"

"Mrs. Fry can't come to the phone right now."

"Is she all right? Tell her it's Meredith. Please, tell her—"

"I'll give her the message. Does she know your number?"

"Yes, yes, tell her—" But he'd hung up.

"Steve is with her," John said.

"You mean a State Department guy like you?"

"Yes."

"Oh God. I have to talk to her. Please, can't you do something?"

"I'm afraid that's impossible," he said.

She slept three hours that night and was up before dawn, checking the dispatches on the Internet, flipping through channels on the TV set in her bedroom, while John presumably slept like a baby on the couch. There were updates on the rescue operation on McKinley but no news about Erik.

It occurred to her to sneak out and drive to Kathy's to see if Kathy had heard anything, but she realized she'd never get past John and his cohort . . . Steve, right.

She suddenly wanted to take her frustrations out on John and his colleagues. But the truth was, for the past year, these same government men were all that stood between the fearful, uncertain public and a very altered, insecure world. God only knew what John and men like him had learned and experienced, horrible things she was best off not even knowing about. It was wrong to blame him for doing his job.

At six A.M., she quietly padded down the stairs and put coffee on. John lay in a tangle of sheets, his face to the back of the couch. He was out cold. She waited while the coffee dripped into the pot, and she stared at him, this stranger who'd taken over her house, her life.

And she'd let him. She must be a coward at heart.

Over her first cup of coffee, her thoughts flip-flopped. Did she really want to go this alone? Her whole being was focused on the rescue, on the hope she held in her breast. Was she really capable of handling the phone and the newspeople parked out front?

He woke around seven and did not seem to notice her when he stretched, scruffed his hands through his hair, and came to a sitting position. He started to rise. He was wearing jockey shorts. Navy blue jockey shorts.

She cleared her throat and set the coffee mug down hard on the counter.

"Oh, you're up," he said.

"Yes, there's, ah, coffee. I'll just go upstairs and check the news on the web again. You can get dressed. All right?"

"Sure, thanks."

She couldn't believe how embarrassed she felt. It had to have been the shock of seeing a half-naked man on her couch, a man who was not Erik. Her embarrassment was followed by a stab of guilt. What if Erik walked in? But of course, he wouldn't. He might never cross her threshold again.

At three P.M., almost forty-eight hours since Erik's disappearance, John hung up on yet one more media hound.

"Would you please get me through to Kathy?" she asked.

He regarded her for a moment, then he said, "What's Kathy Fry's number?"

She told him, then watched as he punched in the digits. After a moment, he said into the receiver,

"Steve? John McCord. Yeah. Here, too. Look. I've decided to let Meredith speak to Mrs. Fry." He paused, listening. "I understand. I'll take responsibility." Another pause. "Okay, put Mrs. Fry on."

He turned to Meredith and held out the cordless phone. "It would be a good idea to keep it short, all right?"

She didn't answer. She took the phone and said, "Kathy? Are you there? It's Meredith."

"Meredith! Oh God, Meredith, this guy's staying here, and he won't let me answer the phone, and I can't go anywhere. This is so fucking awful. Can you come over? Please, I need you."

"What's going on, Kathy?"

Her friend's voice was high and thin, near hysteria. "Chad . . . they . . . He got in this morning, and they were waiting for him at the airport, and, oh God, Meredith, they took him in for questioning."

"Oh, Kathy." Her eyes swiveled to John, but he only stared back impassively.

"And . . . and he called me, they allowed him one call, and I'm trying to locate a lawyer for him."

"Did he . . . Kathy, did he say anything about Erik? About what happened up there?"

"No, he couldn't, he didn't have time. They can't keep him there, can they? I mean, he hasn't been arrested or anything."

"I don't know. I . . . It's all about Kemil, you realize."

"They're crazy! What does Chad know about Kemil?"

"I can't imagine. They questioned me about him. You, too, I guess."

"They want Kemil's ledgers, all my stuff from the computer. I can't . . . I can't give it to them. I don't know what to do." Her voice lowered, strained with tension.

"I'll try to come over. Where are the twins?"

"With a friend. I swear, Meredith, I can't handle this. I can't—"

"I'll be over. Hang in there."

She hung up and picked up her purse, her car keys, her sunglasses to hide her swollen eyes.

John stepped in front of the door. "What do you think you're doing?"

"I'm going to see my friend."

"No." He shook his head.

"No? Am I under house arrest or something?"

"Look. I'm here to help you. Going to Mrs. Fry's house is a bad idea."

"Why?"

"Because a man is dead. Her employer. Your friend is missing. And the only one who can answer the questions surrounding the accident is Mrs. Fry's brother."

"This is crazy. Just crazy. I'm sure Chad's cleared it all up by now, anyway."

His expression bespoke his doubt.

"I haven't done anything wrong. You have no right to detain me."

"I have the right," he said. "You're forgetting Kemil was a Saudi prince. This is a matter of national security, and I assure you, I do have the right."

He seemed to fill the entranceway just as Erik had done. It almost took her breath away.

"I'm going to Kathy's," she said again, and her heart

began to pound. "I'm going," she repeated, the words trembling on her lips.

"Meredith."

"No." She recalled then, remembered how many times Erik had said her name like that: *Meredith.* "No," she repeated. Then, humiliatingly, she burst into tears.

She stood there, holding her purse, tears trickling into the corners of her mouth, her nose running. He moved close to her, put a hand on her arm.

"Take it easy."

"Why? What for? I don't even know if Erik's alive or dead, and you're here, and my life . . . my life . . ." She choked, and she felt John pull her toward him and put an arm around her shoulders. It lay there, heavy and comforting, and she had the urge to lean into him, hold onto him, hold tight to someone she could talk to and hear and touch. Someone who would make her feel as if she were not so alone.

"I know," he said quietly. Then took out a handkerchief and handed it to her.

The storm passed, and she blew her nose and dabbed at her eyes and carefully backed away. "Sorry," she murmured.

"No need to be."

"Can I please go to Kathy's?"

This time he didn't hesitate. "I'll take you."

She was shocked when she first stepped outside and saw all the cars parked across the street from her place. A sheriff's patrol car was there, too, presumably keeping an eye on the media people. The minute she showed her face, car doors opened. There was a news van from a Denver TV station, and a technician with a video camera.

But John steered her to his Blazer swiftly, a hand at the small of her back, until they were safely in his vehicle.

Safe, perhaps, but the newshounds followed his car in a long line—*A funeral,* she thought, *a goddamn funeral procession.*

She sat beside John as he drove, and her tears dried, and she felt bubbles of frustration building in her, then rising to the surface and popping.

"What do you think happened on McKinley?" she asked, trying to keep her voice level. "Tell me, what do you think really happened?"

"I don't know."

"Come on, you have an idea."

"I prefer to wait till the facts are in."

"You really believe someone cut—deliberately *cut*— Kemil's safety rope?"

"The preliminary examination of the rope was quite explicit. But I'll wait for the forensics. We'll all wait."

"Who? Chad? You think Chad did it? Cut the rope and killed Kemil along with his best friend in the world? Or did Erik cut it? But that doesn't work, because he fell, too."

"I don't have answers for you."

"Well, who else was up there? Oh, I know, Kemil cut his *own* rope."

"There's an investigation going on. We'll find out."

"And how does that fit in with Kemil's terrorist friends? Was there someone *else* up there killing people?"

He turned his head and gave her a mild look, then put his attention back on the road.

"And *why?* There's no motive. Do you think Chad

killed Kemil to save us all from terrorists?"

No reply.

"Do you know how crazy you sound? Conspiracy theories, cut ropes, murder, that's what you're getting at, isn't it?"

He remained quiet.

"You won't even let me mourn," she whispered, then she fell silent, too, sucked under by her anguish, trying to hold onto the dwindling hope that Erik could still be found alive.

It wasn't too late. Despite what John said, it wasn't too late. If Erik were dead . . . No, it couldn't be. She was nothing without him.

A contingent of news vans and rental cars from out-of-state agencies surrounded Kathy's house, too. And there was a car identical to John's parked near her front door. The other State Department man's SUV. Steve. The guard.

She got out of the car, not waiting for John, and went to the front door. It was locked. She pounded on the wood, hurting her hand, and then it opened abruptly, almost sucking her into emptiness.

"Meredith," Kathy sobbed.

They hugged and hugged again.

"I'm a mess. I haven't stopped crying in days," Kathy said.

"Me, too."

"Oh God, Meredith, I'm so sorry about Erik. After all those times I told you not to worry."

"I still have hope."

"If anyone could . . . live through that, Erik could."

"I know."

"I finally got a lawyer for Chad," she said, leading

Meredith inside. "He went right down to the police department."

"Good."

"Is that your bodyguard?" Kathy asked.

Meredith looked over her friend's shoulder and saw John talking quietly with Steve, heads ducked, voices lowered conspiratorially. "Yes, that's John McCord."

"The bastards."

"Are the kids okay?"

"I think so. They know about Erik and Kemil, but this other stuff . . ." Kathy turned away and put a hand to her face. "They don't know about it, and I hope they never find out. I'll do anything to protect them from this."

They were still in the entranceway when car tires crunched on the gravel outside, and not bothering to acknowledge Meredith, Steve went past them to the door. "Visitors," he said.

"What now?" Kathy breathed.

Voices outside, Chad's raised in anger, another man's reply.

"Chad," Kathy cried, and she ran out to meet him.

Chad looked like hell. Despite his face being sunburned from the climb, he looked ill, his eyes sunken, his cheeks bristly with whiskers. He wore a pair of jeans and a thermal top, as if he'd come off the mountain and changed his pants, taken off his parka, and caught a flight out of Anchorage. There were two agents with him, the NSA men who had grilled her at the sheriff's department.

"Kathy," Chad said, "my God, are you all right?"

"No."

"Stupid question."

"What did they . . . ?" She glanced around at the government men and cut off whatever she was going to say.

"Thanks for getting Joe Santino for me. He was great. Just waltzed in and made them let me go."

"Thank God," Kathy said.

And then, for the first time, Chad seemed to notice Meredith. His body tensed, and a bitter rictus pulled at his features. He moved to stand in front of her, and his eyes roamed over her face.

"Meredith," he began, but he faltered, unable to come up with any other words.

She saw the misery in his expression, the exhaustion, the unimaginable toll the storm and the loss of his friends had taken on him. And something else—a stutter-step in his reaction to her. Guilt? Fear?

"Meredith," he said again, his voice rough, "I . . ."

Without words, they embraced. He smelled of sweat and weariness, but his arms were strong, and she felt her tears come again.

"I'm so sorry," he whispered. "I'm so sorry."

Then Chad, too, thought Erik was dead, she realized. Was she the only person left who was clinging to a thread of hope?

"I'll make some coffee," Kathy said. "And we'll sit down and relax."

"Sounds good. All I've been doing since I walked into High Camp," he said wearily, "is talking about the accident."

Meredith helped Kathy brew the coffee. She put out sugar and milk, and the whole time she was going through the most commonplace motions, her heart leaped like a wild thing in her chest and her mouth was dry and her hands shook.

It seemed to take forever, the coffeepot dripping, everyone pouring and stirring, the clink of spoon against cup, the settling in the living room. The four men from Washington took cups, solemnly thanking Kathy, then they stood back, holding their saucers, watching, stone-faced.

Meredith forced herself to sit across from Chad and Kathy. Stillness was difficult; her body needed constant movement, as if she could outrun reality.

"Look," Kathy said, her eyes meeting Chad's, "I know Meredith wants to hear what happened, but if you'd rather not go over it again right now, we can—"

But Meredith sat up ramrod-straight. "No, please, Chad, I have to know. It's been hell just stuck here waiting, not knowing, picturing it. *Please.*"

For a long moment, Chad's gaze remained fixed to Kathy's; then, finally, he let out a ragged breath and found Meredith with his eyes. "Okay, okay, I understand. I'm just so damn tired," he said.

"Thank you," Meredith whispered, but she wondered. Did she really want to hear this? Would it rip her to shreds, and she'd never be able to piece herself together?

"It was pretty bad at the summit," he began, and it was too late to stop him. She'd asked for it. "The storm came in sooner than we'd expected. We could see it moving toward us, and we tried to get down as fast as we could. We were making good time, and we reached Denali Pass. But the wind started up. God, it howled. The temperature must have dropped thirty degrees in a few minutes. We couldn't see a thing. It was a com-

plete whiteout, snow and blowing snow. Thank God
we were roped together.

"We decided to keep descending. Erik was sure he
could follow the ridge down. The alternative was to
dig a snow cave and wait it out, but that's always risky.
So we kept going. It was as bad as I've seen it anywhere. And we were afraid that the wind was snow-
loading the cornices, so we might step a few inches to
either side and fall into thin air.

"Jesus, it was hairy. Cold, so goddamn cold. Everest
was never colder than that. So, we're up there, not
really sure exactly where, and Kemil . . . I don't know,
I guess he got disoriented. We were hooked onto the
rope forty feet apart, so you could do that, get too far
to one side or the other. Kemil probably lost sight of
Erik ahead of him. Maybe just for a minute, but it was
enough."

He rubbed his hand across his face and took a deep
breath. "The first thing I knew, I felt a hard tug on my
rope. I followed it, secured my end, Christ, I almost
stepped off the cornice myself, and I got to where
Kemil had broken through. Erik was there by then, and
he secured his end. We couldn't see a thing, only felt
where the rope went over the edge. Then we heard
something, amazing we could in all that noise, and we
looked over the edge. We could make Kemil out,
barely. He'd self-arrested with his ice ax. He was hanging there, dangling over . . . God knows what the exposure was. But alive, he was alive. Then the snow
started blowing bad again, and it was a whiteout, but
we'd seen him. Had a fix on his position.

"Okay, so Erik and I go into rescue mode. We've
done it before; it's second nature, you know? I jammed

in pitons to belay Erik so he could get down to Kemil. Erik looped his rope, checked that he had his carabiner fixed right, routine stuff. Then he began lowering himself over the edge. The rope was around my back and also secured by a couple of ice pitons. I couldn't see Erik because I had to belay him, couldn't get close to the cornice. But I could feel him on the rope, the way it slackened and tightened. I figured he had to have reached Kemil by how much rope I'd let out.

"I also knew what Erik would do as soon as he reached Kemil: check him for injuries, lock his carabiner on the rope, start him climbing up, or, if he was hurt, climb out and help me haul him up."

Chad lowered his head, let it hang. His shoulders heaved in a kind of sob. "But something happened. I don't know, I couldn't see them. The ledge . . . the storm. Maybe Erik slipped, I don't know. Maybe Kemil did. All I know is that I felt a hard tug on the rope then no weight, no weight at all, and I knew they were gone. One or both. I didn't know."

He raised his head, his expression bleak. "Either the rope broke or one of the harnesses snapped or, Jesus, maybe Erik knew he'd take me with him, couldn't hold on, unhooked himself. Or maybe he was just trying to save Kemil and they both fell, and he released the carabiners to save me. I don't know. I've been going out of my mind for two days now, trying to figure it out, trying to figure out what happened down there. But I can't. I can't!"

Carefully, Kathy put her hand on her brother's arm. But Meredith couldn't move. She sat there, the scene Chad had described going through her mind. The wind, snow blown sideways so hard it was like buckshot, the ropes, Kemil falling.

"I don't know how I got down," Chad was saying. "I barely remember it. I almost didn't try, I almost stayed there. Just sat down in that storm and froze to death. I wanted to. Believe me, I wanted to."

"Chad," Kathy murmured.

"But I didn't, and here I am, being questioned like a fucking criminal. And they're dead, two good men are dead."

Dead. The word tolled in her brain like a death knell. *No,* cried her heart. *He's gone,* said her brain. And her eyes met John McCord's for an instant before she looked back at Chad.

She got up, her limbs feeling stiff and unfamiliar, and sat on the other side of Chad, put her hand on his bowed back. "We're all glad you came down," she whispered.

"I'm not so sure myself," he replied.

"What good would it have done if you'd stayed?" she asked.

Then it occurred to her that he had left something out of his story. The piece of allegedly cut rope still attached to Kemil's body.

"Chad," she said, "did you know about the rope being cut?"

"What?"

"Kemil's rope. They think it was cut. Deliberately."

Chad's head snapped up; he glared at his sister, then swung back to Meredith. "What the hell? You're saying—let me get this straight—you're saying someone cut Kemil's safety rope?"

She nodded.

"But . . . that's impossible. I mean . . . Who the hell said that? Why hasn't anyone talked to *me* about this?"

"Our government watchdogs said it."

"Jesus," Kathy breathed.

"No way, no fucking way!" Chad yelled, and he leaped to his feet, whirled toward the four agents. His face was livid with rage. "What are you saying? That *I* cut the rope? Or Kemil did? Or Erik? Are you crazy?"

It was John who stepped forward. "Now, Mr. Newhouse, calm down. It's a preliminary report, and no one's accusing anyone of anything."

"You know what you guys are? You're vultures. You're goddamn vultures circling the dead. You want meat. Dead meat."

John's expression did not change. He was impervious. When it came to his job, he was single-minded and stone cold.

But a half hour later, when she was in the kitchen, John came in and stood behind her as she washed coffee cups.

"That was privileged information," he said.

"About the rope?"

"Yes, goddamn it, yes."

She turned around, resting her back against the sink and staring him in the face. A glimmer of satisfaction swept her when she saw his expression. He was mad as hell. She'd finally gotten through that shell.

"I trusted you." He took hold of her arm, his hand like steel on her. "I trusted you with that information."

"I'm sorry I'm not trustworthy, then. Let me tell you something, John. I have no intention of cooperating with you. And it's wrong to expect me to help trip Chad up by withholding important information."

"There's something wrong with his story. It doesn't hold together," John said.

"Were you up there on that mountain in a storm? What do you know? My God, they were all under the worst duress. Things aren't always logical in those conditions."

"Don't you want to find out what really happened?"

Sudden anger shook her. "We *know* what happened, Chad just told us. And why would he cut a rope and kill his friends? What in heaven's name was his motive?"

"It's under investigation." His smooth façade had slid into place. "It could have something to do with terrorist activities. National Security. That's why I'm here, remember?"

"In this instance, you're wrong. There's nothing sinister going on."

"Well then, have *you* got a motive for Chad to cut his friend's rope?"

"He didn't cut anything. I don't believe it. You're making a tragic accident into something else." She extricated herself from his grasp, folding her arms across her chest, facing him down. She held her ground for a minute, then went into the living room to find Chad pacing back and forth, ranting.

"What am I supposed to do now? You think I'm some kind of murderer, that I killed my friends? And you want me to cooperate? That rope wasn't cut; it couldn't have been!" He flung himself onto the couch, put his head in his hands.

Kathy stood in a corner, white-faced, holding herself. She was trembling. Meredith took in the scene and went to Chad, sat, and put her arms around him.

"It's a mistake. Don't worry," she said softly. "Listen, this isn't your fault. You're suffering survivor's guilt. It'll pass. I swear to you, it'll pass."

"Oh God, Meredith," he choked out. "It wasn't bad enough . . . the accident. But now, now they—"

"Shh," she said. "It will pass. Just hang on."

Then Chad began to shake and weep, wrenching sobs, so difficult to watch in a strong man. Kathy came and settled down beside him, and they both held him while he cried out his torment.

The agents stood, not displaying discomfort or understanding or any human emotion, and observed the man's misery with implacable expressions.

On the way home, they stopped at City Market in Aspen, John insisting they needed food. *She* needed food. While they were in the store, the investigator of the firm hired by the al Assad family tried to corner her. She recognized him right away, because John had pointed him out to her as the man sat in his car with his partner in front of her town house. A big, square head, a blocky body.

"Miss Greene," he said, approaching her in the frozen-food aisle. "I'd like to talk to you about—"

John appeared instantly, insinuating himself between the man and Meredith. "Miss Greene isn't talking to anyone."

"Listen, McCord," the man began, "the family has a right to know what happened."

"Miss Greene can't help you. She doesn't know anything. She's under federal protection."

They stood face-to-face, the investigator taller and broader than John, and Meredith shrank back against the glass doors of the ice cream case.

But it was over in a moment. The big man swore, stepped aside, and said, "She'll have to testify sometime, and you know it."

"Not your problem," John said, and he turned his back on the man and led her out of the store, leaving the half-filled grocery cart behind.

She finally fell into a deep sleep that night, perhaps her mind coming to grips with Erik's death now that she'd heard Chad's story. But the phone woke her, and she lay there, trying to ignore it, nevertheless straining to hear John's voice.

Was he talking to someone? Or was he still saying "No comment" to everyone?

Was there *news?*

She was wide awake in an instant, shoving her arms into her bathrobe, hurrying down the steps.

"Who is that? Is there news?" she got out breathlessly.

He was off the phone, sitting at the counter on a stool, holding a coffee mug, one that had a skier on it, and snowflakes, and the words *King of the Mountain.* "It was Washington." He met her eyes gravely. "They've officially called off the search for Erik."

She found herself on the couch, John holding her arms. She felt nauseous and . . .

"Did I . . . ?"

"I thought you were gong to faint."

"No, no, I'm okay."

"I'm sorry," he said.

"So am I." She took a deep breath, felt the nausea subside. She'd expected this, she'd known it was coming. So why . . . ? Her hand went to the ring around her neck and she clasped it. Her talisman, her touch-stone.

"Did he give you that?" she heard John ask.

She looked up.

"I've seen it around your neck. I assumed he gave it to you."

"Yes."

"You were engaged?"

"Not quite. We were going to get engaged when he got back." Her voice stopped in her throat, and she swallowed. "When he got back from McKinley."

"I see."

"No, you don't," she whispered.

But she didn't cry. There were no more tears left in the terrible hollow place at her core. When she searched inside herself, probing the emptiness, she could not find anyone. There was no identity there. She was no longer dependable Meredith, helper of lost souls, sister to Ann, replacement for her mother. Nor was she the woman with a lover, flush with passion. She realized with stabbing clarity that she had no existence apart from Erik. And he was gone.

SEVENTEEN

Thank God he'd made it out safe and sound, she thought as she lay in bed next to Erik. She was drenched in a relief so profound she could almost not bear it. He was exhausted, beaten up; he'd had a hell of a time, but he was okay.

She'd let him sleep. She lay there, close to his warmth, and dozed and dreamed and woke once again to relief so powerful she almost cried.

He was back, and he loved her, and now she could take his ring off the chain and slip it on her finger. No, *he* would slip it on her finger.

"Meredith," he said drowsily, rolling over to face her.

"Yes?" She smiled, so cozy and warm, so full of love she was bursting.

"Meredith."

"Um."

"Meredith."

Why did he keep saying her name like that? Why did . . . ?

Her body jerked awake.

"Meredith."

No, her mind screamed. *Oh no.*

John McCord stood above her, a hand on her arm, shaking her.

"Meredith?"

"Oh my God," she mumbled.

"Are you okay?"

"No," she whispered.

"You have to get up. I let you sleep, but the memorial service is in an hour and . . ."

"Yes," she said, lying there. Tears squeezed out of her eyes, and a hopeless despair bludgeoned her.

"What's the matter?" John asked. "Do you feel all right?"

She sat up. "I was dreaming. He was here; he was okay." She was surprised at how little she cared that John was witness to her tears, to her disheveled hair and sleep-swollen eyes and the old T-shirt that read *Denver Broncos* on its front.

"Erik?"

She nodded.

"The service . . ."

"Yes, okay, I'll be quick."

She showered and dressed in a khaki skirt and matching jacket, a dark, plum-colored camisole. Sober clothes for a memorial service. Not a funeral—you couldn't have a funeral without a body.

It had been two days since the search for Erik had been called off. Two days of suffering, of John McCord screening her calls, keeping the media at bay, of Kathy phoning her and talking and talking—about Chad and the accident and Kemil and her own watch-

dog, Steve, whom she resented with a seemingly irra-
tional ferocity.

And today was the service.

She went downstairs and poured herself a cup of
coffee John had made hours ago. It was as thick as
mud.

"Do you want breakfast?" he asked, concerned as
always. He was wearing chinos and a dark blue linen
shirt that matched his eyes. His navy sport coat hung
over the back of a living room chair.

"No," she replied.

"You aren't eating enough."

"I'm not hungry."

He shrugged, giving up.

Outside, he hustled her past the vans and reporters
that were camped out across the street. The heavyset
investigator for the al Assad family glared at John, not
even bothering to get out of his car.

They drove to the Aspen Chapel, an elegantly un-
derstated nondenominational building of stone and
glass, its sleek steeple pointing to the sky. Sheriff's
deputies cordoned off the parking lot, keeping the sat-
ellite vans at bay, checking the identities of everyone
who arrived at the service.

My God, she thought, *why don't they leave us alone?*

It was a hot July day, very still, but downvalley, a
line of dark thunderheads were massing. The monsoon
rains would sweep in later that afternoon, cooling and
cleansing, soaked up instantly by the thirsty soil.

The mountains rose on either side of the valley, and
driving into the parking lot she could see Pyramid Peak
twenty miles farther on, a grand sentinel guarding the
end of the Maroon Creek Valley. Next to Pyramid were

the Maroon Bells, where Bridget had died, she thought, musing on the oddity, the finality, the starkness of death.

Bridget . . . Meredith had been so very angry with Erik, blaming him, yes, blaming him. And now Erik was dead, too, and that was all over. It didn't seem to matter anymore.

She sat by herself in a pew across from Kathy and Chad and Randy, the owner of Summit Expeditions. Kathy wanted to talk, she could sense that, but she wasn't up to it. Chad was white and silent, haggard looking.

Kevin and Dan and Jessie were there. And so many others. Friends of Erik's, friends of hers, the entire local climbing community. There were faces she recognized from the books on climbing, craggy, wind-scoured faces from all over the country. And strange ones, people she didn't know.

Women. Lots of single women. Erik's lovers? Or just groupies? Some of them were crying openly. What had his relationship been with them? Not like with her, certainly not. Her hand rose automatically to touch his ring. It would never belong on her finger now.

John remained standing at the rear of the chapel. Kathy's man Steve was back there, too, along with the two NSA men who'd conducted the interrogations. They appeared stiff and out of place, the young NSA agent even wearing sunglasses. Inside.

Hadn't she read somewhere that investigators always attended the funerals of victims to see if the killer showed up? Well, she knew who they were looking for: mad terrorists skulking around, bombers, men who compromised national security. In this instance, they were so wrong.

Down in the very front were two women. Tall, blond, and blue-eyed, one handsome and stalwart looking, her face a feminine copy of Erik's, the other younger, crying into a handkerchief. His mother and a sister?

Had she known he had a sister? And his father . . . Was he even alive? My God, she knew nothing about Erik, *nothing*. The service was going to be nondenominational, Kathy had told her. But now she wondered what Erik's religion had been. She had no idea.

But that was wrong. She did know. His religion had been climbing; the high peaks had been his god. His very profession had been a constant act of worship.

She glanced around, studying the unescorted women once more. All types, tall and short, pretty and plain, dark-haired and redheads and blonds. Some not so young. Even a few with gray hair.

Certainly they were just friends. Acquaintances. There was a short, slightly chubby woman who'd brought her little boy. Pretty face, a long sack of a dress, and big silver earrings. A hippie type. And a stunning tall blond, not young but movie-star glamorous. A petite redhead, with freckles and an uptilted nose, her eyes red from crying.

Erik's women?

She should be mourning, and instead she was distracted by the females who had come to cry over him.

But he'd loved *her* the most. Did any of these women have his ring? No, she did. She had to hang onto that, she had to believe that.

The minister spoke. She tried to listen, but the words

flowed past her in sinuous streamers of sound, and she couldn't stop the flow to understand what he was saying. A few phrases got through to her: "Died doing what he loved best." "His life was so fulfilling." "The brightest light that burns out so fast." "He'll live on in our memories." Clichés.

What would Erik think if he were here? She could imagine him, could almost feel his warmth at her shoulder. He'd laugh and he'd say, "Forget all this crap. I'm dead. So what? Everyone dies." And he'd pull her to him with strong hands and kiss her, ignoring everyone.

She sat there, frozen, seeing little. Later, she would not remember what went through her head.

When the service was over, she saw Kathy and Chad talking to the minister and Erik's Norwegian family. She wanted so badly to go to them and tell them she loved their son and brother, how wonderful he was. But she had no right to introduce herself or hug them or seek consolation in the presence of Erik's flesh and blood.

What could she say to them? "I'm a friend of Erik's." "I'm your son's fiancée." But she wasn't that, either. She could pull the ring out from where it rested against her breast and hold it up and say, "Look, he bought me a ring. He asked me to marry him. See? But, gosh, I wasn't ready to say yes."

Why *hadn't* she said yes?

John drove her to Kathy's after the service. There was to be a gathering of Erik's friends there. Everyone was bringing a dish for a potluck lunch.

But an ugly incident was in progress when they drove up. The NSA investigators were ejecting the al

Assads' investigator from Kathy's house.

John went to help, leaving her in the car; she watched, biting her lip. A nasty confrontation, hard words, stiff-armed shoves. And she heard snatches of the fight. "Knows more than he's saying. My clients . . ." "Under federal protection. You're not going to . . ." "Goddamn feds, we'll see . . ." "Call in the army, why don't you?"

Finally, the big man drove away, John and his fellow agents standing in the driveway, watching him.

The gathering reminded her painfully of Bridget's memorial in the park last summer. The parallels were there, and Erik was the center, always the center.

"How are you doing?" Kathy asked when they got a chance to talk privately.

"Not great," Meredith said.

Kathy looked as if she were about to cry. "And you two were going to get married. I can't believe it, you know? I just can't believe it."

"How's Chad?"

"Terrible. He's a mess."

"It will take some time, Kathy. I keep telling myself that. I learned all about grieving, I've treated patients going through it. I know what the books say. I'm trying to believe they're right. God, I'm hanging onto that."

"It'll get better, I know it will. But now, God, it's so awful. And the mess with Kemil . . ." She stopped herself and tried to smile. "But that's not your problem."

"I miss Erik," Meredith said.

"So do I. Look, do you want to meet his mother and sister? I didn't say anything to them about you. I have no idea if he told them or not. But they're very nice.

His mother doesn't speak very good English, but Astrid, his sister, does."

"No," Meredith said.

"Are you sure?"

"I'm sure." She felt her lips go cold. "Please, Kathy, don't tell them about me."

And then she had to seek Chad out. She didn't want to; his pain was palpable, and she didn't think she could bear it. But she had to ask him something.

She found him sitting outside on a wooden bench, staring up the valley toward Mount Hayden.

"Chad?"

"Meredith." He looked up at her, his eyes sunken into his head, his mouth drawn into a grimace.

"I couldn't find you."

"I had to get away from that." He gestured with his head toward the front door.

"I know."

He was silent for a time. Finally, he burst out with a curse, then said, "Erik would have hated this!"

"Chad . . ."

"You know, I keep expecting him to walk into a room or call me. I keep thinking . . ."

"I know," she repeated.

"I'm not fit company for anybody," he said, turning his face away.

She sat down. "Chad . . ." She felt uncomfortable saying the words, as if the subject were somehow taboo.

"Um."

"Did you . . . I mean, when you were up there . . . and they fell, is there any possibility he could have lived? I know they've called off the search. I know that, but could . . . is there a chance . . . ?"

Chad swiveled his gaze onto her, his eyes bloodshot, dark stubble on his cheeks. He looked ancient. He stared at her for a moment, then tears welled in his eyes, and he shook his head. Shook it slowly over and over.

Her heart gave a sick lurch, then settled back into a steady rhythm. "I . . . I had to ask."

"Never mind. It's okay. I'm just sorry I couldn't . . . do more." He was staring up the valley, a thousand-mile stare, as if he were very far away.

She got the distinct feeling he didn't want her there, he wanted to be alone to mourn his fallen friends privately, but there was one more thing she needed to say.

"The business about the rope. I hope you're not . . . ah . . . worried about it."

He turned on her with sudden anger. "I really don't want to talk about it. It stinks, the whole thing stinks."

"Yes, it does."

And then, fortunately, she was to think later, Kathy came outside and found the two of them.

"There you are," she said. "People have been looking for you. God, Meredith, I thought you'd gone home until I saw your guard dog still here."

"Oh . . . John."

"Yes, John. He's better looking than Steve. Can we switch?"

Meredith forced a smile. "I'll go in, but I'm not staying long. Okay?"

"It's a deal."

She went inside and took a plastic cup of punch from somebody. Looking around for John, she finally located him in a corner of the room, his head bent, cell phone to one ear, hand over the other to cut out the noise. She was moving in his direction to ask him to drive her home, when he looked up abruptly, saw her, hastily clicked his cell phone shut.

"I think we better go," he said when she reached him.

"Yes, fine. But why the hurry?"

"I'll tell you later." He took her arm and steered her toward the front door.

"I should say good-bye to Kathy."

"Not now."

And then she saw what was happening and why John wanted her out of there. Four Pitkin County sheriff's deputies had entered Kathy's house. Kathy was standing in front of them, arguing; Meredith couldn't hear what Kathy was saying, but she looked mad. The deputies were showing Kathy some kind of paper, and Chad was heading over to his sister.

"Is there a back door?" John asked her tersely.

"Wait, what's going on?" she asked.

"I think we should go."

She took her arm from his grasp. "No," she said. "Tell me what's going on."

"Jesus, Meredith, can we leave? I'll tell you later."

"Tell me now."

He looked angry, tense, and worried. "I'm only trying to protect you."

"I'm a grown woman. I'll protect myself."

He regarded her for a long moment. "The forensics came back. Kemil's rope was definitely cut by a serrated blade, the kind found on a Swiss Army knife. The deputies are here to take Chad into custody, where he'll be charged and extradited to Alaska to face criminal charges."

She sucked in a breath. "No!"

"I'm sorry."

"But Chad is innocent! It was an accident."

"That's for the courts to decide."

By the front door, Chad was being handcuffed. Kathy was crying. The guests stared, horrified, frozen in their places, hands grasping plastic cups and canapés.

"My God," Meredith breathed.

"You can't do anything here. Let's go. The news guys are going to be screaming for blood after this."

She went with him, feeling like a thief stealing out the back door. She'd call Kathy later. This would all be cleared up. Chad's lawyer would take care of things. Sure he would.

When they got halfway down Castle Creek Road, the wind began to toss the trees, lightning flashed in the sky over Aspen Mountain, and the rain that had been threatening came down. First only dusty spots on the car's windshield, then a deluge, as if the heavens were weeping for Chad, for Erik, for all of them.

By that evening, she'd spoken to Kathy on the phone three times. Chad's climbing gear had been confiscated and was being held as evidence, especially his Swiss Army knife. And Chad himself was still being questioned in Aspen.

"It's not fair," Meredith kept saying. "He just lost two of his best friends, and they have to do *this* to him." She was pacing, John was sitting on the couch, hands dangling between his knees.

"Take it easy."

"Why is this taking so long?" She stopped and

turned toward him. "Do you know? Are you keeping something from me?"

"No," he said tiredly. "I'm just a lowly field agent. I'm not privy to inside information."

"Can I believe you?"

He simply looked at her.

"Lovely job you have," she muttered, and she climbed the stairs to her room, slamming her door too hard.

She found out what the trouble was the next morning when John drove her into town to run errands.

"I had a call this morning," he began, his tone carefully neutral.

She switched her eyes to his profile.

"I don't like to be the one to tell you, but I guess there's not much choice. You're going to find out anyway."

"What?" Her heart began a leaden drumbeat.

"Look, Chad Newhouse isn't the great friend you think he is." He took his eyes off the road for a moment and glanced at her. "When he was being questioned yesterday, he told the police that it was Erik who cut Kemil's rope, and that Erik fell while he was trying to retrieve it from Kemil's body."

"No," she said automatically.

"I'm sorry, but that's what Chad claims."

"That's insane! My God, you can't . . . No, I don't believe it!" She put her hands over her ears and cried, "No, no, you're wrong. Chad's . . . There's a mistake. Why would Erik do that?"

She was aware that John was pulling the car onto the side of the road, stopping, sitting there with the engine idling. Her mind was full of panicked babble; nothing made sense.

"I'm sorry," he repeated. "I wish you hadn't heard it from me."

"Erik didn't do that," she whispered. "I know he didn't."

"Look, Meredith, there's more going on here than you realize. We're not sure of the exact facts yet, but we'll find out. It has a lot to do with Kemil. Chad said Erik and Kemil had been arguing for a long time, since even before leaving for McKinley. Apparently, the disagreements were over Kemil's terrorist friends. Erik was very angry that Kemil had let him stay at that house in Lahore. It made all of them look bad, according to Chad."

"I told you," she began. "Erik didn't care about—"

"Apparently he cared more than you thought."

"Chad's out of his mind. Erik and Kemil never argued."

"There's more." John seemed reluctant.

"What?"

"Kemil and Erik had words over something else. Chad claims Erik made a remark to one of Kemil's wives. A suggestive remark."

Her reaction was swift. The words were out of her mouth before she thought. "That's a lie! Erik would *never ... never ...* Not to Kemil. My God. I don't know. ... I can't figure out why Chad is telling so many lies. Why is this happening? Why ... ?" She put her face in her hands and drew in gulps of air. She couldn't breathe; something was constricting her chest.

She felt John's hand on her back. The car rumbled, idling, and on the road vehicles streaked by, the wake of their passing causing John's car to shudder. Her mind screamed uselessly. *No, no, it's a lie. It isn't true.*

"Look, Meredith. Either Chad is telling the truth or he's lying to protect himself. We'll find out which it is. I swear to you. We'll find the answers."

Slowly, her breathing came back to normal, her heart stopped its mad beat. And a new emotion took hold, a welcome one that alleviated her suffering. Once past despair, one climbs the ladder to anger.

Chad. The bastard. Blaming everything on a man who was dead and couldn't defend himself. Chad, telling her how he missed Erik, his eyes watering. Oh, yes, he was good at deception, a marvelous actor. She'd swallowed every word, every tear.

Abruptly, a scene appeared in her mind without a bridging thought: that evening back in June when they were all at Kemil's preparing for the climb. *Yes*, she recalled it with vivid clarity. Kemil and Chad arguing outside the door to the big media room, their voices low and vehement. And Erik stepping between them.

It had been Chad fighting with Kemil, not Erik.

EIGHTEEN

It was Saturday morning. An entire week had passed since she'd been at the ranch to work with her equine therapy patients. Seven days. Last Saturday, Erik had been alive. Chad had been a friend. She'd hadn't known who John McCord really was.

One short week.

She hadn't told John yet about the arguments between Chad and Prince Kemil. She hadn't told anyone. She needed to think, to make sense of Chad's wild accusations. If he'd lied about Erik and the rope and Kemil's death, he might have lied about everything. And Kathy: How did she fit into this mosaic of falsehood?

The ground under her feet was unstable, like the crevasse fields on McKinley. Any moment, you could step into a bottomless hole; keen sense, perfect awareness were necessary. She felt so battered, she wasn't sure of her judgment anymore.

She got up, pulled on her robe, and descended the stairs. She'd tried not to go down too early since she'd

ON THE EDGE 243

found John still asleep; it was more comfortable when he was up and dressed.

"I'm going to the ranch today," she announced as she poured herself a cup of coffee.

He was standing by the front window in three-quarter profile, looking out at the bright morning.

"I have my equine therapy kids," she said. She waited a heartbeat then, "Did you hear me?"

"I heard you."

"I need a break. You know, a change of scenery. I need to get away from . . . all this."

"Uh-huh."

"Okay, fine, it's settled then." She sounded belligerent to her own ears. Was she trying to precipitate a quarrel?

"I'll drive you."

"I'm going alone, John."

He turned then and came toward her out of the sunlight spilling through the window, into the shadows. "You know that's not possible."

"I don't need you. I want to get away from the media hounds and the phone calls and this place and Kathy and Chad. I need a break. And those kids depend on me."

"I hear you."

"Well then . . ."

"My job requires me to accompany you."

"Oh, please. No one is going to bother me at the ranch."

"You're my responsibility," he said doggedly.

"This is making me crazy," she muttered.

"Look, you know I can't let you go by yourself. And

to be honest, I'd like to see you work with your kids.
I mean it. I have a sister who has a son with cerebral
palsy. Maybe your kind of therapy could help him. I'd
like to see what you do."

She folded her arms across her chest and eyed him.
"Okay, so first it was a divorce and you were depressed; now it's a nephew with cerebral palsy. *Right.*"

He shrugged and gave her a wry smile. "It's all
true."

"Uh-huh." She let her arms drop. "Oh, what the hell.
Come along. But I'm driving my car."

He raised an eyebrow questioningly.

"My horse stuff is in it."

"Horse stuff. Okay, I'm at your command, Miss
Greene."

Terry and Sean were waiting for her at the ranch.
Their enthusiasm, their enjoyment lifted her and set her
down in another world, a happier one. She almost forgot that John was leaning on the top rail of the fence
around the ring, watching her.

The sun beat down on her head, the air smelled of
sage and dust and horse sweat. A welcome break.

"Okay, Sean," she was saying, "let's try it without
holding the reins. Hands out at shoulder height. Yes,
that's it." She walked alongside Sean, holding his leg
with one hand. His father led Pace, his mother walked
on the other side. Around and around, while Sean did
his "tricks," the movements that aided his balance, in-
creased his muscle tone.

"Oh yes, that's much better than last week. Can you
tell?"

"Yes!" Sean said. "I'm so much better. I want to
trot."

"Hold on there, pardner. Not so fast. Let's try this again. Arms out. Yes. Twist to the right. The left. Okay, now we're going to try it again. Oh boy, are we having fun now!"

Then there was Terry, who was a little more advanced. Meredith had her do different exercises, sitting with both legs on one side of the horse, swinging them around to face the horse's tail, then both legs on the other side then back to the front. Walking, walking, encouraging, loving the children's responses.

Terry kissed Pace good-bye, right on his velvety black nose, as her father held her up.

"Next week?" Terry's parents asked.

"Next week," Meredith said. "See you then."

She was feeding Pace his grain in the barn, John holding the gelding's lead rope, when her father walked in.

"You must be John McCord," he said, his hand out.

"And you must be Neil Greene. Nice to meet you."

They shook hands, sizing each other up in that way men have, and she watched, curious as to how they'd interact.

"Thanks for running interference for my daughter," Neil said.

"It's my job," John replied.

"Her sister told me about you."

She rolled her eyes. This was a typical pointed remark by her father, informing John and her, too, that she hadn't been in touch with him.

"I tried to call you, Dad," she said. "I left messages."

"I know, Merry. I got them. But I kind of wanted to tell you in person how sorry I am about Erik."

"Thanks, Dad."

"It's a terrible thing to lose someone you love," he went on. "I know how you feel, believe me."

It took her a moment to get over her surprise, and then she thought, *Perhaps he does*. He deserved the benefit of the doubt, anyway. She was in no shape to hold grudges right now. God, no.

"You handling it okay?" her father asked.

"I don't know. I'm handling it. What's the alternative?" She tried to smile.

"She's handling it just fine," John put in.

She gave him a look. This, from the man who'd seen her in hysterics, had seen her tears, her rage, her despair?

"Good," Neil said. "She's a tough one. I figured she'd be okay."

"I'm not so sure how okay I am," she said quietly.

"You're okay enough to take care of those kids," Neil said.

"That was pretty amazing," John said. "Seeing how they responded. I was telling your daughter that my sister has a son with cerebral palsy, and I'm sure going to tell her about equine therapy."

"Listen, John," Neil said. "Merry's sister is coming up from Denver—"

"She is?" Meredith asked. "She didn't tell me."

"That's because you kept saying not to come. But she's on her way, and I thought I'd ask you to stay for dinner, so you can talk to your sister."

"Oh, Dad, I don't think John wants—"

"I'd love to stay," John said. "Another Greene sister, huh?"

"Well, Annie's married, and she's bringing her two kids, so it might be kind of hectic."

"The more the merrier," John replied, smiling with charm.

Meredith stared at him.

Ann was dark-haired like her older sister, but her hair was naturally curly. She had her mother's brown eyes, and she was taller than Meredith. Quite statuesque, actually.

"Oh, Merry," she said, the baby in one arm, her toddler daughter hanging onto her denim skirt, hugging Meredith with her free arm. "How are you?"

"I'm okay. Or so they tell me."

"They?" Ann looked around, and her eyes lit on John. "This is John, am I right?"

"John McCord, good to meet you."

Ann shook his hand. "Thanks for taking care of her. She can be pretty ornery, can't she?"

"I won't argue with a pretty lady," John said congenially.

"This is Amanda," Ann said, pulling her older daughter forward. "Named after her grandmother. And this darling boy is Gregory. Say hi, kids."

Amanda hid her face in her mother's skirt, and Gregory gurgled and stared with big chocolate brown eyes just like his mother's.

"They've grown so much," Meredith said. "I can't believe it."

"I know. Amanda's going to preschool in the fall. Aren't you, sweetheart?"

"How about John and I take the babies out to see the new kittens in the barn?" Neil suggested.

"Let me change Gregory's diaper first, Dad," Ann said, "and then they're all yours."

John, a baby-sitter? Meredith thought. It was almost comical. But he went along with the plan as if he were quite accustomed to babies and grandfathers and kittens. But then, she remembered, he had a son. He'd been through this before.

"Well, well, he is quite a good-looking man," Ann remarked when they were alone in the ranch house.

"Who, John?"

"Who else, dummy?"

"Listen, Ann, he got stuck with being my bodyguard or whatever you want to call him. It wasn't as if he *wanted* to do it."

"Hey, all I said was that he was good-looking."

"Don't act the innocent. God, Ann, I just lost the man I loved, and you're—"

"Sorry. Oh, I'm really sorry. I didn't mean anything. But, you know, you never let me meet Erik, and it's kind of hard for me to picture you with him. I mean, it was so fast, almost as if it never happened."

"Oh, it happened."

"Well, sure. But I didn't know Erik, you see what I mean?"

"I never told you, but before he left, he gave me a ring," she admitted.

"Oh my God," Ann breathed.

"He asked me to marry him. Right there in the Aspen airport."

"What did you say?"

"I said—God, Annie, I can hardly believe it—I said it was so soon, I wasn't sure. I said, 'Let's wait.' "

"But . . . but you loved him."

"Yes."

"Then . . . ?"

"I don't know. I'll never know now. I hate myself for that. I should have said yes."

"But it would have ended the same way. It didn't matter what you said."

"It mattered to me."

"Oh, I'm so sorry." Ann embraced her. "It's so terrible, so awful. I wish . . . I wish I could do something."

Meredith leaned against her, smelling the fresh scent of shampoo and soap and a touch of sour baby milk. "I feel like a jinx, Annie. Everyone I love. First Mom, now Erik. They keep dying on me."

"Not everyone. Dad and I are still hanging in there. And all your friends."

Neil, who was very handy in the kitchen, prepared dinner. A big bowl of spaghetti with his own special sauce, Italian sausage, green peppers, onions, mushrooms, olives, and sliced carrots. A salad. Beer for whoever wanted it. Sodas for everyone else.

Meredith noted that John drank a soda, and something tugged at her memory. Something . . .

Garlic bread. And a half-gallon of Medieval Madness ice cream for dessert.

She had steeled herself for an awkward time—halting conversation, crying babies, a handful of mismatched people being forced to make the best of a bad situation. But dinner went remarkably well.

Amanda sat in a high chair, eating messily but enthusiastically. Gregory chewed on a cracker in his mother's lap, then fell asleep. Neil and John talked about football—funny, she'd never considered he'd be interested in sports—and she and Ann caught up on gossip.

"Listen," Neil said, "I happen to know the Broncos have a new wide receiver who's going to be a star this year."

"The Redskins have a better ground game. But they're in a different league. I'm not sure they even play the Broncos this season."

"So, what do you think of San Francisco's new coach? I mean, is he as good as they say?"

"Those men," Ann said. "They sound like my husband."

It could have been a gathering of old friends, Meredith thought. And she studied her father, his creased face animated, his farmwork-hardened hands gesturing. And John, with his open smile and short, neat hair that dipped to a point on his forehead and the crooked lines of his face falling into a pleasing mold. *He'll age well,* it occurred to her. *His features will grow even more comfortable with one another, and his hair will gray at the temples. Distinguished.*

"I like him," Ann whispered.

"You haven't seen him on the job."

"Ooh, scary. Secret agent stuff, huh?"

"It's not like that, Annie."

"Darn."

"Dessert is served," Neil said, and he got out the ice cream and started digging away at it. "Let me help," John suggested.

"Tank oo, gwampa," Amanda said, her eyes big at the bowl set in front of her.

"You're welcome, angel."

It could have been any well-adjusted family, Meredith thought, surprised. No rancorous words, no rebukes or blame. Had it taken Erik's death for her to accept her father more easily?

She felt better than she had in a long time. Despite her sorrow and her loss, she felt as if she were at the starting line of the grueling trip back to normalcy. The moments of tearing grief were, indeed, lessening, stretched out. The psychology books had been right.

Her family, Ann and her father, were there for her. And John . . . even John helped. He was there for her, too, and even though he'd concealed his real identity, he had helped her through the worst of her anguish. *Yes,* she thought, surprised again. It *had* helped to have someone around, especially John.

My goodness, have I learned to accept help? she thought. *Sandra would be proud.*

And all those friends Ann spoke of. She had friends, some from kindergarten, for Pete's sake, a wonderful network of caring friends. But when Erik had been . . . alive, she'd abandoned them. When was the last time she'd hiked or gone camping or shopping in Denver with Darlene or Bobbi or Ellen? She hadn't even returned their calls this past week, even though John had noted each message, each name and number.

She'd neglected them all; she'd lost touch with them, just as she'd lost touch with herself. And now, just today, in the bright sunlight, it was as if she were awakening from a sickness, a kind of coma.

Despite the horror of the last few days, she felt a lifting, a sense of relief. She looked around the table and saw Ann laugh and wipe ice cream from Amanda's face, saw her father lean forward and listen to something John was saying, and she knew suddenly that there was a future for her.

And on the heels of relief came shuddering guilt. How could she so quickly forget Erik? How could she diminish their love? How could she consider a future without him?

She offered to help her father do the dishes.

"You two, go bond," she said to Ann and John. "Or burp the baby or something."

There was a certain relaxation in the busywork of dish washing. She washed, and her father dried.

"Why don't you get a dishwasher?" she asked.

"Oh, what for? There's usually only me. And the well water would just muck it up."

"You're turning into a stubborn old man."

"Yeah, so what?" he shot back.

While he made coffee, she sat at the kitchen table. In an evening of surprises, she was handed another one.

"Look, Merry, I know we don't talk a lot. Not enough. But, that aside, I want you to know one thing. I understand your pain. I understand regret and being alone. The difference between you and me is that I made my own misery. You don't deserve yours."

She sat there, abruptly tense, speechless.

He spoke with his back to her—his back in the faded denim shirt and the jeans that sagged down over his hips—as if it were easier to talk without facing her. "I know I haven't been there for you and Ann. Wallowing in my own pain. And you always seemed so sure, able to take care of yourself. And Ann. Even when you were little. No sense apologizing. Hell, it's too late for that. But maybe we can understand each other better."

"Oh, Dad—"

"No, now wait, I'm not trying to coerce something

from you. I'm just saying it in my own way. Merry, I've wished a thousand times, a million times, I'd never made that drive with your mother."

The coffeemaker burbled, began dripping. Pipes somewhere in the house clunked. From the living room came Ann's voice, then John's.

"I appreciate your honesty," she finally said.

"Okay. Good. We'll leave it at that?"

"Okay, Dad." Was she such a hard person that her own father feared facing her? Maybe. Maybe she was. She'd have to think about it, really put her mind on it. That fist inside her wasn't quite ready to unclench, but maybe in time, it would.

"I've got to go out and feed the horses," Neil said as they drank his decaf coffee. "Can you folks do without me for a while?"

"I'll do it, Dad," Meredith said.

"Now, I didn't keep you down here to do chores."

"I enjoy it."

She left the house and stood for a moment on the creaking porch steps. Beyond the ranch, across the verdant Roaring Fork Valley, Mount Sopris rose, splendid in its three-peaked isolation. She couldn't remember a time in her life when the mountain looked the same. Even in the summer, when the rest of the sky was cloudless, Mount Sopris could be half obscured by billowing cumulous clouds or angry thunderheads.

Behind her, the screen door opened and closed. "Helluva sight," she heard John say.

"Yes, it is," she replied, and for a minute they both stared at the summits of Sopris, which were dipped in molten gold from the setting sun.

"I can see how a person would enjoy life in a place like this," he finally said.

"Does that mean you *don't* enjoy life in Washington?"

He rested his gaze on her. "It could be better, but I'm not complaining."

"Have you ever thought of relocating?"

"Not up to now."

"Um," was all she could say; then, quickly, "Well, I better get to the chores."

"Mind if I tag along?" he asked.

The staid old cottonwoods around the house were filled with their evening contingent of blackbirds, hundreds of them, noisily chattering like a crowd of old lady gossips. The house and the trees cast long shadows. The air was caressingly cool.

She decided then, as they crossed the lawn to the barn, that tonight she'd tell him about Chad arguing with Kemil. She'd tell him despite the consequences, because matters needed to be set right. Erik wasn't here to defend himself, so she'd have to do it for him.

They threw hay to the horses, checked the water tank.

"So this means I'm a certified ranch hand? It's not bad, not bad at all," he said.

"Try doing it in the middle of the winter, with a fifty-mile-an-hour wind, and snow flying sideways, and—"

"Okay, I get it. So, you did this as a kid?"

"Sure. Dad had more stock then, some cattle. He had a couple of hired hands."

"Think he'll ever sell the ranch? You know, retire?"

"No, he'll leave it to us."

"But if you don't live here . . ."

"Maybe I will. Maybe I'll revert."

"Use your psychology on the horses and cows?"

"Very funny."

He stopped and leaned back, propping his elbows on a fence rail of the corral. "I want you to know that I really do have a nephew with cerebral palsy, and I really have a wife that dumped me."

"Okay, so you're human after all." And then she remembered something he'd said in that fake therapy session. Weeks ago, but the words came back to her as clearly as if he'd repeated them right that second.

"Yeah, I'm human," he was saying, but she cut him off.

"You said your wife divorced you when you quit drinking."

He shot her a look.

"What did you mean by that?"

"Am I paying for this?"

"No evasive techniques, please. Answer me."

He didn't say anything for a while. Then he ran a hand through his short hair and said, "Renee and I met in college. We were young, and it was party time. I guess she figured my drinking was the usual kind that all the kids did. And she became an enabler. Of course, neither of us realized it then, but when we graduated, and I was still drinking, she covered up for me. I bet you've seen it a hundred times. Our relationship was based on dysfunction. I think we saw each other as the image of what we wanted, but we didn't really understand each other."

"It sounds like you've been through some therapy."

"Not me. Renee. She's still working on her enabling."

"Your drinking," she urged.

"Yeah, well, it got pretty bad. We had a son, Jack, and I kept on drinking. It was my boss at State that made me see where I was headed. He sat me down one day and told me that I was going to lose my job if I kept drinking. Let me tell you, that sobered me up real quick."

"And you quit drinking."

"Yes. Renee couldn't handle me being in control of myself for the first time in my life, so she divorced me."

"Interesting."

"Not when you're going through it."

"No, of course not."

"Now we're okay with each other, and I see a lot of my son, and Renee has a boyfriend, dumb word, a *male* friend who satisfies her need to nurture."

"And you, do you date?"

"Not really."

"Why not?"

He shrugged. Then he straightened up. "Hey, you're going beyond the scope of this conversation."

"The perils of talking to a psychologist."

"You're a good therapist, Meredith," he said, serious again.

"Well, thank you. But, really, your very brief visit couldn't possibly—"

"I could tell, you're *good*. You understand, you empathize."

His blue eyes regarded her solemnly, and she felt a singular warmth inside, a moment of kinship, of closeness with this man. A man, she suddenly realized, whom she already knew better than she'd ever known Erik.

"We ought to get back," she said, turning away from him, and the fragile strands strung between them stretched and broke.

It was late when they drove back to Aspen.

"I like your family," John said from the passenger seat.

"Ann's great."

"And your father?"

"My dad and I have a few problems. Since my mother died . . . Oh well, you don't really want to hear about it."

"You heard my family history."

"Maybe another time."

Silence fell ponderously between them; then, finally, she said, "You're right."

"About?"

"About you telling me your family history and me keeping mine a secret."

"Go on."

She did. She told him about that terrible day when the State Police along with the local Garfield County sheriff had come to the ranch and told their weekend baby-sitter that there'd been an accident. "I was seven years old. Ann was four. And Dad wasn't even able to come home. He was in a clinic over in Georgetown being treated for a concussion. Mom . . . Well, there was nothing anyone could do."

"Jesus," he whispered.

"Anyway, my whole life I've blamed Dad. Mom was always afraid to drive in storms. I even remember

her telling us as little kids that there's no place you
have to be that's worth risking your life to get to."

"But she went to Denver that day."

"Oh yes. Because Dad bullied her into it. There was
this horse being auctioned and . . . But that doesn't
matter. They went, and until tonight, I never knew that
he suffered."

"Did he say something tonight?"

She nodded in the darkness. "Yes. Finally. After
we'd done the dishes."

"If this is none of my business . . ."

"No. Go on."

"Do you forgive him now?"

"Good question. I'm not sure I know how to answer
that. I've held that anger so close for so long, it's not
that easy to let go."

"But you're trying?"

"I . . . Yes, I think I am."

"Sounds like a good plan."

"Um," she said, and the silence fell between them
again.

"There's something else," he said.

"Something else?"

"You've had something on your mind all day."

She let out a breath. "You read people well, you
know that?"

"So I've been told. Now, why don't you tell me
what's been eating you?"

"Okay," she said, "all right. It's going to complicate
matters for the police, but I really don't care. It's time
for the truth."

"The truth?"

"That's right. It's about Chad and Erik and Kemil.

About who was really doing the arguing."

She heard the rustle of his clothes as he straightened up, and she was aware of his sudden alertness. The headlights of the oncoming cars flashed on them like strobe lights, on and off, light and dark.

"I was there one night at Kemil's, and I heard them arguing. But it wasn't the way Chad described it. *Chad* was arguing with Kemil, and Erik stopped it, calmed them down."

"You're sure?"

"I was there. They were just outside the door of the media room, and I saw them. I heard them."

"What were they arguing about?"

"I couldn't really tell. I only caught a few words." She paused and thought back. "It seemed to be about something that might disrupt the climb. Erik said, and I'm paraphrasing, 'Enough bullshit. We have to concentrate on the climb.'"

"That's it?"

"That's all I heard. But Chad lied about it. Another lie. It wasn't Erik arguing with Kemil, so that business about Erik cutting the rope is a lie, too. Chad is just trying to protect himself. God, I can't believe it, I can't believe he would do that."

"Do what?" John asked, his voice quiet.

"I don't know. I keep thinking about it. Why is Chad lying? To protect himself. But from what? What happened up there?" Then she said, "Look, why don't you tell the police to talk to the others who were there at Kemil's that night? Dan Froberg, Kevin Moore, and Jessie Robertson. Maybe one of them heard the argument, too."

"The police have deposed everyone connected with

Kemil. They talked to the three of them the minute they stepped off the plane."

"Well, what did they say?"

"I don't know exactly what they said about that specific matter. I can try to find out for you."

"Would you?"

"I can try."

Then she burst out, "I can tell you, both as a professional and friend of his—*former* friend—Chad is incapable of killing anyone, much less his best friend."

"Then that leaves Erik."

She didn't say anything for a moment, driving the familiar highway toward Aspen, the mountains dark humps on either side of the road, car lights stabbing at her.

"Erik couldn't have killed anyone, either," she finally said. "And he had no reason, no motive. No, it wasn't him."

Silence.

"I'm not in denial about Erik," she said into the darkness, "and I wouldn't lie, not even for him."

There was a long, pregnant hush, and then she repeated herself. "I would never lie for Erik," she insisted.

The air was fraught with his silence.

NINETEEN

The need to work and set aside her heartache, to be of use again, was overpowering. And so she faced Monday morning with anticipation.

She'd canceled most of last week's appointments; actually, John had phoned some of her patients when she couldn't handle it. She arrived at her office and glanced around, as if seeing the place for the first time, and she felt revived. Maybe now, through work and her friends, she could begin to piece her life together again.

She walked into her inner sanctum, opened the bottom drawer of her desk, and dropped her purse in. A familiar routine, comforting. She checked her appointment book. Maddy at nine A.M. Brenda at ten. Susan at eleven A.M. A full morning. *All right.*

She punched Play on her answering machine, noticed there were nine messages. A lot. Even for a Monday morning, a lot.

The first call was from Brenda. "Hi, Meredith, Brenda Swimm here. It's Saturday. Listen, I want to cancel my ten o'clock on Monday and tell you how very sorry I am about Erik. If you're not up to seeing me later in the week, just call. It's cool, though, if you need more time."

Wow, she thought, taking a step back. Even Brenda, who was from Glenwood Springs, knew about her and Erik?

The next message was from one of her afternoon appointments. "I'm so so sad for you, Meredith. I don't know how to say it right on a machine, you know? Damn. But you take Monday off, hear? I'll stop by or something and reschedule. Chin up. I love you."

Except for one message from a prospective client, a referral from out of town, every message was virtually identical.

She felt herself stepping backward on her road to recovery. Her full day, her day of escaping her grief through work, was ruined. But more importantly, what did the cancelations mean? That not just everyone in Aspen, but everyone in the entire Roaring Fork Valley, knew of her relationship with Erik? Was he a larger icon than she'd imagined? And what had people said about *her?*

She recalled the full pews in the chapel—so many women. Was she considered just another conquest? Tony's words, she remembered, Tony had attacked her in anger, but perhaps there'd been merit to his assertions.

She felt a stab of mortification and the sudden urge to run up and down the streets, showing everyone the ring. She wasn't another conquest, she thought frantically.

Then she heard the outer door of the office open and close, and her pain and confusion were dashed aside.

Her first guess was that it was John. He'd followed her to town in his car, and now he was checking up on her.

But it was Kathy Fry who appeared in the doorway to the inner office. From the pinched, blotched look on Kathy's face, she knew something was wrong.

They've found Erik rushed through her mind. *They've found his body.*

"What is it?" she breathed. "Oh, Kathy, what—?"

"You little bitch," Kathy ground out, and she slammed the office door shut. "You lying *bitch.*"

Meredith was speechless.

"How dare you tell the police that shit? How *dare* you?"

Meredith swallowed; she was so taken aback it took her a moment to respond. "Kathy, I have no idea what you're talking about. The police? You think I said something to the police?"

"You goddamn good and well know what I'm talking about. The fight between Chad and Kemil? You couldn't have forgotten telling the cops that bullshit story, now could you?"

"I . . ." But suddenly she knew. Of course. She'd told John. And he'd repeated her words to the authorities. He'd been compelled to, she realized; it was his job. Hadn't she known this would happen?

"Well, cat got your tongue?"

"Ah, no, no. I'm sorry, it just took me a minute."

"Well?"

"Yes, yes, I did tell John McCord about the argument between Chad and Kemil."

"Oh, really?"

"Look, I could hardly keep that information to myself. Especially after what Chad told the police."

"That's none of your goddamn business."

"It *is* my business, Kathy. Erik isn't here to defend himself. I'm sorry if the information hurt Chad, but it's the truth. I can't change that."

Kathy made a grating sound of dismissal. "So now you're Erik's protector, his champion? Christ."

Meredith choked back a reply. She knew what she'd witnessed, and neither Kathy nor Chad could duck the truth.

Kathy stood facing her, glaring, fire in her eyes. "You know what you are?" she said. "You're a love-sick fool."

"Kathy, I think this has gone far enough."

"No, no, you better hear me out. Your *beloved* Erik, my dear, was not the saint you're making him out to be."

"I want you to leave," Meredith began.

"If you don't believe me, then I think you better talk to Chad. He knows. He knows a lot about Erik the Great, believe me. Or maybe you can't handle the truth."

"Don't worry about that, Kathy."

"Talk to Chad. He's home, at the guesthouse. Talk to him."

Before Meredith could think, Kathy turned on her heel and stalked out. Meredith didn't move for a long time. She couldn't. She felt as if a hand had plunged into her chest and squeezed out all the air.

She drove to Kathy's that afternoon, wondering if she were making a terrible mistake. Chad would tell her just about anything to shut her up. He'd do anything humanly possible to drag Erik's name through the mud to save himself.

The coward, she thought, and she recalled the dozens of times she'd witnessed Chad hanging on every word Erik said, emulating him, idolizing him ad nauseam. But now his revered leader was gone, and he'd say anything to explain away the cut rope. *The goddamn coward.*

She drove out Castle Creek Road, thinking about the futility of talking to Chad, the childish absurdity of her actions. She knew John was following her, but he was the least of her worries.

Then he beeped several times, and actually came alongside her car, nodding, gesturing for her to pull over. Even as her tires rolled to a stop on the gravelly shoulder, she felt anger coil inside her. Anger at John McCord and anger at her compliance.

She rolled her window all the way down when he strode up.

"You're going to Kathy Fry's?" he said.

"Yes, I am."

"That's not advisable."

"Oh?"

"Meredith, look, you have to realize I reported your story about Chad and Kemil arguing to the police."

"Oh yes, I know you did."

"Kathy Fry?" But he answered his own question. "I saw her today in front of your office building."

"You bet you did. And I need to speak with Chad. This whole thing has gone too far. It's out of control."

"I doubt you can right it, Meredith. You might even make matters worse."

"Worse for who? Me? Chad? Or maybe for Erik, but *he* doesn't matter. He's dead."

"Come on, stop this," John said. "You're only going to make yourself miserable. We know Chad's story. Now we know yours. Let the authorities handle it."

"No. I'm going to see Chad. Right now."

He regarded her for a minute. "Is there anything I can say to dissuade you?"

"No."

He let out a breath of frustration. "Then go. See Chad. He's not going to change his story, and I guarantee you're going to be even more upset than you are now."

"I am not upset."

"Of course you aren't," he said, and he stared at her for a moment longer, then rapped his knuckles on the roof of her car. "I'll be parked outside Chad's, if you need me," was his final offer before she drove away, her tires laying a light coat of dust on him.

She parked in front of Chad's, right behind Kathy's house, and was getting out of her car when John pulled in. From the corner of her eye, she saw him signal Steve, who walked out the front door. She assumed the exchange of looks was an okay to allow her entry. She didn't care. One way or another, she was going to see Chad.

With Kathy openly watching from a kitchen window in the main house, she found Chad on the side of the guest cabin. He was chopping wood ferociously, tossing split logs onto a pile. When he noticed her, he went right on chopping.

"Chad," she tried, "will you stop for a minute?"

He paused and eyed her. "You don't want to be

here," he said, and he swung the ax again.

"Listen," she said over the noise, "Kathy told me I needed to talk to you."

"Go home," he said.

"No. She told me you knew the truth about Erik. I want to hear this so-called truth. I won't leave till I do."

He split another log, and a wood chip nearly struck her on the cheek.

"*Chad.* Talk to me."

He finally buried the blade of the ax in an unsplit log and mopped sweat from his neck with a bandana. "Why did you tell them that crap?" he said. "I thought we were friends. I'm in deep shit because you got everything messed up in your head. Hell, my lawyer is fighting extradition right now. They want me in Alaska, they want me because *you* screwed everything up."

She took a breath. "Look, I'm sorry, but I know what I heard that night at Kemil's."

"What you thought you heard. What you *wanted* to hear."

"What does that mean?"

"That, for God's sake, you were . . . you *are* so crazy in love that you never once noticed Kemil and Erik going at it all the time."

"That is just not true."

"The hell it isn't. They argued constantly about Kemil's friends. Erik was pissed as shit Kemil let us stay at his pal's place in Lahore, because the guy rubs shoulders with a bunch of terrorists."

She shook her head. "Erik couldn't have cared less about politics. You know that, Chad, you *know* it."

"Oh yeah? Well, try this on for size. The State Department and U.S. Customs have these computer programs that keep black lists, and by staying with Kemil's pal in Pakistan, Erik and I got ourselves on their shit list. You know how many times we travel out of the country every year? Don't tell me Erik didn't care."

She held her tongue.

"See? You know I'm right."

She recalled suddenly the night Erik had made that obscene gesture toward the dark SUV—toward John, she now knew—but what, exactly, had Erik muttered? Something about the Mideast and terrorism, or had it been politics?

She'd questioned Erik, too, but gotten no answer. So she'd let it go. As she had always done.

"And you pretended not to notice the stuff between Erik and Kemil over one of his wives."

"Oh, please," she said loftily. "How ridiculous. None of us ever laid eyes on Kemil's wives. You know that." She shook her head.

"Think what you want," Chad fired back.

"I will. I will, because I know you're lying. Erik was your friend. And now you're trying to ruin his reputation. To blame him. But in my heart, I know it was you who cut that rope. What I don't know is why. *Why* did you do it?"

It happened so suddenly she almost lost her footing. One second Chad was standing four feet from her, the next he was in her face, his strong hand gripping her wrist, his breath hot on her.

"Wake the fuck up!" he yelled. "Do you really want the truth? Do you?"

She tried to free herself, tried to twist away, but his hold was relentless.

"Let go of me," she gasped.

His face contorted, and his lips pulled back from his teeth. "Take a drive to Boulder," he hissed. "Yeah, do that. Take a drive and pay a visit to Debra, Debra Rosen. And while you're at it, Meredith, why not say hi to Robbie. You know, *Robbie?* Erik's son?"

Every cell in her body was focused on her torment as she drove to Boulder the following morning.

She'd made up a cock-and-bull story for John last night. Something about needing to pick up a couple books at the University of Colorado library there. Maybe, she had muttered, she would drive to Denver and stop at Ann's, visit the kids.

"Really," John had said mildly. He hadn't bought it. Despite her efforts to conceal her misery when she'd left Chad, he'd seen through her. But she couldn't, she simply couldn't voice aloud what Chad had told her.

Debra Rosen. Robbie, the woman's son, Erik's *son*. It just could not be true.

John followed her. She knew she couldn't shake him. She wondered what, if anything, she'd tell him when she visited the Rosen woman. Maybe she'd say Debra Rosen was a colleague, a former classmate? Something.

Did it really matter how much John knew?

And, besides, Chad's story was utter crap. He had been trying to wound her. Maybe Kathy had put him up to it. This Rosen woman story smacked of a female touch—a vindictive female touch. Meredith had put

Kathy's brother in a bad position, and Kathy was into payback.

That was it, of course.

So why, then, did she feel like vomiting?

She drove over Independence Pass, through Leadville, then down past Copper Mountain Ski Resort, the slopes still lush and green; but the sagebrush and scrub oak on the northern exposures were already turning red and orange and ocher, as they always did in the high country by mid-August. Even a few lone aspens were turning to gold high on the forested slopes.

Climbing to the Eisenhower Tunnel, she crossed the Continental Divide at 11,000 feet, then it was down, down past Georgetown and Idaho Springs and the turn off to Central City. All century-old mining towns kept alive by tourism.

She saw little of her surroundings, one of the most scenic and breathtaking drives in North America. It took all her concentration to navigate the interstate and to check her rearview mirror—yes, there was John, two cars back. Her faithful bodyguard until the curiosity of the press cooled, and the al Assad family was satisfied that Kemil's death was a mountaineering accident.

Despite what she'd said to Chad yesterday, she still believed in her heart it *was* an accident. Neither Chad nor Erik had any real motive to cut Kemil loose. The facts would come to light. But when?

What a godawful mess.

Her mind switched to the task at hand. Debra Rosen. She'd gotten the Boulder address from Information last night.

The fact that there was a Debra Rosen in the phone book, that there was a physical address listed, had been a blow. The existence of the woman lent a measure of credibility to Chad's story. But simply because a Debra Rosen existed did not mean there was a connection to Erik. Maybe to Chad. But not to Erik. She would have known, she would have sensed this other woman, and certainly she would have sensed a child.

She turned north past Golden and drove along the foothill country of what Coloradans called the Front Range. Boulder lay ahead, a maverick university town built mostly of red sandstone—the university, the buildings on the downtown Pearl Street Mall, the city and county buildings. Rising above the town to the west were the distinctive Flatirons that jutted from the earth at an odd angle, as if leaning, pressed by the winds of time. No photograph of Boulder was complete without those massive slabs in the background.

Debra Rosen's home.

Is the woman wealthy? So many Boulderites were. Or maybe she's connected to the university. Hell, she thought, *maybe she works at a grocery store or Wal-Mart or is a psychologist.*

"Damn it," she murmured. She shouldn't have come here.

She found the address after a few wrong turns in a modest, lower-middle-class neighborhood of small brick homes with a square patch of grass in every front yard.

Her heart lodged in her throat as she parked. Then she felt sweat dampening the back of her neck, and her fingers were trembling on the steering wheel.

She was vaguely cognizant of John parking a half block away. He didn't get out of his car. Even when she mustered the nerve to open her door, he remained hidden behind the dark-tinted windows.

At least, she thought, he wasn't going to give her any trouble.

The walkway leading to a tiny front porch was only three concrete sections, but it seemed to stretch endlessly before her. She didn't consider turning back, though. She gathered her strength and courage and put one foot in front of the other.

The door. She stared at it as if she'd never seen a front door before. Such a simple thing. Inanimate. Harmless. Yet it seemed all the answers to all her questions, everything she was, everything she had ever believed, awaited her on the other side of those panels of wood.

TWENTY

The boy answered her knock. She almost doubled over at the sight of him, so like Erik, so like his *father*. She struggled against the shock.

"Can I help you?" he asked politely.

He was perhaps eleven years old, on the cusp of childhood, not yet a teenager, slim, with Erik's blue eyes and his mother's dark hair. She recognized the boy instantly, and she also remembered his mother from Erik's memorial service. Yes, of course. How blind she'd been.

"I . . . ah, I'm a friend of your father's," she fumbled. "I . . . I was in Denver visiting my sister, and I thought I'd stop by. I met you and your mother at his service in Aspen, and I . . ." She drew in a breath. "I wanted to say how sorry I am about . . . your father."

"Thank you," he said.

"Is your mother home?"

"No, but she'll be back soon. She has a client right now."

"A client?"

"She's a masseuse."

"Oh yes, of course. Um, do you suppose I could wait for her?"

He hesitated for a minute, then seemed to decide she was okay. "I guess so. Sure."

He opened the door wider to let her enter the house. He wore shorts and a T-shirt from a baseball team she'd never heard of, a kid's team. And white running shoes that looked three sizes too big for him. His calves, even at his age, were strongly molded—like Erik's.

"Do you know how long she'll be, um, Robbie, isn't it?"

"Ah, I guess half an hour or so. She never leaves me alone for long, she's so protective, you know. But I'm very responsible," he said gravely.

"Oh yes, I'm sure you are."

"Well, I'm in the middle of a Caesar game on my computer, so is it okay if I leave you here to wait?"

"Oh, sure, Robbie. Go on."

"There's stuff on TV, and there's some magazines." Politely he showed her the television controls.

"Thanks," she said.

He disappeared down the hall, and she could hear the sounds of a computer game. She stood in the center of the small living room and looked around. Ordinary furniture, a cluttered, mismatched look, as if the pieces had been inherited or bought at the Salvation Army. Dark wood and overstuffed upholstery, melted down candle stubs on every surface. Some prints on the white walls, a bright, woven blanket over the back of a chair, a Navajo rug in front of the couch. A heavy Victorian pedestal table and chairs in the dining alcove.

She was trembling, still standing in the center of the

room, clutching her purse. And John, he was outside in his car, waiting. Well, he'd have to keep waiting.

A faint scent in the air—incense. Debra in the long sack of a dress. A hippie. Incense and an illegitimate child and an Indian shaman print on the wall.

She went to the couch and sat down heavily, as if her legs would not hold her, bent forward to read the names of the magazines on the table. *Prevention, Modern Chiropractic, Massage Monthly.*

She sat there and looked around at Debra's house, drew in the scent of Debra's room, ran a finger along the arm of the dark blue couch, feeling the rough, nubby texture.

Erik had sat here, perhaps exactly where she sat now. He had eaten at that table, gotten a beer from the refrigerator in the kitchen, watched that television set. He had made love to Debra, and they had a son.

And she'd never had an inkling of this doppelgänger world of his.

Why hadn't he told her? Had he *ever* planned to tell her? How many other secrets had Erik Amundsson kept from her?

The floor tilted under her, and for a moment she felt dizzy. Had it all been a lie, then? His love and the ring and asking her to marry him?

The sun spilled in a tall window by the front door and lay in a golden stripe across the coffee table and magazines. Dust motes danced in the light, and she could see a layer of dust on the glass top of the coffee table.

Had he sat there and put his feet up on the coffee table, the way he did at her house? Had his feet rested *there?*

On one wall there were bookshelves filled helter-skelter with books and rocks and ceramic animals and a jade Buddha. And photographs in seashell-encrusted frames.

She forced herself to stand, to walk to the bookshelves, to look at the photos. Evidence of a duplicate life, one she had been completely ignorant of.

Erik holding Robbie when he'd been a baby, maybe six months old. The three of them—Debra, Erik, and Robbie, with mountains in the background.

Her stomach felt queasy, and sweat broke out on her forehead, her upper lip, the back of her neck.

Another picture, of Erik on a mountain somewhere in full climbing gear. Smiling, eyes squinting into the sun.

She tottered to the hallway and called out to Robbie, had to clear her throat and ask again, "Excuse me, Robbie, could I use the bathroom?"

"Huh? Oh, sure." He stuck his head out of his room. "Use Mom's. She says mine is a mess." He pointed to the bedroom across the hall from his.

"Thanks," she said.

But she didn't get past the bed. She stared at it, a queen-size bed, with an East Indian print spread on it, and a heap of pillows at the head, pillows in varied fabrics and bright colors and patterns. Two night tables, one covered with items: a nail file, an incense burner, a clock, an empty glass. The other was bare. Erik's side of the bed.

She tried not to think of them together on that mattress, tried not to let the images inundate her. The questions remained, screaming at her, but she relegated the images to a deep, dark cellar in her mind.

She wiped at her upper lip and wondered at how numb she felt. Grievously wounded but still numb, as if the blow had been so hard, she did not yet register the damage it had done.

She went into the bathroom and splashed cold water on her face, tried not to meet her eyes in the toothpaste-spattered mirror. Used a corner of a towel to dry herself.

There were two toothbrushes in the holder on the back of the toilet. And what looked like a man's hairbrush, although he'd never used one like that with her.

She reached out and picked it up, raised it to her nose for Erik's scent. Yes, it was his.

In the bedroom, she went straight to the empty night table and pulled the drawer open. A paperback book, she couldn't read the title—it was in Norwegian. A pair of cheap reading glasses.

Reading glasses. She had no idea he needed glasses. But then she realized she'd never seen him read. They made love and slept and ate and made love again.

But he'd read with Debra. Relaxed, cozy, familiar. As if they'd been married for years.

She pushed the drawer shut, stood there for a time, her face in her hands, dry-eyed, and then she heard the front door open.

Her feet moved her to the bedroom door, her heart leaping, smoothing her hair nervously.

"Oh!"

"I'm sorry. You're Debra," she said. "I was just . . . Robbie told me to use your bathroom." She felt heat rise to her cheeks. Humiliation.

Debra looked at her for a time, then said, "And you're Meredith."

"How did you know?"

"Someone pointed you out to me at his service."

Of course. Why hadn't anyone pointed Debra out to her? Kathy and Chad had known. And how many others had been in on the secret?

Debra wore a denim jumper over a short-sleeved print T-shirt. Clunky sandals, long, dark hair pulled back with barrettes. Silver loop earrings. A pretty face, a lovely face. No makeup. A little chubby but very comfortable with herself. Very together.

Yes, that's what attracted Erik.

"I knew you'd come here," Debra said. "Sooner or later." She spoke matter-of-factly, with a tinge of satisfaction.

"You did," Meredith said.

"I'm sorry for what you must be going through," Debra said.

"I came here to say the same to you."

Debra smiled, a small, confidential smile. "You came here to see if it was true, if Robbie was real and if I was real."

"Yes . . . maybe that, too."

"We're real, all right."

"He's a darling boy."

"Yes, he is. Thank you." Debra dropped a fringed purse on a chair. "Would you like something to drink? It's hot out. And you have a long drive ahead of you."

She accepted, if only to delay her departure, to have more time to take in this new reality.

Debra poured two tall glasses of herbal iced tea, carried them into the living room, and set them down on the coffee table.

"Sit down, Meredith, please." The woman sat across

from her in an ugly tweed chair. "You're curious."

Meredith was silent.

"Look, Erik and I loved each other. We've been to-gether for twelve years. I expected this someday, his death. I knew, I always knew it could happen. And when I heard, I have to tell you, I was shocked, but I wasn't surprised."

"You aren't sad?"

"Of course I'm sad. The man I loved just died."

She wanted to hate this woman for the control she exuded, but she couldn't. And she couldn't even dredge up hatred of Erik for doing this to her, to Debra, to Robbie.

What exactly did Debra mean to Erik? Okay, so they had a child, and she would think less of Erik if he had ignored his own son and his son's mother. He'd prob-ably helped support Robbie, too. She could accept that. He would certainly have told her about them. When they were officially engaged.

What she simply could not accept was Debra as the love of Erik's life.

"I loved him, too," Meredith said. "And he loved me."

Again the private smile. "He loved a lot of women. Do you think he was faithful to me? He couldn't keep women away." She sounded proud of his conquests. "Look, you were one out of many. Erik loved women. And he wouldn't have been faithful to you, either. It wasn't in his nature."

She looked toward Robbie's room, where the com-puter's squawks and screeches still sounded, and low-ered her voice. "I always thought Erik had to live faster and harder than most men. He knew his life was going to be short."

But he wanted to marry me and live happily every after. Debra was wrong.

"Did you know about me?" Meredith asked.

"Oh, I knew he'd met someone. I could always tell. But he never talked about his girlfriends. He respected my feelings too much to do that." She put her head on one side and studied Meredith unblinkingly. "And then I saw you at the service in Aspen. I was curious, I have to admit."

"I see."

"Consider yourself lucky, Meredith. You had him for a while," Debra said, her tone pitying, condescending. And Meredith recognized a defense system shifting into full gear.

She drank a sip of the iced tea. A faint orange-lemon flavor. Flowery. She sipped again, searching for control, for the next step in this Kafkaesque confrontation. "Do you mind my asking why you and Erik never married?"

"We didn't need to get married." Proudly. "He told me a million times marriage was for ordinary people. Our love was strong enough for us to be free spirits. It was a truly wonderful relationship."

Meredith's hand rose, touched the hard outline of the ring beneath her white blouse. She longed, oh how she longed, to thrust it under this woman's nose, to trump her conceit and annihilate her life as Meredith's had been annihilated.

But what good would that do? It wouldn't bring Erik back to either one of them. It would be a low blow, unworthy of her love for Erik. It would only hurt an innocent young boy. Let Debra cling to her beliefs.

"I better be going," she said, rising.

"I'm glad you stopped by. It's better to know, isn't it?"

They shook hands. "I'm sorry for your loss. For Robbie's loss. What a polite, handsome boy you and Erik . . . well, you have."

"Thank you."

"Say good-bye to Robbie for me."

"I will."

Then she was outside in the hot afternoon, with the everyday sounds around her: birds and cars going by, dogs barking, a child's laughter.

"Meredith?" John's voice.

He was next to her, and somehow she'd walked down the block to her car and was leaning against it, her head hanging, the hot metal scalding her hands where they rested on the edge of the roof.

He turned her around to face him, but she hadn't the strength to meet his eyes.

"Meredith? Are you okay? What in hell happened in there?"

"We talked," she said in a wispy voice devoid of emotion.

"You and Debra Rosen talked?"

She lifted her head sharply. "How did you know about Debra Rosen?"

He looked sheepish, an odd expression for him, her brain registered. "I've known about Debra and her son since . . . awhile."

"Since when?"

"He went to Boulder for three days when you first met. We had him under surveillance, so we—"

"Yes," she said, and she thought, *Those three awful days when he didn't call.* And then, on the heels of that thought, disbelief. "You *knew* about Debra and Robbie?"

"Yes."

"And you never . . ."

"I'm sorry. I didn't think you . . . Well, I guess I felt you didn't need to know, once the search for Erik was called off."

She stood straight. "Why do you keep doing things you're sorry for?"

"Fair question," he said, his eyes holding hers. No evasions, no prevarications, no deception in them now.

"I'm going home," she declared.

"Are you okay to drive? We could leave your car here and go in mine."

"I'm driving my own car home."

She opened the door of her Subaru, ducked in. The captured heat inside pressed on her, and she lowered all the windows. She didn't glance in John's direction, paid absolutely no mind to him. She didn't care whether he followed her or went back to Washington.

She never remembered the drive out of Boulder, along the foothills of the mountains to Clear Creek Canyon, the winding two-lane road that led back to the interstate. She tried not to look in her rearview mirror, but when she could not avoid it, the dark Blazer was there, a few cars back, sometimes in the other lane, sometimes directly behind her. She didn't care.

She drove, but she saw nothing, her mind anesthetized, until she found herself pulling off the highway into the parking lot at the entrance to the Eisenhower Tunnel that pierced the Continental Divide. Stopping the car, she wondered vaguely why she was there, the walls of mountains rising above her, the ugly parking lot with orange State Highway Department vehicles lined up on one side, the gaping hole of the tunnel just ahead.

The tears came suddenly, with no warning. She bent her head to the steering wheel and felt the sobs tear out of her. She banged on the wheel with a fist and cried until her chest ached and her eyes were dry and she was gasping in short breaths like a baby after a tantrum.

After a time, her car door opened, and a hand closed around her arm. Slowly, he drew her from her seat, pulling her to face him, his hands holding her upper arms.

"Better?" he asked.

Her head hung. She didn't want him to see her like this. "Leave me alone."

"No."

"I'm all right now. Just go on . . . go on wherever you need to."

"I need to be here."

Finally, she braved a glance up. The solicitude on his face hit her like a soft blow. "You must think I'm really stupid."

"No."

"He lied to me, and I never even suspected. Not for a second. And I'm supposed to *understand* people. I'm supposed to see through lies. What a joke."

"No, Meredith. You couldn't have known. None of this is your fault."

"He had a *son*," she said. "And I never knew."

"Would it have helped if I'd told you when I found out?"

"Yes. Maybe. At least I would have . . ."

"What?"

The wind tugged at her. It was cool at almost 12,000 feet, even on a summer day. Inadvertently, she shivered.

"I don't know. Maybe I would have asked Erik if he wanted children with me. I just don't know. Or maybe I already knew the answer, and that's why I never asked him. Stupid. How could I have been so stupid?"

"Come sit in my car. It's got more room than yours," John said.

It was not the standard confessional, the gray interior of his car. But she bared her soul as if it were.

"I never felt like that with anyone. I was obsessed. We couldn't keep our hands off each other. Maybe it was sick, I don't know. And I felt, I felt I was lost, like I wasn't me anymore. So much of what I was, my feelings, everything, was invested in him. He was a powerful man. Obviously too powerful."

John sat silently, listening, his expression carefully neutral. Why was she telling him these things?

"I was scared. And I thought I was in love. And then he was dead, but there was no body, and I couldn't believe he was really dead. He was too strong, too careful, just too damn good a climber. I still . . ." She drew in a shaky breath. "I still can't really believe he's dead."

"It's very hard without a body. We see it in those accidents, especially in foreign counties, in explosions, where a family member is far away, and there are no remains. Your reaction is perfectly normal."

She stared down at her hands in her lap, fingers twisted together whitely. Nothing she said penetrated John's professional façade. Nothing. Not even her lurid confession of lust. Yet she knew he liked her, was attracted to her despite it all. He liked her, perhaps too much.

"I . . . I asked Chad, right to his face, if Erik could have lived after the fall. He shook his head. But I still can't . . . quite believe he's gone forever. It isn't real. None of this is real."

"Your mind needs time to accept, that's all."

"Oh, you're the shrink now."

"No, but I've dealt with this kind of thing before. It's my job."

"Not a very nice job."

"I'm beginning to see your point there."

"I'm sorry to dump on you like this." She caught herself. "There I go, stealing your line."

"It's okay."

"Is everything okay with you?"

"Not everything."

"I'm glad to hear that."

"You're feeling better," he said.

"I suppose so."

"Can you drive the rest of the way? Frankly, I'd still rather leave your car—"

"I can drive."

"You sure?"

In answer, she opened the door and stepped out. He got out his side and came around to her.

"We can talk some more when we get back," he offered. "If you want."

"Thanks, but I think I'm all talked out. You're a good listener," she added.

He reached out and touched her cheek lightly with the back of his hand. "And you've had a helluva time."

She felt his touch, and leaned into it, craving comfort. Up there on the windy summit, clouds scudding by overhead, trucks rumbling past on the interstate, she abruptly yearned for a moment of comfort.

He took her in his arms, and she laid her head on his chest, feeling his heartbeat, feeling his warmth. They stood there like that for a time and she knew John accepted her chaste embrace. He was a good person, a good man, and she couldn't help wondering what their relationship might have been under other circumstances. But then, she'd only met John because of Erik.

Her head swam. How could she be thinking about John in this way after the horror of last week? Yet she was thinking about him, feeling his warmth and concern, the pure honesty of his emotions.

He was the antithesis of Erik, who'd never really been there for her except sexually. She saw now, in hindsight, that what she'd had with Erik had not been a relationship. It had only been a sexual liaison.

What she was feeling now for John was quite different.

TWENTY-ONE

The last blow had been devastating. Just when she'd thought she was swimming up from the murky depths, when she could see light above, when she'd been close to breaking the surface and sucking in a life-giving lungful of air, a hand had pushed her head under again.

Debra Rosen. Robbie. The faces swirled in her brain that whole night, a watery kaleidoscope of images and colors. But amazingly, with the dawn, she discovered a strength, a will to survive and go on. Erik was dead. She'd been starstruck by love, struck blind and deaf and dumb, but he was gone now, and it was time to move on. One minute, an hour, a day—the therapist would follow her own advice and manage each step as it came.

At six A.M., she got up, brushed her teeth, washed her face, and drew on her workout clothes, which had seen absolutely no use for months. She dug out her gym bag, dropped shampoo in, a pair of beige slacks, and a black summer-weight top for the office.

She went downstairs, determined to resurrect her former life. Before Erik—she'd think of the time as

B.E.—she'd arrived at her health club in Aspen by seven A.M. a least three mornings a week. She was raring to go. There was just one hitch: the goddamn vultures lurking outside. They'd follow her to town, and they'd besiege her at the health club.

John was on the couch, barely awake. He lifted his head and scrubbed a hand through his hair. "What time is it?" he asked groggily.

She watched him get up, make a cup of instant coffee to go, and she remembered yesterday, that scene at the Eisenhower Tunnel. She was still embarrassed by her meltdown. But she recognized a burgeoning emotion: gratitude. She knew if the roles were reversed, she would not be as patient as John; she would lack his diligence, his steadfast tolerance.

"Let me just wash up, and I'll be ready," he told her, and he strode into the downstairs bathroom.

He'd been right all along, she knew. Right that the death of a famous climber and a Saudi prince—one who lived half the year in Aspen—would draw the media's attention. But now that word had leaked that Prince Kemil's death appeared to be not an accident, but murder, the newshounds had swarmed again. Last night, when they'd gotten in from Boulder, John had been forced to accost a young hotshot from the *National Insider* who'd been parked on her doorstep.

And the reporter was still there, in fact, when they left her town house at six-thirty A.M.

He strode down the sidewalk toward her and shoved a microphone in her face. "Any comment on the rumor that Erik Amundsson cut the prince's rope?"

"Get the hell out of here," John said, shielding Meredith.

"What were Amundsson and the prince fighting about?"

John halted and spun around. "I'm warning you, buddy."

But the reporter was not to be deterred. "Which of Kemil's wives had the affair with Amundsson?"

Then John said something to him in a hard voice, one she'd never heard before. Something low and dangerous that she couldn't make out, and the young reporter put his tail between his legs and slunk away.

What would she have done without John? she wondered, remembering her initial reluctance to have him there at all.

The whole way into town, she pondered their relationship. Unlike Tony, John dealt unfalteringly with the less-than-perfect aspects of her personality. And unlike Erik, there didn't seem to be a closed side to him. She knew she'd miss him when they both returned to their former lives. John back in Washington, or somewhere else, doing for another bereft soul what he was doing for her. And she, of course, would be right here.

Oh yes, she would miss him. His calmness, the solidity of his presence. The lousy coffee he made, carefully spooning too much sugar in it for her. His touch, warm and accepting. So different from Erik's, that was scalding and demanding. She knew full well the components of good relationships—it was her job to know. And she knew that what she'd had with Erik—or with Tony, for that matter—had not fit that definition.

How, exactly, would she define her relationship with John? Friendship. Yes, they'd grown to be friends. But wasn't it a little more than that now?

She spent an hour working out at the club, then showered and dressed and found John still waiting out front.

"You should have gone for coffee or something," she said.

"I'm fine. I'll get some later. How was your work-out? Feel any better?"

"Yes," she said, walking toward her car. "But I was thinking, what happens now? I mean, how long will the reporters hang out?"

"Till the story dries up, I assume."

"And when will *that* be?" She dug her car keys out of her gym bag.

"Of course I can't say for sure, but I have to assume that the police are going to want Chad to take a lie detector test. At that point, Chad's lawyer will advise him not to. There'll be some back-and-forth posturing, but in the end, the cops will be forced to file Chad's statement and shelve the case." He shook his head. "Too bad, because we'll never really know what went on up there on that mountain."

"Don't they believe Chad and Kemil were arguing?" she asked. "Do they think I made that up?"

"Whether they believe it or not, it's your word against Chad's. No one's come up with a reason for their alleged argument. So—"

"And Erik and Kemil are both dead and can't testify," she said, suddenly dejected.

"Yeah," he agreed. "That they are."

"It's not right. Damn it, it's so unfair." Then she caught herself. "You have no idea how many times I've told patients that *fair* has nothing to do with life."

John parked in his usual place on Main Street, across

from her office. By now she knew his routine as well as her own. He'd watch the building until her first patient arrived and then, figuring she was safely ensconced, he'd walk a block to Zele's Café for coffee, buy a newspaper, then appear back at his car, where he'd remain until lunchtime. Twice she'd gone to lunch with him. Mostly, she got takeout and caught up with office work: typing, filing insurance papers, returning calls. Since the accident, though . . . since Erik's . . . death, she hadn't been in the office much.

She began the morning by calling patients. The ones who'd so thoughtfully canceled their appointments. They needed her. And she sure as heck needed them.

She dialed Nancy Randall's number, and while the phone rang, she swiveled in her chair and peered through the wooden slats of the shade. There was John. Getting out of the Blazer, most likely on his way for coffee and papers. She recalled something he'd once told her about leaving State when this job was over. He certainly liked Aspen. Would he relocate here? He knew enough about security to get a good job with one of the local agencies. And if he did, would she see him again?

"Hi, Nancy, it's Meredith Greene," she said to the machine that answered, and John was forgotten.

By nine-thirty, she was filling out insurance forms, an ungodly task, when Sherry, the architect's secretary from next door, knocked and came in to tell her she had a long-distance call.

"A what?"

"I know, it's weird. But they asked for you, said your phone was on the fritz."

"Oh damn." She rose and followed Sherry. Did that

mean her patients couldn't return her calls? And it
sometimes took days to get the phone repair guys.
Damn.

Sherry showed her the phone, told her to punch line
two, then disappeared into one of the architect's of-
fices. Still standing, Meredith picked up the receiver,
pressed the blinking button. She'd call the phone company as soon as she hung up.

"Hello?" she said, impatient.

"Meredith."

The world stopped short, her blood froze in her
veins. Her brain flared once, then was dead, a piece of
wood. "Meredith?"

Then life exploded again, lurching crazily, and her
knees went rubbery and she felt her way around the
desk to sit down hard in Sherry's chair.

She tried to reply, but her throat was paralyzed. A
croak emerged.

"Yes, it's me," came the voice. "Are you all right?"

"Erik?" she breathed.

"Yes."

"But—"

"No, don't say it. Let me talk. Do you understand?"

"Erik? Is this a—?"

"Is anyone there?"

"Y . . . yes. No . . . Sort of."

"Don't talk. Just listen. Can you do that?"

"I . . . what . . . ?"

"I can't give you any details. Not now. I'm in Washington State. At a friend's. I'm all right. But I need
your help. Do you understand?"

She propped her elbows on the desk, her head sunk
between them. She tested the sound of his voice in her

ear. Yes, it was him. She wasn't dreaming. "I understand."

"Tell no one. This is the most important thing. Not Chad, not Kathy, no one. I need you, Meredith. You have to come here."

"I don't—"

"No, no, not now. I'll tell you everything, but you must come. Do you understand?"

She nodded, then realized he couldn't see her. "Yes."

"Write down these directions. Can you do that? Write them down and come to me. Today, if you can."

"Yes," she repeated.

When she hung up, she had scribbled the directions on a notepad of Post-its. She was to fly to Seattle, rent a car, tell not a soul where she was going, make sure no one followed her.

"Thanks, Sherry," she called, rising.

Sherry poked her head out of a door. "You're welcome. Anything important?"

"Oh, just, you know, just one of my patients, lost my number, crazy idea to call you," she got out and went back to her office.

He is alive. That was all she could think. She stood lost and bewildered in the middle of her outer office. *Alive. He is alive.*

And he needed her.

What to do? What to do first? *Tell no one,* he'd said.

Her brain began to spark. Slowly, then with urgency. Could she get to Seattle today? Maybe. Yes.

Her patients? Her father? She'd have to have a story . . . John. *Oh my God, John.*

She rushed into the other room and looked down

onto the street. He was in the Blazer. Window down. She could see him reading the paper.

"Okay, okay," she said, panting as if she'd run a race. She hurried to her answering machine, thinking furiously, and recorded a new message on it. "I'm sorry, but I've been called out of town on an emergency. . . ." And then she phoned her father, leaving a message on his machine—thank God he wasn't home. "It's only to help a friend, no big deal. I'll ring you when I get back. Say hi to Ann if she calls," she put in, thinking how clever, how ordinary and unsuspicious she'd sounded. Or had she? Had her voice been quavering?

John. She'd never be able to fool him. And after all he'd done for her . . . *No, no,* she thought, she had to concentrate on Erik. John would be okay. But Erik needed her.

She stood with one hand on her hip and the other on her brow. If she couldn't fool John with a story, she'd have to evade him.

Okay, okay. Her car was parked out back in the alley. She might be able to pull onto the side street undetected . . . or not. Probably not. For all his laid-back demeanor, John was always alert.

A taxi. She could take the back fire escape steps, cross the alley, go through the Alpine Bank building and onto Hopkins. Her car would be in its normal spot all day. When she didn't appear for lunch, he would worry, though, and he'd come up to her office to check on her. But just because she wasn't in wouldn't mean too much. He'd assume at first that he'd missed her going out. She could even pin a note on the door. Or maybe he'd see through that. And what if he eventually thought to call her machine? He'd know she left town.

But he wouldn't do that for hours and hours.

She finally told herself to hell with it. Once she was on a plane, it would take time to trace her. By then, she'd be in Seattle. In a rental car. Impossible to trace.

She decided there was no way she could afford the time to tell a cab driver to stop at her town house, plus there would be a few media guys hanging around, so she'd go dressed as she was. She wouldn't even have to stop to get her gym bag in her car, because she kept a toothbrush and deodorant in the cubbyhole bathroom of her office. It would have to do.

Erik. Alive. Her mind rebelled at the notion and refused to fit itself around the concept as she grabbed her toothbrush and dropped it in her shoulder bag. In the mirror, she caught her reflection: hair a mess, eyes wild and bright, furious patches of red on her cheeks and neck.

She almost laughed hysterically.

Deciding against the note on the door, she pulled it shut and locked it. Then she clattered down the back fire escape steps, her heart pounding. Across the alley. Sweat trickled between her breasts. Through the Alpine Bank building. *Wave at that person. Who is he?* Her pulse leaped. *Chuck. He works here. Okay. Out onto Hopkins. A taxi? Not here. Up by Rubey Park, the taxi stand. What if John . . . ? But why would he break routine and leave his car? He wouldn't. But what if for some reason he did?*

The cab driver wanted to talk on the ten-minute ride to Sardy Field, but she said little. She kept glancing out of the back window, looking for a dark Blazer. Ridiculous.

Then she was pierced with a stab of guilt that pinned her to the back of the seat. What she was doing to John was unconscionable. He did not deserve this, not after everything he'd done. And now, the way she felt about him . . .

She pulled herself together. Later, she'd deal with John later.

She gripped the strap of her bag tightly, shutting her mind down, not thinking. She just had to get there. To see Erik, touch him, really believe he was alive.

She talked her way onto the 11:25 flight. A death in the family, she babbled. And she must have been convincing, her face white and frozen, her voice shaky. Then she spent most of the time before boarding in the ladies' room in case John had somehow already traced her to the airport. It was impossible, she kept thinking, but she stayed in there, alternately hiding in a stall or combing her hair in front of the mirror as other women came and went, came and went.

At Denver International Airport, she headed straight to the United customer service office and used the death-in-the-family routine again.

She had to wait an hour and a half in Denver, nervously casting about for John, knowing he couldn't be there. They put her on standby for the 2:10 flight to Seattle, but she knew she'd get on it. She had faith. Nothing could keep her from going to Erik.

Had John tried her office yet, wondered about her absence and the locked door? He'd wait awhile, because her car was there, then he'd call her office number, her friends, her father, and eventually Neil would give him her message. John wouldn't believe it, of course, and he'd figure out she had ditched him. He'd check flights, check car rental agencies. He'd find out where she went, but if she were lucky, it would take him all day. And once she hit Seattle, well, the North-west was huge, and following her exact movements would be impossible.

Maybe he wouldn't even try to follow her. Maybe he'd assume she flipped out—he'd seen her on the way back from Boulder—and decide she needed time on her own. After all, he had no way of knowing Erik was alive.

No, he'd follow her. John was nothing if not tena-cious. She admired that tenacity, and she had to admit she had benefited from it. What would have become of her without him these past weeks?

Yes, she knew he'd follow her. Was she running to Erik, knowing John would dog her footsteps? Knowing he'd be there when she needed him?

She pictured his face when he caught up with her. She felt a pang in her heart just imagining his disap-pointment. But he'd be there, waiting. No matter what. And the notion comforted her.

Lunch was served on the flight. She picked at it, ate the stale-tasting cellophane-wrapped cookie. The man on her right fell asleep and snored, the one on her left worked on his laptop the whole time. She sat wedged between them with her mind working overtime.

How had Erik survived? And why in God's name had he let her suffer all this time? Let his friends and family, even Debra and his son, go through hell?

He was dead. Then he was alive.

A curious and unsettling emotion swept her, and at first, she couldn't quite decipher it. Despite her shock and relief, there was a part of her that was experiencing qualms. She had resigned herself to the loss, to life without him, to moving forward again, and now . . . She racked her brain for a meaning to her misgivings.

She felt for his ring between her breasts, warm from her body, its outline hard. Could she bear to love him so deeply again? In spite of everything—Chad and Kemil and Debra and his son—could their relationship ever return to what it had been?

She thought again about John. Pictured him in her town house, in her kitchen and bath and stretched out on her couch. He fit so easily. She couldn't imagine her place without him.

At Sea-Tac Airport, she got on the first car rental van that pulled up to the waiting area. She ended up renting a silver Ford Neon, the most nondescript car on the lot. By four P.M. Pacific time, she drove out of the airport and began to follow the directions Erik had given her. Her palms were slick on the steering wheel.

She turned onto Route 7, passing through rolling, green farmland. So very green after the late-summer brown of Colorado. It was an overcast day, warm but gray. Ahead of her, she could see the flanks of Mount Rainier rising, dark green, covered with fir trees, but its snow-covered summit was hidden by clouds.

Elbe, she'd written down. The name of the town nearest to where Erik was staying. And more directions for her to follow once she was past Elbe. Dirt roads that led up toward Rainier.

And all the time, she put her mind and her feelings on hold, like a videotape stopped at the climax of a movie. Stopped dead, the actors frozen in their spots, all emotion stamped on their faces without the ability to change.

Erik needed her.

She found the isolated dirt road in her directions, the abandoned apple orchard and broken fence on the corner, and turned onto it, bouncing over ruts that still held muddy water from the last rain.

Towering Douglas firs rose on either side of the road, transforming the afternoon into twilight. Around a last curve, splashing through mud, the car rocking on its springs. And there was the cabin, exactly as he'd described it. Small, made of chinked logs, a chimney, a porch, with two steps down to the needle-littered ground, deep in the shadows of the forest.

And there he was, standing on the porch. Her whole being, her life, narrowed down with the precision of a laser to the tall, fair man who awaited her.

TWENTY-TWO

She had no memory of turning off the car or opening the door or getting out. No recollection of Erik crossing the space between them. He was suddenly there, in front of her, studying her face for a heartbeat, then two, then taking her in his arms.

She clung to him, pressing down her doubts, trying so very hard to convince herself her misgivings stemmed from her fear that he'd vanish into wisps before her eyes.

He spoke her name over and over and kissed her hungrily. Her body responded, but her mind wrenched itself apart, as if she were watching some other woman cupping his face in her hands, returning his desperate kisses.

"Is it really you?" she breathed against his lips. "Why, why did you let us all think you were dead?"

"Yes, it's me. God, how I missed you, Meredith." And he pulled her hard against him.

"Do you know how it felt to believe you were dead?"

"I had to let you believe that. Do you think I enjoyed it?"

"I can't go back," she said, almost to herself, and she knew suddenly and irrevocably that she could not make love to this man, not anymore.

"We *can* go back. I'll take you there," he said.

She moved out of his embrace and looked up into his beloved face, scored now by lines of pain. "Tell me everything."

"Soon. Come here."

She shook her head.

"All right," he said, "all right. But inside. You're cold. You're shaking."

She smiled faintly then. Yes, she was cold and, yes, she was trembling. But, as always, his hands holding her arms were warm.

They walked side by side toward the cabin, and she felt almost as if she couldn't breathe. For a moment, she was afraid that once the door was closed behind them, she'd lose her resolve. He'd see her falter, and she'd be lost.

No no no, she thought. *You're okay, you can handle this.* What was the mantra Sandra had given her? *What was it?*

He opened the door, waited for her to go in. God, what if the past weeks had been nothing more than a bad dream? What if she'd never met John? Then she could . . . *No one can take me over,* she remembered, and she desperately repeated the words in her head.

The interior of the cabin was rustic, even for the mountains. In the dim light of a single lamp that sat by the couch, she saw a tiny corner kitchen, narrow

cupboards, a Formica counter on one side of a sink—
water dripping from a faucet—a small gas stove on the
other side, a refrigerator. In the center of the far wall
was a potbelly stove, its door half open, ashes spilled
on the tiles under its legs. A plank floor with a dingy
braided rug in the middle. The couch, a blue expedition
sleeping bag thrown across it. A split log on legs for
a coffee table. On a peg by the front door was one of
Erik's parkas and a plaid shirt she recognized. Beneath
the pegs sat his rucksack. His duffel bag was nowhere
to be seen. Of course not, she realized, it had been
brought home from Talkeetna, where he'd left it before
the climb. Before his death.

But he wasn't dead.

She lifted her gaze to his. "What happened up
there?"

He looked at her gravely and searched her face.

"Tell me, goddamn it, Erik, tell me."

For a moment longer, he stared at her, then finally
he let out a sigh. "I will tell you everything. I promise
you that. But first I must know what Chad said."

"Okay," she said, "okay." She related Chad's story
to him, skipping the details of the assault on the summit and the storm because he already knew all that.
Then she came to the accident. The *so-called* accident.
Here she paused, something inside her warning her to
hold back, to gauge his reaction before she revealed
everything.

"What did Chad say about Kemil?"

"That Kemil stepped off a cornice in the storm, and
Chad lowered you down, belayed you."

"And?"

"Chad claims you just let Kemil go. He said it was

because you and Kemil had been arguing about Kemil's friends in Pakistan."

"Jesus," Erik said, and he began pacing.

"And he said you'd made an advance to one of Kemil's wives."

He stopped and whirled to face her. "Chad, that coward," he rasped. "He told the authorities this bullshit story?"

"Yes, he told the police."

His skin seemed to take on the color of the ash beneath the stove. He swore again.

"So," she said, "what really happened?"

He began to pace again, back and forth, as if he were a caged animal. She saw that he was limping and held one arm stiffly. He'd been hurt, and she hadn't even noticed.

"Erik, please, I need to know the truth."

"The truth. The fucking truth."

"Tell me."

"I don't know where to start," he said harshly.

"At the beginning."

"The beginning." He maneuvered to the chair and lowered himself carefully, one leg straight out in front of him. "That fucking Chad," he ground out.

"Forget Chad."

She sat, too, but on the edge of the couch, pushing the bright blue sleeping bag aside. She folded her hands in her lap and set her gaze on him.

"All right, all right," he said. "The day we made the summit bid . . . Goddamn that Chad."

It took a while. Getting Erik to voice his memories was like pulling teeth. But she was good at this. Helping people admit difficult things was her job.

"We reached the summit, and we knew we had to hurry," he said.

"The storm?" she prompted.

"Yes, yes, the storm. We could see it coming in a line of gray moving toward us. We thought we had time."

"Yes?"

"It simply blew in too fast. That bastard of a mountain," he reflected.

"Go on."

"Yes, all right. The wind was bad up there, you could hardly stand. Only a few minutes, then we started down. If we could get below Denali Pass, we'd be okay. It wasn't far, we had time. We were all in good shape."

"Yes?"

"We were roped together, me leading, Kemil in the middle, making good time, but the fucking storm, Christ, it struck us so fast, just as we were descending the pass. You couldn't see. The snow hit your face like needles. Well, I've been there before. So had . . ." He frowned. "So had Chad. Kemil depended on us, but he was good. He was still strong."

"And?"

He rubbed his beard. "We could barely hear one another, just kept on, one foot at a time, very careful not to go wide, because the wind built up cornices along the edge of the trail, and if you stepped on one, it would give way. But, of course, we were roped together."

He paused, going inside himself again. Remembering.

"Erik, what happened then?" she urged.

His expression filled with disgust. "I can hardly believe it, even now, I felt the rope pull, and I stopped and turned to look. It was like a bad dream, Kemil and Chad struggling, fighting. And the wind blew so hard I couldn't see them for a minute, and I thought it must be my imagination, but there they were, fighting on Denali Pass in the storm."

He met her eyes and shook his head. "I rushed back, and only Chad was there. I followed the rope to the edge. The cornice was broken, and I knew Kemil had fallen. But he was still on the rope. Chad hadn't meant for him to fall, I was sure of that.

"I screamed at Chad. 'What were you doing? What the hell were you doing?' But I couldn't hear his answer. I remember I lay down and looked over the edge. The wind died for a moment, and I saw Kemil, dangling, hanging by his ice ax. I don't know whether he saw me, but I knew he couldn't hold on much longer. If he fell, he could take us both with him.

"We knew what to do. No need to talk. Chad belayed me, hammering in two ice pitons, bracing himself, letting out the rope as I climbed down toward Kemil. The wind knocked me off the face and I hung there, thrown back and forth, but I managed. And then I had almost reached Kemil. He looked at me. I saw him look at me. He tried to smile. He knew I'd save him. But the storm, the snow. We couldn't talk. Christ, Meredith," he said.

"Erik, go on."

"I can't even stand to think about it, much less talk about it."

"You have to."

He swore.

"Tell me."

"I guess I pulled on my rope, I remember I needed more slack to reach Kemil, and then," he paused, his gaze inward, "and then, I can't believe it even now, I thought it was some mistake of my eyes, in the storm. I felt the rope go slack, but too much, too much, it fell down the face like a snake, that long loop of bright yellow rope. I can still see it." He closed his eyes. "And then I looked up and I knew what he had done. I knew, but I couldn't really believe it." He stopped and ran a hand over his eyes. "Chad had unhooked the rope from the carabiner on his harness. He'd unhooked it and taken it off the pitons and thrown it over the edge. He'd left us down there with no way to get back up to the ridge. *He'd unhooked it.*"

"Chad tried to . . . kill you?"

His clear blue gaze swung around and came to rest on her. "That is what he did."

"But he—"

"Yes, I wondered what he told you, what he told everyone. I should have guessed."

"How did you get down?"

"I tried to get closer to Kemil. We were still roped together, and I thought, I thought, maybe we could climb down; I had a few pitons on my belt. We could hook up and get down that way, but it was too bad, the wind, and after a time, I don't know how long, Kemil looked at me and he, God, his lips moved, he said something I couldn't hear, and I saw his hand slide off the shaft of his ax. I saw it slide, and then he fell, just disappeared into spindrift, and the end of the rope slid through my carabiner, so fast, the loose end slid out, and that was it. He was gone."

He paused, then said, "I held on as long as I could. I climbed down a few hundred feet. I had my ax but no rope, so I couldn't anchor myself. I was very cold by then, very cold. And tired. I fell. I don't remember it. But I fell and I woke up later, I don't know how long had passed, and I was wedged into a narrow slot. It saved my life. My knee was wrenched and my shoulder, but I was so cold I didn't notice. Then it was morning, and I climbed down to where it was not so steep, a glacier on the north side of the mountain. I walked, down and down. Just walking. Christ, I don't know how long. And then there was the valley and a cabin. Some people, a couple who live there, and I woke up. They said it was three days. Three days. I remember nothing. No, excuse me, I remembered Chad's expression and the rope falling and Kemil's face when he could hold on no longer.

"Goddamn it, Meredith, I still can't believe it. Chad is my best friend. We've saved each other's lives so many times. I need to figure this out before I see him. I have to understand, so I needed you. You see, Meredith, don't you? I needed you to tell me what Chad said."

She stared at him. "Yes, of course you did."

"I don't know who to trust. Except you. I can trust you. And then I'll know what to do."

"That's quite a story, Erik." She studied him for a moment longer, then took a deep breath. "A very good story. There's only one problem. Kemil's rope didn't slide through your carabiner. It was cut. It was cut with a knife. Now, would you like to tell me what really happened up there?"

She watched the gamut of emotions swirl across his

face. At first he stared at her in disbelief. Then it was shock, then horror, then anger, and finally he turned hard and cold, his eyes flinty. She'd seen that look. Never directed at her. But she'd seen it. Her heart began to pound. If he'd murdered Kemil, could he kill again?

Silence cocooned them, and all she could hear was the dripping faucet, dripping more rapidly, it seemed, in time with the beat of her heart. Louder and louder. And that look in his eyes.

The silence stretched out, the beat in her breast accelerating, until finally he let out a groaning sigh and sagged in his chair. "So they knew the rope was cut. *What* would you have me say? What can I tell you?"

"The truth."

"So simple. Just the truth?"

"Yes. No more lies. Were you really involved with Kemil's terrorist friends? Did you have an affair with one of his wives? *Did you? Did you cut Kemil's rope?*"

He lifted his head and stared, and then he laughed, a short, bitter bark. "Chad really said I did something with one of Kemil's wives? That's very good. Very clever. I've never even seen one of Kemil's wives. But who would know that, once Kemil and I were both dead? The terrorist crap? Yes, I knew the government was watching us. They watched us for a long time. We all made jokes about it. And whenever we left the country, they'd make us go through such red tape, searched us when we came back to the States. It was a routine. We laughed. It was very funny." He pushed himself out of the chair, awkwardly, and it wounded her to the very core to see him fallen from his godlike perfection.

He paced unevenly across the cabin, limping, gazed out of the streaked window, then moved back to stand in the small circle of light. "Do you remember I told you about Kathy's child having leukemia?"

"Yes, Brit. And she's fine now, and—"

"It was always about Kathy." He abruptly slashed the air with a hand, and she winced. "Everything. Kathy had no insurance. She was desperate. Brit needed a bone marrow transplant, and Kathy's ex-husband wouldn't help. Chad gave her some money, but he didn't have enough. I tried to help, but it was beyond our resources. So she stole from Kemil. You say, cooked the books? He didn't even miss the money for three years. Then he found out. Last spring. He said he wouldn't turn her in to the authorities if she paid it back. She tried to get a loan, but she couldn't. Tried to sell her house, but the mortgage was too big. Her ex, that son of a bitch, he wouldn't do shit. She had nowhere else to go. She begged Chad for help. He went to Kemil and tried to reason with him, but it didn't work."

Of course, the argument she'd overheard that night.

"And then, naturally, Chad came to me."

She waited, her pulse ticking in her ears.

He held her gaze, his turning as cold as ice, as hard as marble. "Do you really think *Chad* had the guts to cut Kemil's rope?"

Everything slid into place. Chad's dependence on Erik. *Erik* had cut the rope. *Erik* had tried to retrieve the damning evidence off Kemil's body, and in so doing, he himself fell. My God, Chad's story had been the truth. She put her head in her hands.

"It wasn't that hard," came his voice, relentless, pounding at her. "Accidents happen. Eventually, most climbers, if they don't quit, die on a mountain. Kemil pushed the limits. I push the limits. What the hell difference does it make?"

What difference does it make? The difference between an accident and deliberate murder.

"No." She shook her head. "No. You can't mean that."

"Oh, but I do. I . . . I've seen so much death. Too much."

"You aren't that hard. You aren't," she insisted.

He laughed bitterly.

"I can't believe you're a . . . murderer. I just can't."

"Maybe I'm not. Kemil was almost gone, anyway. You see that, don't you? He was hanging by a thread. I may not have been able to save him. I merely quickened the process. Murder? Maybe. But the real murderer is the mountain. Any mountain. Anytime. I did it for Kathy and Brit and Timmy. I did it for Chad. The mountain helped me."

She looked up sharply. "Did Chad make you fall? Did he . . . ?"

"No. It was all my doing. I was afraid Kemil's body would be recovered with the cut rope. So I decided to climb down, remove the evidence. But, my dear Meredith, the mountain had other plans. You see, when I reached Kemil, my rope slid out of my carabiner, and I was no longer attached to Chad. A small miscalculation. Call it fate. Call it my punishment. There was no time to get his rope, because I slipped. I fell. I should have died along with Kemil. The rest you know."

The minutes crawled by, unhurried by her desolation. Neither of them spoke. She sat on the edge of the couch, trying to fit her mind around Erik's words: The mountain had killed Kemil, Erik had merely hastened the inevitable.

She drew in her breath, filling her lungs with the damp air.

"Tell me you forgive me," he said softly, his voice a low rumble in his chest.

"I don't know," she said slowly.

"You always know, Meredith."

She looked straight at him. "What about Bridget? And the men on Aconcagua? Did they die because of you?"

"They died because of the nature of climbing."

"So you hold no responsibility?"

"I have come to terms with my responsibility."

"And?"

"There's nothing more."

He displayed no guilt whatsoever. But then she'd known he wouldn't. It had never occurred to him that he could have told them no, he wouldn't guide them up a mountain that, given the right circumstances, could kill them. Erik believed in free will. If they wanted to climb a mountain, if they trained and conditioned and met the requirements, he absolved himself of responsibility, so long as he did his job to the best of his ability.

And Kemil. No doubt Erik believed from the bottom

of his heart that in the end, with or without Erik's involvement, it was the mountain that took the prince's life.

And this was the man she thought she had loved. A man that, even now, after everything she'd suffered, after everything he'd suffered, was still a stranger.

She focused her eyes on him. And then she had to know. "Did you ever really love me?"

He didn't hesitate. "Yes. I still love you. You believe me, don't you? Now that I've told you the truth. And to prove how much I love you, I offer this to you. I have a son, Meredith. And his mother and I—"

"I know about Debra and Robbie," she interrupted.

"Ah, I see,"

"I went to Boulder. I met her. We . . . we talked."

"Who told you about them?"

"Chad."

"The bastard," he said without rancor.

"She said she knew about me, and she said you'd never been faithful to her, and you wouldn't be faithful to me."

"I never asked Debra to marry me." With great effort, he kneeled in front of her and held her face between his hands. "Did I?"

"No," she whispered. But she was numb, empty inside. Suddenly weary from the long day, her worry, the truth. The truth that she had chased so assiduously every day of her life, but had not caught up with until now.

She sucked in a quick lungful of air and sat back as if pushed. She'd been an addict, a junkie, blinding herself to reality in the pursuit of pure pleasure. She'd denied all along that Erik had a certain moral carelessness, even while she'd known something was terribly wrong. She'd even gone to her colleague Sandra, but nothing had stopped her or cured her until this. Until his confession.

A sense of utter humility swept her, combined with gratitude that she'd come through this fire not destroyed but tempered. Suddenly, she craved John's presence, his composure, his surety of right and wrong. He'd know what to do in this situation; he always knew what to do. She felt his absence like a void.

"So what happens now?" she found herself asking. "What happens to you? To Chad and Kathy?" *To me,* she thought.

TWENTY-THREE

They must have talked for hours, and then they sat
there wordlessly across from each other, the two of
them held in the embrace of four rough-hewn walls,
while outside, the overcast afternoon dulled to evening.

Fog curled relentlessly in from the Pacific Ocean and
snaked through the ferns and moss and tall firs, ebbing
and flowing around the cabin, muffling all sound. The
night grew inky black, the stars disappearing one by
one into the fog. The silence between them lengthened
and deepened.

"I want you," Erik finally said.

She didn't answer. She stared into the shadows beyond the couch and felt the steady pulse of her heart,
and she knew she'd remember till she was very old
this cabin and Erik and the way the water dripped mo-
notonously in the kitchen sink and the smell of damp
ash beneath the potbelly stove.

"Meredith?"

"Do you think," she said, "that we would have been
happy?"

"We were happy. We *are* happy."

"Are we? Would I ever have been truly happy if I couldn't have known you?"

"We were happy. I asked you to marry me."

"That's not what I mean. I could never have known you, not really, and without knowing you—"

"We were happy," he insisted.

She pulled her gaze from the shadows and met his eyes. Until that moment, she had believed that her judgment, her sense of self, who she was and where she was going, had left her. But now she knew she hadn't lost her way, only discovered a new element of herself, which had frightened her because it was unfamiliar and different. But it was only one of the facets of the human psyche, with potential for either good or bad; it was, in the end, what you made of it. He had set her free in many ways, and for that she would be forever thankful.

She wanted to tell John what she'd discovered about herself. She yearned for the chance to explain everything to him. Would he understand?

She cringed, remembering confessing her lust for Erik to him. Yet, even then, he'd treated her with care. And respect.

Where was he now? Closing in on her trail? She needed him here.

"You know," she said, "I was so afraid in the beginning. I thought I'd lost myself. I thought you'd taken me over, body and soul."

He smiled into the dimness.

"But I was wrong. It was me, all along. Even from that first night at your place, it was me. No," she thought suddenly, "before that. At Bridget's memorial. I was the one giving off all the signals, wasn't I?"

"Yes."

"Even then? Could I have wanted you even then? I was sure I hated you."

"You wanted something. Perhaps someone to free you."

"Maybe . . . yes. But not just anyone."

He shook his head. "Meredith, there is no such thing as one man for one woman on the face of the earth. You were ready. It took you longer than most, perhaps."

"I'll always believe it was you."

Did Erik truly love her? Had he truly loved her? Or perhaps it had been the idea of her he'd been seeking. She guessed in the end it no longer mattered.

He tried a last time to persuade her to make love. And one last time, she couldn't. "I'm sorry," she said, reaching for his hand. "I'm so sorry, Erik, but I've given you everything I have to give. There's nothing left."

"I see," he said, but she knew he never would.

They talked awhile longer, and then he stuffed his belongings into his rucksack and stood at the open door.

"Kiss me?" he said.

She kissed him in the mother-of-pearl dawn, held him tightly as he held her and tasted him and sadly ached for the man he could have been.

"Good-bye, Meredith, my love," he told her, and she watched as he crossed the drive, until the fog encased him and closed back around his form, blotting him out.

"Good-bye," she whispered.

• • •

The rain began at midmorning, a dreary Pacific Northwest rain, heavy pewter clouds hugging the sides of the mountains.

She drove through the downpour to the airport and felt as if the past twenty-four hours had been a dream. In a while she'd be home, and she knew none of this would ever seem real. Except, perhaps, for the cabin, the water dripping from the faucet, the scent of pine and ash and Erik's blue eyes, the distant stare—her Viking scanning the horizon, accepting its peril.

John found her at the car rental agency. She was waiting for the airport van, sitting on a bench, the rain trickling from the eaves onto her shoulders. She didn't notice him at first. She didn't notice the rain or her soaked clothes. She was staring at the fog-enshrouded mountains that circled Puget Sound, and she was thinking she'd never see the top of any mountain. She was simply too grounded.

"Jesus, Meredith," she heard, and she forced herself to look up.

"Here, put this on." He draped a raincoat over her shoulders.

"You found me," she said tonelessly.

"Where in hell have you been?" He stood over her in the soaking drizzle, his raincoat protecting her while he rubbed her arms. "We checked the airlines, then the car rentals here. There was an APB put out on the car."

He was there, just as she'd known he would be. He'd found her. Now she could let go, give in to her weariness. She leaned forward and rested her forehead against his chest.

"Meredith?"

"I'm so tired," she whispered.

He put his arms around her, gently brought her close. "You saw him."

"Yes." She closed her eyes and drew in his scent, damp wool and starch from his shirt and his own unique essence. She sighed.

"Are you okay?"

She nodded against his chest.

He held her, stroking her back.

"I knew you'd come," she said.

"But did you want me to?"

"Yes, oh yes."

"What you did was dangerous, crazy."

"I had to."

He said nothing.

"You won't find him," she said.

She couldn't tell John the truth yet. She had to give Erik time. Thankfully, John did not press the issue.

It wasn't until he had her safely on a flight back to Colorado that he finally said, "I want you to tell me now."

She had a blanket wrapped around her, and she was leaning her head against the window. "I'll tell you," she said. "I'll tell you everything. It was never what you thought," she began, "it was never about Kemil and his terrorist friends or anything even close to that."

"Go on," he said, his voice so familiar to her, a voice she trusted.

She told him everything, from Brit's leukemia to Kathy Fry embezzling from Kemil to Chad trying to intervene for his sister to buy her time to repay the theft. And then Erik became involved.

"In the end, though," she said, "it was Erik who took action. It was Erik who cut the rope and let Kemil fall.

It was never Chad." She shook her head. "I didn't believe it when he told the police it was Erik's doing, but he was telling the truth. Chad never had the guts. I should have known that. The only detail he left out was the motive." She looked at John. "Money."

"And all us feds have mud on our faces," John mused.

"Everyone was wrong. Everyone. You, me."

"So it would seem."

"What will happen to Kathy now?"

"I don't know. It'll be up to the al Assad family to decide, I suppose. If they want to press charges they can, of course."

"But they may not want all the publicity. They've had enough as it is."

"No," he said, "most likely they won't, especially if it would mean opening up Prince Kemil's books for the world to scrutinize."

"And Chad? I mean . . ." She frowned. "Can he be charged? Maybe as an accessory?"

"I doubt it," John said. "If Chad didn't cut the rope, he may not even have known what Erik was up to. Either that, or he'll claim he didn't." He let a moment pass. "Okay," he finally said softly, "so where exactly *is* Amundsson?" Then, "Meredith?"

She tucked the blanket under her chin and gazed out the window. She suddenly wanted to think about it. To remember. To share everything with John.

"I'm leaving at dawn," Erik had said, the lamplight gilding his beard, his eyes fixed on her, waiting. Did he think she would try to stop him? Or call the authorities?

"Do you recall," Erik went on, "that solo climb I

always wanted to make? Chad and I used to talk about
it a lot. Even Kemil . . ." His face darkened. "But that
doesn't matter now. Tirich Mir in the Hindu Kush."

"My God," she breathed.

"That's right. A beautiful mountain. A peak every
climber dreams about."

It took her a very long time to find the words, and
then she whispered, "You said, you told me that was . . .
suicide. Erik, you can't, you *can't.*"

He didn't reply. One corner of his lip turned up very
slightly, and his gaze grew distant. He was already on
that mountain. In the background, the water dripped,
and she felt the cold breath of morning on her skin.

"Please," she got out, "there has to be another way.
Erik, please."

He laughed suddenly. "Don't you know me? Don't
you know how every cell of my body longs to make
this climb? All I ask is that you allow me the time.
Allow me to go before you tell the authorities. Will
you do that for me, my love?"

The water dripped and her heart beat and the fog
curled around the cabin.

"You still have the ring?" he asked then.

"Yes, of course." Her hand went up to it automatically.

"Will you give it to me?" he asked.

She lifted the chain over her head, and he took it
and hung it around his neck. "There," he said with
satisfaction. "You will always be with me."

And in the end, she let him go, because she knew
she could not stop him, and she knew she should not
even try.

"He lived by the sword," she said, her gaze fixed

out the plane's window. "He'll die by the sword. I let him go."

Her eyes were dry. She had done the right thing; there was no question in her mind. "He couldn't have stood being judged and condemned and imprisoned," she finished.

John reached for her hand, finding it under the blanket and clasping it in his.

He did not call the authorities when they landed in Denver, and he did not call them an hour later when their next flight touched down in Aspen. She had almost wanted him to—surely Erik could still be stopped—but in her heart, she was grateful that John understood. He always understood.

Her car was still parked at the office where she'd left it yesterday—a lifetime ago. John drove her home. It was very dark and very chilly out, and she still wore his raincoat when he unlocked her door with her key, and she stepped inside.

"I have to stay here," he said.

She turned and looked at him. Without hesitation, she said, "Yes, I know. And I . . . I don't want to be alone tonight."

He nodded and closed the door behind them.

"I'm going to bed, all right?" she said, handing him his coat. "Maybe a hot shower and then bed. I'm very tired."

Again, he nodded. And then he smiled faintly. "I have to make that call," he said. "Do you understand?"

"Yes. It's okay now. Really."

He moved toward the phone, and she moved toward the stairs. Then she paused. "What happens now?"

"I don't know," he said. "The one thing I do know

is that I want to see you again. I want to be with you."

She met his eyes for a moment, and despite his measured tone, she recognized the heartfelt emotion in his gaze. Warmth filled her, banishing her tiredness, her sadness, her doubts.

"I'd like that, too," she said almost shyly.

He smiled then, a carefree smile that lit up his face as if he were a boy. She went to him, and they embraced, and she felt the promise of the future unfold inside her.

USA Today

Bestselling Author

PATRICIA
POTTER

"Is a master storyteller."
—Mary Jo Putney

BROKEN HONOR 0-515-13227-6

Long ago, in the wanning years of World War II, a Nazi train was captured by Allies. Its cargo––a fortune in stolen art and gold dust––vanished. Now, two strangers are about to become engulfed in its tantalizing mystery...unexpected passion and inescapable peril.

THE PERFECT FAMILY 0-425-17811-0

In this compelling contemporary novel, a woman confronts past secrets and present dangers when she travels to Sedona, Arizona, to attend a family reunion.

TO ORDER CALL
1-800-788-6262

(AD #B601)

New York Times Bestselling Author
Nevada Barr

Deep South

Park Ranger Anna Pigeon stumbles upon a gruesome murder with frightening racial overtones in the latest installment of the award-winning series.

An Anna Pigeon novel that "takes your breath away." (Cleveland Plain Dealer)

"Suspenseful." —Publishers Weekly

"Surprising." —Booklist (starred review)

**To order call:
1-800-788-6262**

0-425-17895-1

(ad #b600)

PENGUIN PUTNAM INC.
Online

Your Internet gateway to a virtual environment with
hundreds of entertaining and enlightening books
from Penguin Putnam Inc.

*While you're there, get the latest buzz on
the best authors and books around—*

Tom Clancy, Patricia Cornwell, W.E.B. Griffin,
Nora Roberts, William Gibson, Robin Cook,
Brian Jacques, Catherine Coulter, Stephen King,
Ken Follett, Terry McMillan, and many more!

**Penguin Putnam Online is located at
http://www.penguinputnam.com**

PENGUIN PUTNAM NEWS

Every month you'll get an inside look at our upcoming books and new features on our site. This is an
ongoing effort to provide you with the most
up-to-date information about
our books and authors.

**Subscribe to Penguin Putnam News at
http://www.penguinputnam.com/newsletters**